Long Way Back

Long Way Back

DAVID BOWRA

IGUANA

Publisher: Cheryl Hawley
Editor: Paula Chiarcos
Copy editor: Toby Keymer
Front cover design: Jonathan Relph

ISBN 978-1-77180-637-4 (hardcover)
ISBN 978-1-77180-634-3 (paperback)
ISBN 978-1-77180-633-6 (epub)

This is an original print edition of *Long Way Back*.

For my grandchildren: Ryan, Lauren, Zachary, Jason and Jack. You make life special.

Prologue

November 27, 1983
Eastern Townships, Quebec

Alan Davis didn't want to go to the meeting. At 4 p.m. it would be almost dark, and no one would be around. The summer was long gone, but snow had yet to arrive. He watched his breath and heard his own footsteps as he crunched along the frozen path. The trees were bare, and he could smell the smoke from the last of the burning leaves. It usually took him an hour to walk around the large lake. So how did they know which park bench to meet at? They knew. Of course they knew.

He arrived early, and there was already a light mist on the lake as he walked past the designated bench. No one was around. He walked on for a bit and then turned back and sat down on the bench. Five minutes to four. He heard footsteps and could make out shadows. And voices, at least two of them. As they got closer, he stood up. The small figure was Walter Pigeon; he didn't recognize the taller guy.

Pigeon smoothed his jet-black hair with one hand as he approached. "How you doin'?" His squeaky voice and beady black eyes reminded Davis of a rat. "Tony got tied up and asked me to come along instead. This is Harry Parker."

Davis nodded to Harry, who looked uncomfortable, edgy, as if he had better places to be, then focused back on Pigeon.

"The boss asked me to pass on a message, make sure there was no misunderstanding." Pigeon paused to rub a tooth with his tongue, then began again. "You do know who we are, don't you? I'm sure Dennis told you everything?"

Davis nodded. His employer had been quite explicit about who these guys were and what they would expect.

"You need to understand where you fit in," Pigeon continued. "We've checked you out..." Pigeon looked like he was expecting a reaction. He scratched at his jaw as he considered his next words. "The boss thinks you're the right guy. In my book, you need to work with someone a long time to gain their trust. I'm damn good at smelling a rat, and you need to know what we do with rats."

He turned to Harry. "What do we do with rats, Harry?"

Harry didn't seem to know.

"Come on, Harry, speak up, tell him what we do with rats."

"We deal with them, boss."

"That's right. We crush 'em because they're vermin."

"Yes, boss."

Pigeon put his hand in his pocket and took out a gun. He looked at Davis as he moved the gun from one hand to the other, feeling the butt of it in the palm of his hand. He ran the forefinger of his left hand along the barrel and pointed the gun at Davis. He smiled. "This is how we deal with rats," he said.

Chapter 1

Five months earlier

Davis sat back in a worn-out leather armchair by the fireside in his old farmhouse and gently swirled his glass of single malt whisky. He thought back to when this had all started, when his old adversary from the Vancouver RCMP had turned up at the fishing lodge he was working at in Miramichi, New Brunswick. Davis hadn't heard from Pat Lossan since going into witness protection more than two years earlier. Lossan told him that some people from the RCMP Security Service in Montreal wanted to meet him. He claimed they wanted his advice on gang crime at the Port of Montreal. Davis was sure there was more to it than that. Reluctantly, he'd agreed to meet them in Quebec.

He'd spent three days in Montreal, listening to a senior RCMP Security Service representative and a couple of RCMP Organized Crime officers who'd lived and breathed gang crime in Montreal for the last fifteen years. They talked about organized crime in the port city and wanted his views on their latest plan to tackle crime on the docks. The older guy, a grey-haired fellow named Vincent, said that given his previous life, Davis would be an ideal candidate to help them. They wanted his advice on how to go after the gangs.

They explained how one of the gangs, led by a man named Tony De Riggi, had contacts that went deep into Customs, the Montreal Police Service and even the Quebec Sûreté. They estimated that the dollar value of drugs arriving at the port had tripled in the last five years. The gangs controlled the docks, where they loaded and unloaded large quantities of hashish and ecstasy coming in on ships from Pakistan, via Rotterdam or Antwerp.

One of the cops had held up a satchel about eight by ten inches. "Believe it or not," he'd said, "you could hide a million dollars' worth of drugs in this."

Most goods were stored in large shipping containers, which were controlled by longshoremen and checkers. A few of the gangs had strong ties to these two groups; some of them were gang members themselves. Employees were often told to stay home or take a sick day so that somebody else could take their position on the day a particular container was scheduled to be unloaded. In one case a container supposedly loaded with 1,500 kilos of hashish was being watched by an RCMP surveillance team. Within ten minutes of them sending a fax to the terminal to have the container picked up, it disappeared. With more than a thousand containers in a terminal at any one time, hiding one forty-foot container was child's play.

The truckers that picked up the containers played their part too, even though most of the time they weren't aware of who the merchandise belonged to or who they were dealing with. Most of them knew they were doing something illegal, but they were getting well paid and didn't ask questions. And there were no police in the Port of Montreal, just a security agency under contract to the Port Authority.

Davis asked why the port couldn't control employment at the docks, and why employees weren't subject to criminal background checks. He already knew the answer though. It was no different in Vancouver. The docks had a law unto themselves, and the port authorities across the country just lived with it. The agent had stared at him in disbelief, muttered something in French and then in broken English said, "Been like that for years. Port administration turns a ...

blind eye. Drugs"—he shrugged—"This is just a fraction of what comes into the port. They'll never shut down for this reason. Even where the authorities control who works on the docks, like in Rotterdam, drugs still find their way to Montreal."

At the end of the third day, Vincent stood up, walked to the window and looked out. He then turned to Davis and said, "So, will you help us go after the gangs? Develop a plan that will penetrate their network, find out what's really going on, who's pulling the strings and how we can stop it, and then…"

Davis had stopped listening. He had a lot of questions. They wanted more than just advice. They planned to put someone on the inside, and an undercover cop would soon be discovered. They wanted him to penetrate the gang.

Davis stood up. "You're planning a major operation that could take years. I need time to think about it."

"I understand," said Vincent. "But you will think about it?"

Davis's eyes gave nothing away.

"I'll be in touch when I've made a decision."

***

Davis had gone back to Miramichi to mull over their proposal. He'd even talked to Tidby, the old lodge manager, about whether he thought someone bad could change and do some good. The old man was a good listener and never judged him. When the old man had hired Davis at the lodge, he'd known Davis was running from something, but he never asked. Davis even talked to Lossan on the long drive back from Montreal. Both knew the plan was full of holes— the idea to have Davis infiltrate the gang by pretending to be a drug dealer wouldn't work, they'd smell him a mile off. He'd needed to find a different way to get into the gang.

Dennis Hatfield's trucking company had been the perfect opportunity. It had operated close to the city's Racine and Cast port terminals in east Montreal for nearly forty years. Hatfield wasn't a gang member, but a few of his drivers were. And Hatfield never asked what was in the containers he shipped for the gang; he didn't want to know.

It wasn't hard for Davis to slip into the role of a logistics expert hired on the recommendation of a friend of Hatfield's, one who knew that the old man needed to change his ways. The business was in trouble. And even though the gang paid well, way over the odds in fact, it wasn't enough in the cutthroat trucking business. Hatfield hadn't invested in technology. His fleet was old, and half the trucks should have been replaced years ago. He also kept manual records and had never used a computer. The old man should have sold out and probably knew his days were numbered, but at seventy-two, he wasn't going to change. Sooner or later, the business was going to fail.

Davis had been working there for a few months now, getting to know the business and the people. He'd been most surprised by the lack of security at the docks. Massive containers, stacked one on top of the other, dominated the landscape. The place reminded him of Midtown Manhattan, but instead of high-rise office and apartment buildings, it was a large Legoland village of multicoloured metal containers—earth red, grey, white, brown and maroon. There were long and narrow spaces between them, one lane looking just like every other. And even though the dock was less than two miles long, Davis saw how easy it would be to hide a container here. Without some form of tracker, you might never find it again.

He decided to live in a little cottage in the Eastern Townships, where he could stay under the radar. The village he'd picked was less than an hour's drive east of Montreal. He'd always been a loner, and this quiet place allowed him to keep to himself. The cops had told him it was a good spot and that there were always people arriving from out of town and staying for a few months—he wouldn't look suspicious.

Davis took a sip of whisky and slouched back in his chair. Finding a new haulier to manage the gang's business would be difficult. It would be easier for them to take over Hatfield's business. That was the endgame. Davis knew he had to go slow. Montreal was like Vancouver; the locals were suspicious of outsiders. Hatfield needed to think it was his idea and that Davis was the right guy to help. He had to become the son that the old man never had. Hatfield had to be the one to convince the gang they should take it over and that Davis could run the business.

There were always risks to a plan like this. The gang might want to bring their own guy in to run the business. They might even get onto Davis. It was moments like this that he wondered why he was helping the cops. Something about wanting to set the record straight, he remembered. Proving to people there was some good in him after all. Not that his ex would care. And he doubted his daughter remembered him; she was only a toddler when his wife had walked out on him.

Davis came out of his reverie with a sigh. The empty whisky glass was on the floor by his feet. He picked it up, lifted himself from the chair and headed off to bed, hoping to catch some sleep before meeting his two handlers the following morning.

Chapter 2

Davis's RCMP handlers, Paul Primeau and Bernie Lacroix, were an odd couple. Primeau was a brash, thickset Montrealer in his late forties. He still had all his dark hair, and by afternoon he had a five o'clock shadow. Born and raised in Montreal East, he was third-generation Italian. His swarthy looks reminded Davis of a gang member he knew from East Vancouver, who used to work on the docks. Lacroix was in his late fifties, about five foot nine, slim, with glasses and a pale complexion that made it look like he spent all his time in the office.

And while Primeau had been gung-ho for the operation to start, Lacroix had been hesitant. He was the one who warned Davis about life undercover, as though he was hoping to dissuade him from continuing. He told him he'd have to forget about his past and develop a whole new persona, change his appearance and always be on his guard. Dennis Hatfield would check him out when he hired him, and so would the gang who used Hatfield's trucking business. If they ever found out who he really was, he'd be a dead man.

Over those first months working for the RCMP Security Service, Davis had been amazed at the lengths to which Lacroix went to help him establish his new identity. There was a driver's licence, a social insurance number, credit cards, doctored family photos of a woman in her mid-forties with a young girl, clearly meant to be the ex-wife and daughter whom he hadn't seen in years, a personal history going back to his childhood, even a diploma from the high school he had supposedly graduated from when he was eighteen. When he looked at his new driver's licence photo with his grey moustache and salt-and-pepper goatee, he doubted that even Lossan or Tidby would recognize him, let alone any of the old gang back in Vancouver.

They'd discussed a name change and worried that neither Alan Davis nor Dennis Kelly, the name he'd been given for witness protection, would work. Even though the likelihood of him running into someone he knew was remote, there was always a chance.

Davis had insisted on using his old name. He'd spent the last few years using the name Kelly, and now they wanted him to assume yet another name? He knew he needed to keep it simple and the more he could step back into his real life, the easier it'd be.

"Come on, guys, that's hardly going to happen to me. I lived in Vancouver for over thirty years, and I've been on the other side of the country for the last three."

Lacroix shot back, "You'd be surprised. And we've invested a lot of time and money in this operation. You got to assume anything can happen and plan for all possibilities. Reduce the risk. Remember, you'll be out there on your own, and I guarantee you'll be under suspicion the minute De Riggi or any of his guys meets you. Montreal may be a big city, but it's a small town, all the gang members know each other, and they know all the crooked cops. They'll be checking you out eight ways to Sunday. They'll set traps, they'll put you under pressure in ways you can't even begin to imagine."

Lacroix had talked a lot about what the gang might want him to do and warned him that if he had to take part in a crime, the activity had to be approved in advance. Dealing in narcotics was to be avoided, not only because it was illegal, also because he could become addicted. If he were ever called to testify in court, it could damage his credibility as a witness.

As he drove home from the city, Davis laughed at Primeau's response to Lacroix's demand that he not do anything illegal. The big man had just rolled his eyes and laughed. "Jesus Christ, Bernie, how the hell do you expect him to act? He's gotta be like one of them all the time, of course he'll be exposed to criminal activity, of course he'll be expected to do drugs, he's joining a bloody gang for Christ's sake."

Davis flipped on the wipers. Primeau wasn't completely dumb after all. He knew there'd be times when Davis would have to act on his own and that there wouldn't always be time to run it by his handlers. Isn't that what *undercover* meant? Davis thought back to the time in Vancouver when McVittie, the gang's boss, had ordered him to get rid of George Koehle. He'd lied and pretended he was going through with it, even to the point of making up an elaborate plan to dispose of the body. Davis thought that assuming a different personality wouldn't be as difficult as Lacroix made it out to be. He knew that in a way he'd assumed a different persona for over thirty years while he was in the gang back in Vancouver.

According to Lacroix, the ideal undercover agent was someone who made friends easily. "You can only fake so much," he'd added. "You spend enough time with people who like and trust you, doing what they do, you're likely to develop some affection for them, even though what they do goes against your moral principles. Then when the time comes for you to betray their trust, it's not so easy…"

Davis had wondered if his handler was speaking from personal experience.

Months ago, when Davis had first started working at the trucking company, Lacroix told him they weren't to meet in person for at least a month, expecting that Davis would have a tail. And he might have been right. Davis had been thoroughly grilled by Hatfield during their first meeting. The old man had seemed overly suspicious of outsiders. Maybe it was just that he wasn't used to taking advice and didn't want to admit his business was in trouble. The police cover and the background they'd given him in the trucking industry seemed to convince Hatfield that he knew the business. Davis could still tell the man didn't like change.

Davis pulled up to the motel where his handlers were currently stationed. They'd told him a black pickup truck would be parked outside their unit. He noticed a few motorbikes parked outside one of the units and breathed a sigh of relief; they weren't Harleys. At the very end of the lot was a black pickup. Davis drove the length of the parking lot and parked his truck in the overflow area at the back of the motel, then slowly walked back and knocked on the door with the pickup out front.

Lacroix opened it. Primeau, who'd been seated at a table behind him, stood up. He was anxious to hear about Davis's recent trips to the Racine terminal and to Toronto.

Davis shrugged. "The usual."

Primeau was disappointed. "Look, I know it takes time to establish a legitimate cover, but it's been months since you started working at Hatfield's and we've gotten nowhere. You haven't even met De Riggi for Christ's sake!"

Lacroix pushed his glasses up and glared at his partner. "You know, Paul, sometimes you can be a real ass. Who cares what Vincent wants; this guy's life is on the line! What would you have him do, go to De Riggi's house in Saint-Henri, knock on the door and ask to join his gang? No. For now it's enough that he's working with Hatfield and they're starting to trust him to carry out their business. We must be patient and stick with it."

Yves Vincent, the Quebec head of the RCMP Security Service, had invested a lot of time and money in this operation and was anxious to get results. And Davis worried that Primeau would start to push things and expose him to even more danger.

"How patient? Another four months, six months, a year maybe? Christ, they'll shut us down before that. We need some results, and soon."

Lacroix didn't seem to be listening, and for a moment they were all silent with their thoughts. Then Lacroix looked at Davis. "You said you don't think Hatfield can survive for more than a few months at the rate he's losing money."

"Yeah, that's right, maybe less. Unless…"

Lacroix raised his eyebrows.

Davis shifted in his seat. "I've been thinking about a way to … speed things up."

Primeau leaned forward. "Well, let's hear it."

"What if something was to happen to the business?"

Primeau looked confused. Lacroix's eyes lit up. "What were you thinking?"

"Create a crisis. Have Canada Revenue Agency to do an audit. And then hit the company with a big fine and penalties, get a judgment against them, maybe garnish their bank account."

Struggling to keep up, Primeau looked doubtful. "Do they have a tax problem?"

"They do now," said Lacroix, rubbing his hands together. "We need to find a way to make Hatfield go to the gang cap in hand, explain what the taxman has done, tell them if they don't step in he's going to have to shut down the business." Lacroix took off his glasses and polished each lens with the corner of his handkerchief. He put them back on and smiled at Davis. "We'll have a word with some people we know and have the tax guys investigate. I'm sure they'll find something. Even if they don't, they can make something up. Just to make sure it looks legit we'll get them to audit some other truckers at the same time." Lacroix looked gleeful. "Just leave it to us."

Primeau looked at the two of them. "You guys really are pieces of work," he said.

Chapter 3

That Sunday morning, as usual, Tony De Riggi dropped his wife off at mass at Saint Patrick's Basilica. He kissed her goodbye and told her he'd be home after lunch. He watched her walk up the steps to the church holding her umbrella against the light drizzle and greet one of her friends, who was waiting for her at the top of the steps. The two walked in together as he pulled out into traffic on Sainte-Catherine Street West and headed across town to the Auberge du Vieux-Port hotel to meet up with the manager.

De Riggi met with Josie Chouinard at 9:30 a.m. almost every Sunday. After a quick recap of the events of the previous week at the hotel, they'd spend the next hour in bed. Josie was a good manager. She was an even better lover. She knew what he wanted. She was used to men like him. At forty-five she was still an attractive woman with a fine figure. She knew her best days were behind her and she had to use her brains, feminine charms and guile to survive. She remembered one of the tales her mother used to read to her when she was a little girl, of Scheherazade, the storyteller from *One Thousand and One Nights*. Josie was no storyteller. She was a good listener though. She gradually became De Riggi's confidante and was surprised at the secrets he'd shared with her.

They'd first met when the gang had acquired the hotel a few years back. Originally a small inn located in Old Montreal with some views of the old port, the hotel had seen better days. He didn't take long to figure out her role at the hotel, or the fact that it was nothing more than a brothel. Josie looked out for the young girls who were employed there. Most of them were under twenty-five, all worked part time in some capacity or other and all of them were escorts, as she liked to call them. De Riggi saw no reason to change things.

And Josie saw the advantage of being with a powerful man. The previous owner had treated her like a piece of meat, would often punch her where it didn't show and ridicule her in front of other men. De Riggi was different, gentler, and he treated her with respect. Maybe he was just a romantic. While she knew it was always about the sex, he took the trouble to make her feel special. She'd often have to help him get an erection, and like most of her clients he would come almost immediately and that was the end of it. Slowly she'd taught him to take his time, and he listened as she described the various ways he could pleasure her. After only a few weeks of knowing her, he'd insisted that she no longer entertain regular customers. And she knew he had ways of checking up on her.

That morning De Riggi stayed longer than he'd intended. She could tell there was something on his mind. She didn't press him, having learned that if a man wanted to share something with you, he'd do it eventually. Suddenly he got out of bed and headed for the shower. He dressed in silence and then embraced her. Putting his forefinger to her lips, he said, "*À bientôt, mon cherie.*"

He was late for his call as he left the hotel on Rue St-Hubert and headed back downtown to his office in his dirty old black Chevy. He could have afforded the latest Caddy, but he always preferred not to draw attention to himself. The cops knew who he was and he didn't want to give them another reason to stop him.

There was little traffic at that time of day. The lobby was empty as he entered the elevator of the old office building. He walked quickly into his office on the tenth floor and sat down at the desk. He called the number his contact had given him. The phone rang and rang. He let it ring for three minutes and then hung up.

Exactly ten minutes later he called again. The contact picked up on the third ring.

"You're late."

"I got delayed. Did everything go according to plan?"

"The cargo arrived safely and has been unloaded. I will call you once it leaves port. Good day, Mr. De Riggi." The contact hung up.

De Riggi wasn't used to such disrespect and was about to tell the guy who he was, but he knew the guy was just some agent in Rotterdam that the mob had used to arrange shipment. Besides, he'd hung up on him before he'd gotten to say anything.

So far, so good, De Riggi thought. He was glad that New York had given them a chance to handle the shipment. If it worked out the way he hoped, they could expect a lot more business, as well as a chance to get a piece of the action going forward.

He looked at his watch. He knew where he'd rather be. Josie would be busy though. And anyway, he was expecting another call. He also needed to meet up with Pigeon and talk about their problem. One of their dealers was claiming some of their drugs were bad. He needed to get to the bottom of the story.

Another call came through, and De Riggi smiled after he put down the phone. Today was a busy day at the docks. The longshoreman had assured him that everything had gone to plan: the shipment had just left the Racine terminal and was on its way. One of several hundred containers unloaded and leaving the terminal that day, it was probably the only one that contained a large quantity of hashish. The container had arrived a few days earlier on a ship from Europe. The manifest described the cargo as machine tools. It wasn't a big shipment, and normally he wouldn't be concerned. Still, this was a new customer, and De Riggi was always cautious when dealing with a new customer. He'd vetoed deals in the past, suspecting the supplier was part of a police sting. Every few years the Montreal police or the Sûreté tried to place one of their own at the docks. They never lasted.

Once the gang discovered who they were, they were either badly beaten and never showed up for work again, or they disappeared. The gang had ties to the construction industry and knew how to get rid of a body for a price or a favour. The police were always hoping to trap them and catch the guys at the dock. This time they were merely ensuring safe passage, for a fee.

The gang had developed a reliable supply chain for their drugs and dealt with a limited number of suppliers. That hadn't always been the case. In the past the gang had imported hash, meth and fentanyl and then sold it on. Occasionally deals went sideways; either the quality didn't meet their standards, or the quantity was overstated. Then there was Customs and the police, always trying to shut them down. He'd known they had to change their business model. Now they offered safe passage for illegal drugs coming through the port rather than buying the drugs and taking all the financial risk.

Establishing their stronghold at the port had been a challenge at first, infiltrating the longshoremen and checkers ranks at the port, fighting off rival gangs, bribing port employees and management. De Riggi had been running the Montreal gang for over fifteen years and had steadily increased their influence at the docks. The gang were able to charge up to twenty-five per cent of the value of goods and take payment in product, never in cash. The only people that paid cash were the police. He wondered how the gang hadn't been caught more often. One of his police contacts told him that Customs checked less than three per cent of all containers passing through the port. There could be up to one thousand containers unloaded daily at the dock. Even when the police knew a container contained drugs and phoned Customs to have the container picked up, within ten minutes of the call the longshoremen would arrange for the container to disappear amongst the hundreds of others. Even when the port installed cameras at the docks, the longshoremen knew where they were, and were able to avoid them.

At their lawyer's prompting, the gang had started to use legitimate businesses to hide the proceeds from the drug trade. They even leased some office space downtown. When the lawyer told him to hire a professional to manage the business, De Riggi drew the line. He didn't like outsiders knowing his business, and he laughed when the lawyer suggested hiring an accountant, until he realized he was being serious. And while he knew he could control his lawyer, because of what he had on him, hiring an outsider to run the business was a different proposition. Business was family, and only family should run it.

***

De Riggi made a stop at the clubhouse in Pointe-Claire before heading home. As he sat back in his chair, waiting for his second-in-command, he reflected on the last five years. He was only fifty-five, but he was worn out. He ran his large hand through his short black hair, touched the small scar just above his right eye and exhaled. He'd put on thirty pounds and had started taking sleeping pills. Though he knew they didn't mix with alcohol, he needed a drink to get through the day. It wasn't just the constant battle to maintain the gang's presence in the port, fighting off the other gangs who were trying to encroach on their turf, paying the right people to keep them happy or look the other way, or making sure he was always in the know when the police had a new initiative to target port crime; there was also his wife of thirty-five years. He'd promised her he'd slow down, be more attentive, lose weight, exercise and spend more time at their place in Florida. Over the years his arthritis had gotten worse, a casualty of the long, cold Montreal winters. He had some good business contacts down there and had even toyed with the idea of managing the business remotely. Though he wasn't sure he wanted to spend the rest of his years with his wife, nor whether his number two could take over.

After about half an hour, De Riggi decided Pigeon wasn't coming and headed home. It was unlike Pigeon not to be there. The guy had no life other than the gang. He needed to get out more and live a little. He'd catch up with him later and bring him up to speed.

Chapter 4

Davis wasn't surprised when Hatfield told him a few days later that he wanted to chat about the business somewhere privately and suggested they go for a beer after work. The bar in the east end of Montreal was almost empty when they walked in the door at 5:00 p.m. The loud music drowned out any chance of them being overheard.

Hatfield went to the bar and brought back two beers, then slid into the booth across from Davis. The old man took a slow breath, his veined hands wrapped around his stein. "Quebec Revenue called today," he began. "They're conducting a sales tax audit."

Davis feigned surprise. "Has anything like this ever happened before?" he asked.

"About eight years ago, the bastards were here for a month. Claimed we weren't recording our sales tax properly. We fought it, but at the end of the day, what with penalties, interest and God knows what else, it cost us about fifty grand. I never really did understand what we did wrong. Shoulda had a decent accountant, I suppose. It's robbery, that's what. I can't afford no lawyers, and I sure as hell don't have the cash to pay another fifty grand this time."

"What are you going to do?"

"Don't know. Bank says there's no more cash. Every nickel I have is tied up in the business, and I'm never gonna see any of that back."

Davis put his beer on the table and looked Hatfield in the eye. "There's no easy way to say this."

The old man ran his hand through the few strands of white hair he still had left on his head and bit his lower lip. "What do you mean?"

"The sales tax audit is the least of your problems."

Hatfield swallowed hard and took another swig of his beer.

"Your fleet is old, your technology is years out of date and if it weren't for one client, you'd have been out of business years ago. At your age you should be retired, sitting on a beach somewhere, not worrying about how you're going to last another week."

"Come on, it's not that bad."

"Dennis, you can barely make payroll. You need at least half a million just to survive. You've got one month before you go under, and that's if you're lucky. The audit, that's just another bill you can't pay."

"What are you saying? Shut down the business? I can't do that, everything I have is in the business."

Davis felt sorry for the old man. His whole life was tied up in the sorry little trucking company. This was his chance. "Have you ever talked to anyone about buying the business?" he asked.

"Who'd buy it? Especially if it's as bad as you say it is."

"What about customers?"

He waited while the old man reflected on his business going down the pan, and his life with it.

Hatfield, who was about to say something, hesitated. For a few minutes he appeared deep in thought, eventually deciding to keep whatever thoughts he had to himself.

"I'm sorry to be so blunt," Davis said. "I thought you needed someone to tell it to you straight."

Hatfield stared at him and finally spoke. "You're right, and you're not the first one to tell me. I was surprised when you joined us. I guess you didn't know how bad it was, did you?"

"The company has a good name, but the days of customer loyalty are long gone, and you're competing on price for every contract. There's nothing unique about your business."

As he finished speaking, he noticed a change in Hatfield. As if a light had gone on. He resisted the temptation to say anything more.

"Well, there is someone …" The old man stared down at his beer.

"What is it?" Davis pressed, though gently.

"Ah it's nothing, just an old man with a silly idea. It wouldn't work, they'd not be interested, I'm sure."

Davis went to the bar and brought back two more beers. He realized it was up to the old man; there was no way he could force him to do anything. What if he didn't go to the gang? What if the gang said no? The months of planning and undercover work would've been a waste of time. There was nothing he could do but wait. Try as he might to get Hatfield to open up, it was as if the old man had decided he'd said too much and wasn't going to say anymore. Davis realized he'd done enough. The rest was up to Hatfield.

Chapter 5

Walter Pigeon was at home in his old house in Saint-Leonard. He was born there and had grown up among the many Italian families it was home to. He'd inherited the run-down old place from his mother. It was about the only thing she ever gave him. He remembered the beatings from his father. The old man took an unnatural interest in him as a small boy, and Walter grew up not knowing that what his father was doing to him was wrong. Like most kids with no future, the gang was the only way out, and through hard work and doing what he was told, he'd not only survived he moved up the ranks. He had always dreamed of taking over from De Riggi, but he knew it was a long way off. He'd proved his worth many times over, and he thought De Riggi viewed him as his loyal lieutenant. He'd cultivated some good business contacts along the way, and one of them, Dennis Hatfield, had proven damn useful over the years. The relationship went back thirty years.

Lately he'd sensed a change. Hatfield had become more distant and kept avoiding his calls. When Pigeon finally confronted him, it all came out. His business was in trouble, had been for some time, and he wasn't sure if it'd survive. He needed money, big time.

Pigeon was more worried about his boss's reaction. The trucker was key to their operations. This hadn't happened overnight, and he knew that he'd dropped the ball. De Riggi would be furious. He'd swear, shout, maybe even shoot somebody. Eventually, once he calmed down, he'd ask Pigeon what he thought they should do. Pigeon knew from experience that you didn't sit on bad news, his boss hated people that did that. So he called De Riggi and told him about the call he'd received from Hatfield.

"Dennis is running out of money, the taxman is all over him, going through his books."

"Why's that our problem?"

"He's struggling to meet payroll and if the tax guys hit him with a big fine, he'll have to shut down."

De Riggi was silent for a few moments. This was the last thing he needed. Sure, he could get another trucking operator to help in the short term. Longer term he needed someone who knew the game. Once other gangs heard about this, they'd be telling customers that he couldn't guarantee delivery of product.

"We've always paid him over the odds, what's he done with the goddamn money?"

"Boss, he's been struggling for a while. Dennis is an old man, he's probably taken his eye off the ball. He wants to meet; claims he has some ideas on how we can help."

"We? Let me guess, he wants us to give him money?"

"Boss, maybe we should carry on this conversation somewhere else. Why don't I meet you at the usual place and we can get into the details?"

De Riggi shared his number two's paranoia about their phones being bugged, and they'd pre-arranged a place to meet whenever there was a crisis. The time was always ninety minutes after they'd hung up.

"Okay, usual time."

"Yes, boss."

***

They met in a room in the Auberge du Vieux-Port in Old Montreal. The gang had acquired the place a few years back as part of the settlement of a turf war. They used it as a place where the girls who worked at their strip clubs could make a little extra money. Sometimes the girls made money offering their services to people that De Riggi dealt with. City officials, planning officers, Port Authority officials, members of the Sûreté and undercover cops on their payroll used from time to time. While most people knew the hotel belonged to the gang, what they didn't know was that there were hidden cameras in certain rooms. The gang didn't always have to use the pictures, but it was handy if somebody needed a little prompting.

The hotel was busy in the summer months, when unsuspecting tourists flocked to the old town and didn't seem to be put off by some of the more scantily clad young ladies that came and went at all hours of the day and night. There'd been complaints by other operators, claiming the place was nothing more than a brothel. De Riggi's lawyer told him he needed to clean up his act or they'd lose their hotel licence. The boss ignored him and had one of his guys pay a visit to the city's licencing office. He suggested the licencing officer see for himself and stay at the hotel for a few nights, free of course. The licencing manager was no match for De Riggi. It wasn't just the free accommodation, food and alcohol. The old guy couldn't resist the attractive young lady whom De Riggi introduced as the hotel manager. Of course, the boss would never have allowed the real manager to take part in the charade. After the first drink, De Riggi was called away on urgent business, leaving the two of them to chat over dinner about the complaints from the local hoteliers.

No sooner had they finished dinner than the poor guy started to slur his speech. His companion needed to get the hotel porter to help him up to his room, where he was undressed and laid on his bed. The young woman decided to join him in bed. In the morning he woke up with a hangover, naked and alone. There was a note on the desk with an envelope containing some very revealing photos of him and the "manager." The note said that management hoped he had a wonderful stay and that he should feel free to come again anytime, and next time be sure to bring his wife. De Riggi never heard from the licencing department again.

Then there was the time he wanted to expand the twenty-room hotel but was running into difficulties with City Hall. The old town had certain restrictions on what you could do with an old building. He was told that the fellow in charge of building permits was a miserable old sod, never left his office, did everything by the book. He thought about his problem for a few weeks, knowing the guy wouldn't fall for the usual trick.

There'd been a recent scandal involving the mayor of Quebec City, who was alleged to have taken bribes for political favours. When the mayor proclaimed his innocence, photos appeared in the local paper showing him receiving an envelope from a known gangster. While nothing was ever proven, the mayor was forced to resign.

De Riggi arranged for one of his men to leave a package addressed marked "Private & Confidential, Mssr. Jollivet" at the official's office at City Hall. Inside the package was a large amount of cash. The package also contained a photograph showing the bureaucrat in charge of building permits shaking hands with Walter Pigeon, along with another photo, blurry but discernibly of Pigeon handing him an envelope.

A month later, to the surprise of most staff in the planning department, planning approval was granted.

He had other reasons for expansion. The gang was moving into human trafficking and wanted a place to house newly arrived young girls from Ukraine. They were told they could make new lives in Canada; they believed it when they saw photos of the Old Montreal hotel where they'd be staying for the first few months until they found employment. Though the gang's prostitution business had grown, clients were looking for something different. Canadian girls were too soft, De Riggi thought, didn't do what they were told and were ungrateful for the new starts that the gang had given them. Many of the girls were from rural Ontario or small-town Quebec, attracted by the bright lights and allure of the big city. He figured girls from a faraway country would be less likely to complain. They'd owe everything to the gang for getting them into Canada and were unlikely to be taken seriously by the cops, especially since most of them couldn't speak English or French.

Madam Josie, however, wasn't happy, even though he'd told her it was short term. She knew he was lying but couldn't do anything. However, it marked a change in their relationship, and set them on a course that he could never have anticipated.

De Riggi was seated in a chair by the window looking out onto the street when Pigeon knocked on the door. "It's open," he called out.

Pigeon walked in and sat in the chair across from his boss. "Hatfield's panicking. He can't handle the pressure, he wants out."

De Riggi blew out his cheeks and threw his hands up. "So, what does he wants us to do?"

"Well … he wondered if we might be interested in … taking it over."

"Why the fuck would we do that if the goddamn thing is losing money!"

"There's only one reason."

"I'm all ears."

"Boss, if we want to continue getting product through the port, we need a trucker. Simple as that." He stopped and assessed his boss for a moment. "Maybe we could buy the company. Make it look like he's still the owner."

"So what you're telling me is because of your fuck up, we now have to buy the business."

While De Riggi had always liked the way his number two didn't hold back, his mouth had gotten him into trouble too many times, and he had the scars to prove it. Too many bar fights with the wrong people. He was never afraid to take someone on, no matter their size. This time he'd dropped the ball big time.

"So what are you saying? That this could be an opportunity?"

"I'm not saying we take it over right away. But we should look at it. He'd give us the company for a buck. We'd just have to fund it."

"How much?"

"No idea, boss. We need to have someone look at the books, figure how bad the trucks are and what it'll cost to get new ones. And then we'd need to find someone to run it."

"Where are we going to find an operator?"

"Don't know, boss, maybe Hatfield has some ideas."

"Let's get the old guy in for a chat."

De Riggi decided to talk to Sean Dunphy. The gang's lawyer had been telling them to diversify for years, expand their business interests and find ways to launder their drug money. Maybe taking over the trucking business wasn't such a bad idea.

Chapter 6

When Davis arrived at the trucking company a few days after his conversation with Hatfield, the old man's office door was closed. The receptionist said he was in a meeting. Davis left his door slightly open then he sat down at his desk. He could hear shouting, and as it grew louder he got up, pretending to shut his door. That's when he saw a rough-looking man in his mid-fifties coming out of Hatfield's office. Dennis looked upset as he followed him out into the yard.

Davis looked out the window as the two men headed toward a pickup truck. Hatfield was trying to catch up to the other man and it appeared as if he was pleading. The shorter man turned on him with a raised hand and was about to strike him when he noticed people watching from the office. He waved the old man away, got into the truck and drove off.

Hatfield threw his hands in the air and turned to head back to the office, when he noticed staff looking at him through the windows. He turned around and headed to his truck parked by the gate, got in and drove off.

Davis asked receptionist if she knew who Hatfield was meeting with.

"I'd rather not say." She walked back to her desk, at which point the other three people looking out the window turned and headed back to their offices.

He decided he would catch up with Hatfield outside of the office. Around one o'clock there was a knock on his door. It was Hatfield. "Let's go for lunch."

As they drove to the restaurant, Davis looked over and asked him who his visitor was.

"A customer. I've asked them to buy the business."

"I take it the meeting didn't go well."

He hesitated and with a tremor in his voice said, "You know … I'm way too old for this game. These guys … you don't want to mess with them."

"What are you talking about?"

"Come on, Alan, you're a pretty smart guy, you must have figured things out by now."

"What are you saying?"

"Those guys, they're important customers. They pay damn well. There's a reason for that.… They're one of the big biker gangs in the city. We move drugs for them. Some of our drivers know what's going on, they just turn a blind eye. Safer that way. The customer doesn't like being pushed into a corner, and that's where they are right now. I've told them I'm going to shut down the business. They'll have to find another trucker, and that's not going to be easy."

They were both quiet for the next several kilometres, but Davis had to know. "Do you think they're going to do it?"

Hatfield pulled into the parking lot and parked before answering. He turned off the ignition, looked at Davis and said, "They're thinking about it. If they do, they're gonna run it their way, and I don't want to be around when that happens."

"What do they know about the trucking business?"

"Nothing. They'll just run more drugs through it. That's how they'll finance their investment."

Davis said, "Come on, let's go eat."

Over lunch the old man was constantly looking around the bar and he spoke in a quieter tone. Davis wondered how much of a secret Hatfield's gang connection really was. On the few occasions he'd been for a drink or had lunch with Hatfield, he noticed that people gave him a wide berth.

"What are you going to do if you don't stick around to run the business?" Davis asked. "They're gonna have a tough time finding someone. Can you say no to these boys?"

"I gotta stick around, I don't have much choice…"

"What do you want me to do?"

Hatfield's large puppy dog eyes and frown told him everything. Davis sighed. "Why would I stick around and run the business for them?"

"They've given me two weeks to find someone. They've made it clear that if I don't come up with someone, they're not putting any money in. And they'll take care of me … permanently."

"Why the hell would they agree to me running the business? They don't know me, I'm a stranger, and I've been here just a few months."

"Anyone I hire will be a stranger to them."

"How involved will they be?"

"We didn't get into the details. They're going to keep a tight handle on the cash. I don't see them getting involved in the day-to-day operations. As long as their shipments go through and they're able to keep losses to a minimum, they won't care."

"Do they know they're going have to spend a bunch of money on new trucks and technology? I'm assuming these guys still wanna make it look like they're running a legitimate business, so no one comes snooping. Do they understand all that comes with running a trucking operation, all the regulations, the licences and permits, both here and in the US?"

Hatfield looked a little sheepish.

"What's the matter?"

"I gave them your report. They said they'd pass it on to their lawyer. Figure out what they needed to do to protect their investment.

You're right though, the last thing they'll want to do is draw attention to themselves, so I doubt that they're going to be actively involved in operations."

Davis didn't know Hatfield had read the report, let alone shared it with the gang. He wondered what the gang had made of it. Would they be suspicious? Would they wonder why there was stuff about Hatfield's financial situation? Would they start to wonder who Davis really was? Or would they assume that this is what a logistics guy would look at?

It didn't matter now, the report was in their hands. He'd have to think of a story about where he'd gotten his financial knowledge and experience.

"Don't kid yourself, Dennis; they're going be more involved than ever."

Chapter 7

"Boss, Hatfield's scared. I told him what we were going to do. I wasn't gentle," Pigeon said.

De Riggi looked at him. "'Course he's scared. The question is, who's going to run the business? They're gonna figure out who we are in no time. The old man's probably already told this logistics guy. If the guy's got half a brain, he's figured it out. I'll be suspicious if he sticks around." De Riggi ran his forefinger up the side of his face ending up at the scar just above his right eye and gently rubbed it. "We need to check out this Davis. Is he really who he says he is? I'll get Dunphy to check into his background, find out if he's got a record."

"Should I pay the guy a visit, boss?"

"Nah. Let's do some digging first. We'll meet Hatfield next week, and if this Davis guy checks out, maybe we tell him to bring him along too."

As he left the club house, Pigeon wondered whether the boss was getting a bit soft. Pigeon had known Hatfield for years and knew how to manipulate him. He was going to find out more about Davis but not tell the boss. In the meantime, he had some unfinished business. A small-time dealer had failed to pay for the product he'd bought from the gang, and Pigeon needed to deliver a message in person. It didn't pay to sit on things. If word got out that nothing was being done, then soon all the small-time scumbags would be doing the same thing. One of the boys had picked the dealer up few days ago in a downtown bar, took him to one of their safe houses and locked him in the basement. Like most dealers he needed a fix on a regular basis, and that was usually the easiest way to deal with these guys. And anyway, they'd had some complaints about the quality of the product lately. Some of it had been suspect. Like someone was cutting it with something. Pigeon had told his guy to try it on the dealer, see what happened.

Pigeon showed up at the safe house a few miles east of the clubhouse, close to the docks, and banged on the door. It was opened by one of the gang members. "How's he doing, Tommy?"

"He's out of it, Walter. I gave him those pills like you told me too. He's barely moved since."

"How many did you give him?"

Tommy looked away.

"How many?"

"Just a couple, honestly."

"How many is a couple?"

"Uh, maybe five or six."

"When did you last check on the little shit?"

"A few hours ago."

They headed to the basement and even before Tommy opened the door, the stench hit them. The dealer had shit his pants and was laying down on the floor in the corner curled up in a ball. For a moment it reminded Pigeon of when he was a kid, just after a visit from his dad. His mother always cleaned up after him and put him to bed. She never made any attempt to stop her husband and never said anything.

The single light bulb didn't throw out much light, but as Pigeon approached the dealer, he could see he was soaked in sweat and not moving. The dealer was supposed to be just a kid. He looked about fifty. Sunken eyes, a thin, pasty yellow face.

"What'd you do to him?"

"Nothing, I swear."

Pigeon kicked the dealer in the back a few times, then bent down and smacked the back of his head. No reaction. The kid's eyes were closed. Pigeon held one hand over his nose and leaned closer. He pulled back one of the kid's eyelids. The pupil was dilated. He was out of it all right.

"Goddammit." Pigeon started back up the stairs. "Don't give him anymore pills, no matter how much he begs. And when he wakes up make him eat something for Christ's sake. I need to talk to this guy before we waste him."

He left the house and got back in his truck. His mind turned to Davis. Who was he, where did he come from? He decided to pay Hatfield a visit at his home. Why hadn't the trucker told him about his business problems? Maybe he was scared, maybe he didn't care anymore. He had everything tied up in the business, it was his life. Had he done enough to check this new guy out?

Chapter 8

Tony De Riggi was a patient man. Doing business the right way had earned him money and a reputation in the community as a successful businessman. Most people had never heard the name Sean Dunphy. Even fewer understood just how important the gang's lawyer was to De Riggi's operation.

Now things were going sideways with their connection at the docks, and De Riggi knew it was time to bring Dunphy in. De Riggi was still pondering his next move when the door to the boardroom of the lawyer's office opened and Dunphy strode in with his arms extended. De Riggi never had much time for lawyers, always covering their backsides with legal words that meant it was never their fault if something went wrong. Still, De Riggi had to admit, Dunphy got results. The man had a knack for legal loopholes, and he could be counted on to come up with ideas to make the gang money while keeping his nose out of their daily business.

"Tony," Dunphy said, kissing the gang leader's cheeks in greeting. "Do you need anything? Coffee? Scotch?"

De Riggi waved the offer away and the two men sat down.

"I read through the reports you sent over," Dunphy said, one hand stroking his bright-blue silk tie. "Hatfield's in big trouble all right—if what this Davis character says is true."

De Riggi placed his hands palms down on the table. "What I wanna know is, if we take over the business, how much it's gonna cost me. And if it can ever make any money." He felt his blood pressure rising and remembered his wife's warning to stop eating so much pasta. Damn. He needed to calm down, and this Hatfield business was not helping. He took a breath. "And I wanna make that money without the goddamn feds on my back."

Dunphy started to laugh, something that immediately irritated the mob boss.

"Tony," the lawyer said smoothly, "the cops already know you guys are involved in Hatfield's business; they've just turned a blind eye."

"What are you saying? We can continue, business as usual like?"

Dunphy leaned in and his thinning brown hair fell forward onto his shiny forehead. "It's not that complicated, actually. You keep Hatfield in place, I'll get someone to look at the numbers and find out what's involved in transferring the licences. We keep your part in all this under the radar, so to speak. And this Davis, well, I think he might be the right guy, but I need to dig a little more. You'll be betting the farm on him if you let him run things. So let's make sure he's legit first."

De Riggi leaned back in his chair and nodded to himself a few times. Finally, he said, "I'm only prepared to lose so much money. I want you to find out if Davis has a record, where he lives, where he came from"—he stroked his chin—"and if he can be bought." De Riggi fell silent, as if he was holding something back.

Dunphy fiddled with the ruby ring on his right hand, watching De Riggi. What was he thinking? Finally the lawyer broke the silence. "Is there anything else I need to know, anything you haven't told me? Because—"

"Nah, that's it."

De Riggi stood up abruptly and Dunphy followed suit. As they moved toward the door, Dunphy told him he would hire an accountant he'd used in the past to go through the books, and someone with a trucking background to find out if Davis could run the business. He would also arrange for a general background check.

De Riggi wondered who he would use. Probably some private dick or an ex-cop. *Someone with access to police databases who can dig up the dirt. Nah, I don't wanna know*, De Riggi thought. The less they knew of each other's plans, the better.

After De Riggi left his office, Dunphy sat back in his chair. He'd been the gang's lawyer for over ten years. At first it was to pay the bills. It had led to a life of luxury he now wasn't willing to give up, even though an old school pal had warned him about De Riggi years ago. He knew he was taking a chance. There was no going back now. He remembered an old judge's words in a case involving a bankrupt lawyer: "When you lie down with dogs, you get up with fleas."

Maybe someday he'd find a way to get rid of De Riggi. Dunphy sighed. *I'd have to change my name and get the hell out of Canada*, he thought. He remembered hearing about a defence lawyer who had acted for an East End gang for years and tried to get out. "The gang fed his lifestyle, nice house, trophy wife with expensive habits, shopping weekends in New York, holidays in Florida. It was a life the lawyer couldn't really afford but couldn't give up if he wanted to keep the wife." At least Dunphy didn't have that problem. He'd been divorced twice and wasn't looking to go through that ever again.

Dunphy had looked at his old friend. "What happened?"

"He told the gang he wanted out. They told him there was only one way the relationship ended. He stopped returning their calls. Then one day, they came for a visit. Let's just say it wasn't a social call. And a week after that, before the bruises had even healed, his wife found him dead in bed. Said it was an overdose, even though the guy never took drugs. In the end, the police didn't bother to investigate. They knew who did it and they knew they'd never get them on it."

***

Ten days later Dunphy met with the accountant he'd hired to look at Hatfield's business on behalf of the gang. He'd used John Smith on numerous occasions, and he liked the way the man operated—he knew the way the game worked; he knew who his client was and why he'd been hired. His biggest asset was discretion. At five hundred bucks an hour, he was pricey, but he was worth every dollar.

"What have you found out?" Dunphy asked.

Smith settled his lanky body into a chair and crossed one long, skinny leg over the other. "A lot of this is not going to come as a surprise to you," he said. "The trucking industry is very competitive, low margins, capital intensive, and even good operators struggle from time to time. The report you gave me from this Davis was helpful. Whatever his background, he knows the industry." Smith adjusted his thick glasses and cleared his throat. "To put it plainly, it's going to cost your client at least two million to upgrade the fleet and the information systems. Not all that money needs to be spent right now—certainly over the next eighteen months to two years. Based on the projections that he came up with, it will probably take six months to a year before this business is cashflow positive. That means they could easily burn through half a million dollars or more. Then they have a working capital deficit of at least half a million, which they'll need to address now or they won't be around in three months. So they need to find another million to fund operations."

Dunphy just listened and made some notes, looking at the list of questions he'd prepared, crossing them off as the bean counter dealt with them.

"The operating licences are valuable; he's had them for years and they're difficult to get these days. The problem he's got is that he's stuck in the middle between the big boys and the small guys. He needs to decide what he's going to be; either focus on the high-end long-haul market or the local market."

The accountant went on for another ten minutes, getting more into the details. Dunphy had heard enough.

"Yeah, yeah. What can you tell me about management?"

Smith looked a little put out at the interruption, but he only said, "If I were your client, that's where I'd spend my time and money to start. Without the right management it's never going to work. They'll be throwing money away."

"Anything else I should know?"

"Well…" Smith uncrossed his legs and bit his lip. "There is one thing—and this is only gossip—are you aware of the rumour … that one of Hatfield's clients is an East End gang? Supposedly ships containers out of the port. Containers of *illegal substances*."

"Yeah, my client heard that too. It's just a rumour, right?" Dunphy snorted.

Smith looked over his glasses at the lawyer. "Of course, there may be nothing to it. I just thought you should know. I spoke to a few people who know the industry, on a no-names basis obviously."

Dunphy appeared deep in thought for a few moments. Then he looked up at Smith. "If this thing is going to see the light of day, I wanna make sure I'm protected." He leaned forward in his chair. "The rumour about the gang, that's just between you and me. Understood?"

"Of course." The two men shook hands before the accountant got up, carefully wiped his hand with a handkerchief and headed for the door.

Chapter 9

The following week, De Riggi and Pigeon were on their way to the clubhouse. Located in a light industrial area, the building looked more like some high-end tech business, with security cameras and a large gate surrounded by a seven-foot-high wall. When the small businesses nearby discovered who their neighbours really were, many began moving out. Despite complaints to the landlord and numerous visits from the police, they were told that the owner of the so-called security business owned the land as well as the building and there was nothing they could do about it.

The clubhouse was empty when they arrived, and Pigeon had to punch in the security code to open the gate. He looked along the street at the other businesses and wondered what they must think of their "security company." It was still early so he wasn't surprised that none of the gang was there. The four vacant buildings gave him some ideas for how they could expand their business. He wanted to give it some more thought before he shared them with the boss. Maybe he'd run them by Dunphy.

De Riggi was in a pensive mood. The information he had gotten from his police contacts hadn't told him anything. It looked like this

Davis guy was as clean as a whistle, had worked in Toronto for fifteen years in the trucking industry, met a girl from Montreal a few years ago, then split up. He sounded like a bit of a hermit. Nothing was ever as it seemed though, and if they hired him to take over the business, De Riggi intended to keep a careful eye on him.

Pigeon's voice pulled De Riggi from his thoughts. "Boss, we got a lot riding on this Davis guy. For all we know, he could be a snitch."

De Riggi stared at his second-in-command's profile. "What are you talking about?"

Pigeon glanced away from the road and caught his boss's eye. "Don't you find it strange that this guy shows up from nowhere, out of the blue?"

"He used to work in Toronto, then he moved here. Something about a woman. It happens, Walter."

"If you were working in the trucking industry, why would you move from Toronto? And why would you come from Toronto to Montreal just for a woman? I'm not buying it, there's more to this guy than meets the eye." Pigeon knew his boss liked to work things out for himself and if someone else had a differing opinion, it might take a while for him to come onside. He had to keep presenting the evidence. "What if he's undercover? Sometimes it's better to walk away. It would sure save us a lot of money and cause us a lot less grief. At least use the time to check him out."

De Riggi sat back in his seat. "You're starting to think like a boss, my friend. One step ahead." He was quiet for a few moments. Maybe there was something to what Pigeon was saying. They couldn't be too careful. Losing the business at the docks would be catastrophic. Hiring a snitch would be ten times worse.

"Okay. Check him out," De Riggi said finally. "Call our friend at the Sûreté, see what they can dig up."

Pigeon smiled and rubbed his hands together. Finally the boss was starting to make some sense. There was no way they were going to get into bed with some guy without knowing anything about him. If the guy had half a brain, he'd know who he was working for. He'd rather know up front whether the guy had a problem with them. Just in case, they should be looking for another trucker. Sometimes you had to let the chips fall where they may, even if it meant delaying a few shipments.

Pigeon was still feeling bad for dropping the ball. Hatfield was his baby, his relationship, and he should have been on top of it. There was a balance between staying in touch and getting too involved. Maybe the old man was scared to let him know he was having problems. Whatever the case, he wouldn't make a mistake like that again.

De Riggi stared at his second-in-command and almost chuckled. *Pigeon trusts no one*, he thought. A grumble from his stomach drew his attention. Damn diet. How could a man survive on half a plate of pasta with no sugo or panini? This was no way to live. But if they moved to Florida … if he got out of this life, he wouldn't have so much stress. Maybe his heart would settle down and he could eat again, damnit.

De Riggi shifted in his seat. "I'm getting tired of all this, Walter. The fighting with police, the other gangs, the constant grind. I need to slow down."

Pigeon's forehead creased. This was what had been worrying him for a while now. His old friend was getting soft. He felt genuine shock when he heard the boss's next words.

"You interested in taking over?"

Pigeon opened his mouth and closed it again. "The gang's my life, what else would I do, boss?" He glanced at De Riggi. "You're gonna be around for a while, aren't you?

"I don't know, Walter. The wife keeps going on about spending time down south. I've been promising her for years we'll take a long holiday. Trouble is there's always something going on, you can't take your eye off the ball for even a minute. This business with Hatfield…" De Riggi blew out his breath, and Pigeon felt a twinge of guilt. "I'd like to stay involved, but going down to Florida for three months … how's that gonna work?"

"You never know boss, maybe you could make some contacts down there that'd be good for business."

He hadn't told his boss that he'd already been tracking Davis for a couple of weeks. He almost mentioned it then but held back. De Riggi liked to give the orders. He didn't like to find out his underlings were going out on their own.

There was a lot to follow up on. Davis had a small farmhouse near East Farnham, just outside of Bromont in the Eastern Townships, a one-hour drive east of Montreal. It was a strange place to live. The village had a population of five hundred.

Pigeon had a guy keeping an eye on the place. He had even followed Davis into the local village one morning. The village only had a dozen or so stores, two small restaurants and a few taverns. He had to be careful not to walk into Davis. When he finally saw Davis walking in his direction, he was carrying a bag of groceries. He turned around and walked back the way he came. When the guy told him he thought he'd been spotted, Pigeon smiled. He liked the idea that Davis knew he was being watched.

Chapter 10

November 27, 1983

Davis hadn't wanted to come to this meeting, especially now when it was almost dark and no one was around. He sat on the designated bench and rubbed his hands together, thinking about everything that had happened over the past few weeks. The gang's attempts to tail him were a joke. He'd been followed more than once. Most recently, a car followed him for at least thirty miles as he headed home back to the Townships one evening. Maybe they wanted him to know he was being checked out. Either way, it wasn't very subtle. Neither was the way they ransacked his place. Not only did they leave a mess and not find anything, but a few things were stolen. Things that wouldn't have meant anything to most people, like the fake photo of his ex and a couple of philosophy books. Even the fake letter of recommendation from the Toronto trucking company was missing.

Davis let it all roll off him. He wondered how long it would go on. He thought about what he'd do if he were De Riggi or Pigeon. Of course, he wasn't thinking the way they were thinking. They would threaten him, maybe even beat him up. He, on the other hand, would probably have just sat down one on one and explained the facts of life and the choices he had. Either he'd cooperate, be part of the team and be well rewarded, or not. If not, there would be consequences.

There might be a test. They'd want to know if he could be controlled and would turn a blind eye to what was going on around him. The test would involve violence against someone close to him or someone that he worked with. They might target Hatfield. That thought made him feel a little sick. He'd come to respect the old man.

Five minutes to four. Davis stared at the mist on the lake, and for some reason an image of his daughter—perpetually a toddler—suddenly took over his mind. He wondered if he'd ever see her again.

Footsteps crunched on the frozen path and Davis turned toward moving shadows, straining to hear the voices—there were at least two of them. He stood up.

Tony De Riggi's second-in-command, Walter Pigeon, was coming toward him with a taller man Davis didn't recognize. Apparently De Riggi had better things to do than be at this meeting. *This is it. They either accept me or I'm dead.*

Pigeon's squeaky voice cut through the fog. Davis felt his heart pick up pace as Pigeon told him they'd been checking him out.

"The boss thinks you're the right guy," he said. "In my book you need to work with someone a long time to gain their trust. I'm damn good at smelling a rat, and you need to know what we do with rats."

He turned to the other man. "What do we do with rats, Harry?"

Harry didn't seem to know.

"Come on, Harry, speak up, tell him what we do with rats."

"We deal with them, boss."

"That's right. We crush 'em because they're vermin."

"Yes, boss."

Pigeon took a gun from his pocket and moved it from one hand to the other a few times. Then he pointed it right at Davis's head and smiled. "This is how we deal with rats," he said.

He turned, swinging the weapon toward the taller man, and put two bullets in his forehead.

Harry fell back and hit the ground, a stunned look on his face.

Davis forced himself to look away. Pigeon had taken out a handkerchief and was wiping blood spray from his face. He glanced at Davis as he folded the handkerchief and pushed it into his pocket. Davis thought he could feel splatter on his face too, but he stood frozen to the ground, willing his hands to unclench as they hung by his side. Pigeon half smiled and gave him a mock salute before he turned. "We'll be in touch," he said as he walked away.

Davis's heart jumped and he took a deep breath. He stood there for what seemed like several minutes. He didn't need to check on Harry. The man was lying spreadeagled, grey and white brain matter a few inches from where he fell. The bullets had gone clean though the back of his head.

Davis managed a few steps before he doubled over and threw up on the frozen path. He needed to get out of there; someone walking their dog might have heard the shots.

Before he drove to his farmhouse, he stopped in the village and made a call from the local telephone booth. "You need to check out the park, near the lake. There's a guy by one of the benches, name of Harry Parker. Pigeon just put two bullets in his head. We need to meet. Usual place, tomorrow, nine a.m." He hung up.

Back at the farmhouse, Davis's heart was still pounding as he'd poured himself a whisky and tried to relax in his leather chair. The meeting with Pigeon was making him question his decision to go undercover more than ever.

He kept replaying it in his mind—the gun pointed at his head, the blood splatter, the grey matter, his own vomit—he'd witnessed too many killings, and no matter what people say, you never forget them. He kept replaying the moment in his head until finally he dozed off.

***

"So who was Harry Parker?"

Primeau pointed to a chair and Davis sat down. "Harry was a small-time gang member. Rumour has it he was shortchanging the gang on drug deals. That's not what got him killed though. He was leaking information to the Montreal police."

Davis shifted in his chair, then looked up at his handler. "About what?"

"It doesn't matter. The gang found out what was going on and decided to deal with him. And they brought him along to the meeting to show you they mean business."

Lacroix had begun pacing, and now he turned and stared at Davis intensely. "What did Pigeon say when you met?"

"Just that they checked me out. De Riggi seems comfortable, but Pigeon, that guy doesn't trust anyone. I think the little man is gonna keep tabs on me. He went on about rats and what they do with them, then pulled his piece and shot poor Harry, as calm as you like. And just smiled at me and walked away."

"That's some warning," said Primeau.

Davis shrugged. "Pigeon's a psycho. I've seen it before."

"So have I," said Lacroix, back to his pacing. He turned suddenly toward them. "And I'm sure this wasn't sanctioned by De Riggi."

"Yeah, well, Pigeon might be the one in charge soon," said Davis.

"Why do you say that?" Lacroix asked, stopping in midstride.

"Hatfield. He said De Riggi's getting tired of all the hassle, the infighting with all the gangs, increased police surveillance. The old man wants to step back, spend some time down south."

Primeau rubbed his chin. "So how do we handle Pigeon?"

"That depends." Lacroix looked at Davis. "Are you still prepared to carry on? There'll be no turning back."

Davis nodded. "I've spent almost a year building this cover with Hatfield."

"Okay. Well then, we need to discredit Pigeon in the eyes of the gang," said Lacroix.

"What are you thinking?" Primeau asked.

Lacroix's eyes were sparkling as he looked back and forth between them. "Something that'll get De Riggi's attention, scare him. Like a rumour that he's an informer..."

Davis stared at him. "You start a rumour like that, his reputation is shot. Not only that—he's a dead man."

Primeau shook his head. "Nah. He's been a member for over twenty years. Now suddenly he's a rat? Who's going to believe that?"

Lacroix turned to Davis. "We've got to tap into the gang's contacts, someone De Riggi trusts. A port official, someone in the Sûreté. First we share it with someone we know is not on the take and have them pass it on."

Primeau rolled his eyes. "You lie awake at night thinking up this stuff, Bernie?"

Davis didn't listen to Lacroix's comeback. He was busy wondering if this had been their plan all along, and if sidelining Pigeon was just the first step. Davis looked up. "You wanna take out De Riggi next, is that it? I show up out of nowhere and five minutes later take over the gang? That's a long shot."

Lacroix looked distressed. "That was never the plan. Right now we take out Pigeon—and this is as good a way as any. There's no one else there that could take over; most of those guys can't tie their own shoelaces, let alone think for themselves."

Davis wasn't convinced. Why take out Walter Pigeon unless they planned for Davis to take his place? He was quiet for a while, running a bunch of ideas through his mind as his handlers exchanged glances. *Their endgame isn't taking down the gang. It's finding out who the gang's contacts are at the port, the City and the Sûreté. Having someone at the top of the gang would be a dream come true. It'd make me indispensable to De Riggi. Then something happens to De Riggi, an accident, whatever, and I take over.*

Davis wasn't sure how he felt about this, nor what it meant for him. And if they took care of Pigeon and found a way to sideline De Riggi, he'd become a high-profile gang leader.

Davis knew that meant he'd be exposed to dangers from other gangs who saw a chance to eliminate the competition and take over their turf. Then there'd be De Riggi's gang members, likely pissed off that an outsider took over, not to mention the police and other agencies who weren't privy to their plan. *Who'll be covering my back?*

Davis frowned. He'd been the RCMP's pawn all along, and an expendable one at that.

Chapter 11

De Riggi and Pigeon met at Sean Dunphy's office half an hour before Hatfield and Davis were due to arrive and went through the list of questions the lawyer had prepared. Dunphy could tell that De Riggi wasn't prepared and, as usual, was planning on winging it. He also worried about what Pigeon would say. Pigeon had made it clear he had no time for Davis, claiming he couldn't be trusted despite the report from Dunphy's accountant and his own guys, who'd apparently been watching Davis for some time now.

After his conversation with De Riggi, Pigeon had had one of his guys park his camper van half a kilometre away from the farmhouse, just off the main road, to keep an eye on Davis. For two days Gagnon reported no activity. Then early one morning Davis left the farm and headed along the road east toward Montreal. A perfect opportunity to check the place out. Gagnon had walked around the outside and checked the outbuildings. The place appeared deserted. He knocked loudly on front door, knowing the place would be empty. He waited sixty seconds and then forced the lock. There was a small living room, a tiny kitchen and two bedrooms. The place was tidy but bare. There was no TV, no photos of girlfriends or kids. He found a small desk, unlocked. Mostly bills, a chequebook in the name of Alan Davis, and some old correspondence with Davis's Toronto address.

Tidiness wasn't something Gagnon was used to, so everything felt wrong to him. He ran his eye along the bookshelf. Apart from books on the city of Montreal and the Townships, there were a few mystery books by a guy named Blunt and two books on philosophy by a guy named Kant. Inside one of the books was a photo of a woman in her forties. Not unattractive.

He reported this back to Pigeon, who wasn't sure what to make of it all. Pigeon had Gagnon check out this Kant at the library. It turned out he was a philosopher from Germany who'd been dead for two hundred years. Pigeon became even more suspicious. What kind of person read stuff like that?

Dunphy didn't pay much attention to Pigeon's report and told them how he planned to run the meeting. De Riggi just nodded, anxious to get on with it.

When Hatfield and Davis arrived, they were shown into the lawyer's boardroom. Shortly after, De Riggi, Pigeon and Dunphy joined them. After the introductions were made, Hatfield suggested that Davis give them an overview of his report.

Davis briefly looked down at his notepad, which was full of handwritten comments, and then looked up. Slowly and methodically he talked them through the key issues as he saw them. While he was talking, De Riggi noticed Pigeon staring at Davis. He kicked Pigeon hard under the table, not caring if anyone noticed.

Pigeon grunted, interrupting Davis's explanation, then looked at Hatfield. "So who's gonna run the business? This guy?" He jabbed a thumb in Davis's direction. "I mean, let's face it, Dennis, you're done."

Dunphy cringed. Davis noticed that De Riggi was showing no emotion. Hatfield seemed overwhelmed by the thought of losing control of his business. The old man was staring blankly at the table, his eyes glassy.

Davis cleared his throat. "Dennis is the face of the business," he said. "It's important to keep him in place, especially if we don't want to draw any attention from our customers or the licensing authorities." He turned to Hatfield and his voice was gentler when he said, "Slowing down will be good for you, Dennis. Maybe even take a vacation, once things settle. I'm happy to step in and run the business until things have turned around." He looked directly at De Riggi. "I need to know who I'm working for and how involved you'll be."

De Riggi wasn't sure why he liked this guy, apart from the fact that he wasn't pulling any punches. He was starting to think he could work with him.

Pigeon was still glowering from the other side of the table. *Why does this guy want to stick around?* He leaned forward and pointed a short finger at Davis.

"What we'd like to know is where you're from, your background, your plans. And just how long do you see yourself running this company?"

Davis sat back in his chair and silently observed the little man across from him until finally Pigeon sat back too, an ugly look on his face. Davis shrugged, glancing at De Riggi and Dunphy. "I can't tell you how to run the business. All I can tell you is how *I* would run the business. You'll require regular reports, I get that. At the end of the day, it comes down to the cash in the bank, and the bottom line."

De Riggi was nodding along. He really liked this guy's no-bullshit style.

Davis looked around at them all. "I'm not saying it's going to be easy, and if it were my money, I'd go slow. Invest enough to keep it afloat, upgrade the fleet over three years or so. You give me some capital to operate over the next twelve months and we go from there. That gives you the option of cutting your losses any time."

Pigeon was about to say something when De Riggi put his hand up. "I like your style, Davis. But it's like this—see, we got a lotta business interests. I'd like to think of us as hands off, so to speak. I'm not interested in day-to-day management." He shifted forward, leaning his forearms on the table. "We might pay you a visit now and then"—he glanced at Pigeon with a half smile—"but running this business, well, that would be down to you, or someone like you. We need someone with industry experience and an eye to the future."

Dunphy smiled to himself. De Riggi sounded more like a businessman than a gangster. Maybe the boss been listening to him after all. And while De Riggi was doing a good selling job, Pigeon was an open book. He didn't like Davis and made no effort to hide it or his doubts about the venture.

Dunphy was afraid that the man's attitude would undermine things. A break was in order. He stood up. "Let me get my secretary to bring in some sandwiches or something."

Leaving Davis and Hatfield in the conference room, De Riggi and Pigeon met privately with Dunphy in the lawyer's office. The boss stood by the window, looking out on the street below while Dunphy sat at his desk eating a sandwich. He turned and looked at Dunphy. "Walter has made it clear what he thinks of Davis. What do you make of him?"

Dunphy took a sip of his coffee. "Tough to tell, Tony. I guess the real question is, why would he stick around and run this failing business? He's obviously a smart guy, I'm sure he knows who you are and what Hatfield's been doing. He knows what he's getting into."

Pigeon, who'd been lurking by the doorway, jumped in. "This joker is too good to be true, Tony. Shows up out of the blue. References check out, but so what? Probably fake."

De Riggi looked at him. "It's clear to everyone what you think. I bet you don't even trust your goddamn mother."

Dunphy said, "I have to say, it's a healthy attitude to have, especially in your line of business."

De Riggi looked at the lawyer. *The man shouldn't wear such colourful shirts*, he thought. "Don't you mean *our* business, Sean?"

"Yeah, yeah, our business. And just to be sure we can do some more digging on Davis. Put Walter's mind at ease."

"And if he's a rat?"

De Riggi looked from his second-in-command to his lawyer. "What do you think, Sean? The police aren't that smart, are they?"

Dunphy smoothed the purple pocket square in his breast pocket. "It's hard to believe they'd go to all this trouble."

De Riggi nodded. Pigeon was bursting to say more. De Riggi put his hand up. "Walter, you're never gonna trust him. I get that. But when you take over, you've gotta learn to trust *somebody*."

Dunphy looked from the boss to his underling. This was the first he'd heard about Pigeon taking over. "You're retiring, Tony?"

"Nah, just planning to spend a bit more time down south. Don't you worry. It's important to build for the future, Walter knows that just as much as anyone. Right now, if we're gonna take over Hatfield's business, this isn't a good time for me to go anywhere. Maybe in a few months, once we've figured out whether this is gonna work."

Dunphy had more questions but decided that the less he knew, the better. He was already in too deep, and Pigeon might want a different lawyer once he took over. Dunphy set his coffee down and adjusted his tie. "Lemme dig a little deeper on Davis, get the accountant to go through the books more thoroughly, figure out how big the hole really is."

Back in the boardroom, Hatfield was eating a sandwich. Davis wasn't hungry; he was too busy thinking about De Riggi and Pigeon. Pigeon's cynical approach was probably just the way he was—it was hard to believe it was just an act. He clearly had problems relating to anybody. He wasn't sure how he'd be able to work with him. For all the bad things he'd heard about De Riggi, he came across as almost friendly. The lawyer was just a go-between. Likely he'd gotten in over his head and couldn't get out. He'd seen it before. A lawyer would get gang members out of jail, the pay was good, then suddenly he was trapped and there was no way out.

Davis looked at Hatfield. "How do you think the meeting's going?"

Hatfield swallowed a large bite and wiped his mouth with a napkin. "They're sizing you up, trying to figure out if they can work with you, deciding whether you're your own man or not—and whether they can control you." He took a drink of water and looked at Davis thoughtfully. "They don't have many options, Alan. In the end, they'll probably choose to work with you. Just understand, getting into bed with these guys … it's a big price to pay."

"Too late for regrets now."

Hatfield looked pained. "I turned a blind eye for too many years. I always knew what they were doing, but … hell, we needed the money. It was easy to pretend not to notice. I never asked any questions. Then … it was too late." A look of understanding passed between the two men. "It's not too late for you, Alan. And once you're in, there's no way out."

Davis had heard those words before. "You're sure they're going to take it over?"

Just as Hatfield was about to reply, the door opened.

De Riggi and Pigeon came in, followed by Dunphy, who was carrying a fresh pot of coffee. His clients sat down opposite Hatfield and Davis. Dunphy placed the coffee pot in the middle of the table and sat down next to De Riggi.

"Okay, Dennis, this is what we're gonna do." De Riggi looked over at Davis and then Hatfield, his dark-brown eyes darting between the two. "We're going to fund this thing for the next few months and see how it goes. We'll check out the numbers, figure out what new trucks really cost, the whole deal. We'll also get an idea of how long it'll take me to make money." He stopped for a few seconds to pour some cream into his coffee, then looked up again, his eyes focused on Davis. "It also gives us a chance to get to know Mr. Davis here. See if we can work together." He glanced at Pigeon, then faced Davis again. "And like I said, we're hands off. The less we're involved in the business, the better for all concerned."

Davis silently held the man's gaze.

Finally, De Riggi smiled. "If that works for you and we like what we see, well, there shouldn't any problem. If the business can get back on track, and"—he looked over at Hatfield—"things don't go off the rails…"

There was an awkward silence. Hatfield had been told, and Davis had been given, the boundaries. Davis sat back and crossed his arms. People often said too much, feeling they needed to fill the silence with idle chatter. He always learned more by just sitting back and saying nothing.

Hatfield, on the other hand, needed to end the silence. "What plans do you have for me?"

De Riggi looked at Pigeon, as if the question had been anticipated, and said, "That depends on you, Dennis. We'd like to think you're still part of the team, sticking around in the background, and if things work out, who knows. Walter tells me you need a bit of a holiday, somewhere in the sun. So maybe we'll find you a nice little place down in Florida, somewhere you can go for a few months."

Davis wondered what De Riggi meant by "taking a holiday." The old guy was on his own and it wouldn't take much to get rid of him, especially if the gang wanted his silence. Maybe it was something they could hold over Davis. If he stayed, Hatfield would be protected. If they did want to get rid of the old man, Florida was far enough away, accidents happen. They could just as easily happen in Montreal though, and they probably had ways of making sure he disappeared without a trace.

De Riggi interrupted Davis's thoughts. "So what do you think? Interested in sticking around, see if this thing can make it?"

Davis took his time replying. He leaned forward and looked at De Riggi, "As long as you understand what you're getting into, how much it's going to cost to fix the business, and how long it could take. Remember, there will be bumps along the road." He paused, trying to gauge De Riggi's reaction, and then continued. "You don't have the luxury of time. You're going to have to put your hand in your pocket, catch up on the old bills and deal with the taxman."

Davis sat back in his chair. Had he overplayed his hand, painted too bleak a picture, or even come across like it was his way or the highway?

De Riggi smiled. "We know this thing's bleeding like a pig. But if it can make money in the longer run, we won't interfere."

Dunphy decided it was time to move things along. "Okay, any more questions?" When no one responded, the lawyer turned to

Davis. "We'd like a budget for the next three months, so we can arrange short-term funding. I'll prepare a list of next steps and I'll be in touch with you before the end of the week. Oh, and yes, all communications will go through me."

Davis and Hatfield got up and walked over to the other side of the table. De Riggi, who was smiling, stood up and held out his hand. Davis shook it. Despite his large hands, De Riggi's handshake was firm but not crushing. Meanwhile Pigeon was sharing something with Hatfield that he couldn't quite hear. De Riggi guided Davis to the door, resting his powerful hand on Davis's shoulder. Davis looked him in the eye, wondering how much they had in common. *If only he knew*, he thought. A moment later, Hatfield followed him out the door.

De Riggi watched them leave with a frown. He had a large shipment coming from Antwerp and it had to clear the docks. He had a lot riding on it, and he'd do anything to make sure everything went well. New York had a lot invested in the deal and would hold him accountable if anything went wrong.

Chapter 12

A few weeks later Davis was sitting at his desk at Hatfield's reading *La Presse*. He reflected on recent events. He'd been impressed by the people that the gang's lawyer had hired to look at Hatfield's operation. They clearly knew the trucking industry, and Davis could tell they didn't think much of the state of Hatfield's finances or the financial controls. They also asked him a lot of questions about his background and whom he had worked with while in Toronto. One of them even mentioned some people who'd worked at Davis's old company. Davis told him he'd never heard of some of the people. The handlers' story that he'd worked at just one company in Toronto made it easier for him to follow the script. He'd done his homework and knew his lines, knowing that some of the names the guy had come up with had been a trap.

He still hadn't heard anything from De Riggi since they'd met in Dunphy's office.

A knock at the door pulled him from his thoughts. Davis looked up as Hatfield walked into his office. "Good news. That was Walter on the phone. Mr. De Riggi wants to meet."

Davis set the paper he'd been reading down and leaned back in his chair.

"He wants to have a little chat," Hatfield continued. "Make sure you understand the rules. Make sure it's clear: it's their business, their money, their way of doing things."

Davis felt the strange combination of relief and trepidation for the future. Apparently the gang hadn't found any red flags—they'd bought his cover. And that meant he was going to be getting even deeper into this mess.

"Said he wanted to meet on the weekend," Hatfield was saying. "A place in the Townships. He said you'd know it, a lake near a village just outside of Bromont. Mean anything to you?"

Davis nodded. "It's where I live. De Riggi's been having me followed for some time now."

***

The following week, Davis sat in his office at the docks with the door shut and paper scattered uncharacteristically across his desk. The meeting with De Riggi had been as short as he'd expected. The gang boss had greenlit a million dollars in funding so Davis could start to turn Hatfield's trucking company around. He'd also made it clear that if anything went wrong, it was on Davis's head. Since then, Davis had barely had time to sleep, and finally the big money transfer was coming through. Things were happening fast, maybe too fast.

Davis picked up his phone and called Dunphy. He'd need to meet the lawyer to work out a few more details now that a cool million dollars was being dropped into his lap. And Davis wanted to know more about the gang's role. He doubted they'd want a paper trail and would keep communications to a minimum. They'd put someone in the business so they could keep an eye on things. He needed an understanding with Dunphy.

Davis headed out just before lunch and parked close to the lawyer's office, not far from McGill University. There was a park there where they could meet. A lot of people were coming and going. It had been an unusually cold winter morning. He sat on the bench waiting for Dunphy, his parka shielding him from the cold wind. He couldn't understand why the youngsters were dressed only in jeans and a jacket. Most of them were students on their way to classes or to the nearest pub for lunch. Dunphy came alone and waved to him as he approached. He waved his newspaper, motioning Davis to catch up with him as he carried on walking.

It was difficult to see if they were being watched. The lawyer didn't seem to be bothered. Wearing a brown woolen coat, a stylish red scarf and shiny brown boots, Dunphy slowed down to allow him to catch up.

"Let's keep walking, Mr. Davis. It's too cold to be hanging around." For a small man Dunphy walked quickly, his thin brown hair blowing across his pale forehead that was turning pink from the cold. "I'll keep this simple. You'll be hiring a John Smith to act as our eyes and ears. You'll find him quite knowledgeable. Mr. Hatfield will execute a transfer of his shares in Hatfield to a numbered company. The transfer will be held by me in trust on behalf of my client. All communication will be through Mr. Smith. I doubt you'll meet with me or Mr. De Riggi on a regular basis. Mr. Pigeon seems to have made you his special project." The lawyer smiled despite the frigid wind cutting across them.

"I can only apologize for his behaviour. If it ever gets to a point where the situation becomes unworkable, let Smith know." Here Dunphy stopped and faced Davis. "We'll meet again in a few months unless you need to meet sooner. Any questions?"

"What does your Mr. Smith know about the trucking industry?"

"Absolutely nothing. He's a qualified accountant and, most importantly, very discreet."

He had more questions, but the lawyer, who was practically dancing on the spot to maintain some warmth, cut him off. "I'll say goodbye now. Good luck."

Dunphy turned and fast-walked back in the direction he'd come from.

Davis stood there watching him. Then he looked around to see if anyone was watching either of them. He didn't see anybody.

Chapter 13

Over the following months, Hatfield's company continued to bleed cash, but slowly things started to improve. The gang ran more shipments through them, and Davis acquired more trucks, took on more business and started doing longer hauls.

Never once did any member of the gang show up at the company's operations. However, on regular occasions Davis saw Pigeon and other people that he believed worked for the gang in the village of Bromont. None of them ever made any attempt to engage him. On one occasion he saw Pigeon seated at a table in the local pub. The small man made no attempt to acknowledge him. Davis didn't react, assuming it was his way of reminding him that he knew where he lived and was keeping an eye on him.

Then one late afternoon in early March, Dunphy surprised him by showing up at his office at Hatfield's. He looked slick as usual in a shiny suit, heavy winter coat and fur-lined winter boots. He asked Davis if he had any whisky. After Davis had poured him a drink, the lawyer settled into a worn-out leather chair in the corner of the office. Davis was wary. Dunphy had never come to see him here before. Was the gang unhappy with the results? Had they changed their mind? He couldn't imagine what he wanted to talk about. Had they found another trucker?

"You seem to be getting to grips with the trucking company. Think you can do the same thing with other businesses?"

"What other businesses?"

Dunphy finished a generous swallow of scotch before answering. "Oh, you know … From time to time my clients come across business opportunities." He paused, waiting for Davis to react. "And I'm guessing this day-to-day grind is gonna bore you before too long—if you aren't already there."

"Hatfield's isn't out of the woods. There's a long way to go before it starts making money."

Dunphy waved this away. "Yes, yes…" He leaned forward in his chair. "Would you be interested in at least looking? And maybe even managing one of them if Tony decided to … take it over?"

Davis smiled to himself. Dunphy and the gang had decided that he could make a far bigger contribution than just running Hatfield's. "Who would I be reporting to?"

"Mr. De Riggi, of course." Sensing Davis's hesitation, Dunphy added, "I believe Mr. Pigeon would be involved too."

"Right now the best use of my time is to make sure Hatfield's survives. Then I'll need to find someone to take over the day-to-day operations. At that point, if all goes well, I should have some time to look at other opportunities."

"Makes sense, of course, but I wonder…" Dunphy lifted his briefcase onto his lap and flipped it open. "In the meantime, I wonder if you could look at some other business opportunities my client has been considering?" The lawyer's polite tone masked what was really a demand, and before Davis could respond, he pulled out some folders and laid them on the desk. "Go ahead, have a look."

Davis opened the first folder. There were brochures on several motels, financial statements and operational reports detailing average room occupancy, room rates, gross profit and net profitability. The only thing they had in common was they all seemed to be losing money. The second folder held information on a mortgage investment company. The third contained background on a construction company, along with a list of contracts, history of revenue and profitability.

"They're buying all three businesses?"

He smiled. "Maybe. This is where you come in. We want you to tell us what you think. What makes sense, what doesn't—"

"I can't just drop everything and spend time looking at other businesses."

Dunphy waved away his concerns. "Hatfield's is heading in the right direction. And with opportunities like this, sometimes it's better to act quickly." He set his glass down and stood up. "I'll leave the files with you," he said as he walked to the door. "Thanks for the drink."

Chapter 14

That evening De Riggi was seated by the fireside sipping a glass of grappa in his home office. While he wasn't a solitary person, there were times when he just wanted to relax with his own company. He needed to slow down but had too many things on the go. He had been reflecting lately on what made him happy and had realized that spending time with Josie was what got him through the week.

Even at home he couldn't unwind. His wife was unhappy, and so was he. There was no way he'd be happy with her down in Miami, or anywhere else for that matter. He had trouble remembering a time when they had loved each other. Looking back on it, maybe if she'd been able to have kids it might have been different. It wasn't to be. And for decades, she'd put up with his lifestyle, never complained and was probably aware of the women who'd come in and out of his life. *Am I going through a midlife crisis? No. I just want more out of life.*

And then there was Pigeon. De Riggi took a slug of his grappa and grimaced. He had to be honest with himself: it was becoming clear that Walter just didn't have what it took to lead the gang. He didn't have the vision, pissed off too many people and was just too difficult to deal with. He didn't have a filter and didn't know when to let something go. Even in their business there were times when you had to compromise. His biggest problem was his paranoia. It made sense to be cautious in their line of business, but sooner or later you had to learn to trust somebody or deals simply could not get done.

De Riggi poured himself a little more grappa and ignored the voice telling him he should drink less. Would he still be involved with the gang in ten years? While he didn't want to give it up completely, what if there was a way? Could he bring someone on to take over while he spent more time down south? He'd never been much of a planner, more of an opportunist, seizing the moment, taking risks along the way. And he liked being in control.

He leaned back in his chair and held the shot glass just below his nose. He loved the citrusy aroma, the heavy fruit of the brandy. De Riggi sighed. He wasn't sure what to make of Davis. He had to admit he was impressed; the guy was smooth, didn't seem to get upset, no matter how much pressure was put on him. He wondered what he would be like to work with. Of course, Walter didn't trust him. Walter didn't trust anybody though. Or maybe it was jealousy. Either way, they had to move forward. Their drug business was growing and they needed to find more ways to launder the money. That meant acquiring businesses. And this Davis guy seemed to have a keen eye for fixing up a loser.

De Riggi took another sip and let the heat fill his chest, his eyes closed. *Forget Walter's worries*, he thought. *If Davis can get us more businesses, he's okay in my book.*

***

A few days later, on a whim and wanting to escape for a few hours, De Riggi decided to go to the Auberge hotel in Old Montreal. He wasn't planning to meet Josie, just sit and have a coffee. When he bumped into her in the lobby and she suggested they have a coffee in the restaurant, he couldn't say no, even though he kept glancing around to see if anyone was watching them together. De Riggi knew he was being stupid. Everybody at the hotel was aware of their relationship. And it's not like anyone here would be talking to his wife.

"You came to see me," Josie said when they were seated at a table in the corner. She was staring into his eyes.

De Riggi nodded. "Yeah … Well, actually, I got some business nearby…"

Josie's face reddened. She'd rehearsed what she was going to say at a moment like this many times but had never had the courage to go through with it. She let go of his hands and leaned back in her chair. "Tony… I can't carry on like this. We only see each other once a week while your wife's at church."

De Riggi looked at her and said in a quiet voice, "Keep your voice down, there are people working here."

Josie looked at the waitress, who was standing by the entrance to the restaurant, pretending to look busy. "You think they don't know? Everybody knows about us."

"'Us?' What are you talking about?"

Josie felt like she'd been slapped. "Do I mean nothing to you? A quick screw once a week?"

De Riggi rolled his eyes. "Look, we're not going to have this conversation here."

"You're right, we're not, cos we're done." She stood up and turned to leave. He grabbed her wrist.

"I didn't mean it that way, honey," De Riggi said. "You know I care, it's just … complicated."

"What's complicated? The fact that you're married, or that your wife might find out?"

"I thought you were happy. What is it you want from me, Josie?"

"You told me you loved me, or was that just words, the sex talking? I can't carry on like this. Either this relationship is going somewhere, or it ends here and now."

He was about to laugh but there was nothing funny about the look on her face. And he felt his blood starting to rise. His tone was like nothing he had ever used with her before when he spoke. "I'm not used to people threatening me. It's usually the other way around."

Josie was having trouble keeping it all together. She could feel the tears coming. Something softened in him when he saw her like that. "What is it that you want from me?"

"You told me you were going to leave your wife, run away with me. You never meant any of it, did you?"

He glanced around and saw a few people were standing still, likely listening in. "We can't talk here." He had to end this before it became a story. "Look, why don't we go away somewhere for the weekend, just the two of us? Maybe Boston or New Hampshire."

Josie wasn't sure how far she should push him. He seemed more concerned that people could hear them arguing. Was he trying to shut her up with more lies?

"Give me a few days and I'll sort something out. I promise you we'll go away somewhere nice."

"When?" She asked, her chin now up, her eyes glistening.

"This weekend."

People were starting to come into the restaurant for an early lunch. Josie decided she had gone as far as she could; the rest was up to him. She'd been there before. Falling for a married man, an undercover cop of all people. He'd promised her the world. And then one day he disappeared. A few weeks later she asked another cop if he'd seen the guy. He told her he'd been transferred to Quebec City.

"We'll see," she said.

"I promise, this weekend for sure."

She tried not to smile.

He kissed her on the forehead. "I've gotta go."

As he walked through the lobby of the restaurant out onto the street, he was of two minds. On one hand he was shocked that Josie had spoken to him like that. On the other, he couldn't help but be impressed by the spunk she'd shown. Whether it was over or not, he didn't know. It made him realize he couldn't carry on the way he had been. Things had to change. Going away for the weekend with her wasn't such a bad idea. He needed a break and so did she. He'd never spent any time with her away before. She was a good listener, good in bed, fun to be with and, up until now, didn't argue. He knew one-sided relationships never lasted. That's what he had with his wife and that was over years ago. What made him think this thing with Josie would work?

It had never occurred to him that opening up to her was a bad idea. What could she do? She could call his wife and tell her about the affair. Then she'd be out of job and maybe worse. Was she worried about herself? He'd read somewhere that as women age, they look for different things in men. With men it was always about the sex, whether they were sixteen or sixty. With women it was more about security and companionship. Did she really want to spend time with him, or was it just security?

He pulled the truck out onto the street and smiled to himself. She wasn't scared of anyone.

Chapter 15

Davis treated himself to a rare lunch out at the local bistro, and almost as soon as he walked in his attention was taken by the beautiful waitress who approached him. It had been a long time since anyone had affected him like that. He sat at the corner table and returned her smile when she gave him a menu. She was about five feet eight with short dark hair, somewhere in her mid-forties he guessed, with a slim figure and stunning eyes. As she brought him water and coffee, she said, "I haven't seen you in here before. You must be new."

"Yes, this is my first time."

"Well, I'm Helene. I'll be your server today."

"Alan, pleased to meet you."

"I recommend the Croque Monsieur. Or if you're hungry the steak and kidney pie."

Davis scanned the menu. "What about the chicken salad?"

"I'm not sure it's very filling unless you add a bowl of soup. It's tomato bisque."

"Okay, chicken salad and tomato bisque it is. Thanks."

She smiled again as she left the table and headed back to the kitchen. Davis couldn't help smiling back. As he waited for his food, he looked around the small restaurant. There must've been room for about thirty people. A small group wandered in and sat at a table in the corner. They seemed to know Helene, as they all kissed her on both cheeks. A few minutes later she reappeared carrying his tomato bisque and some bread. There was that smile again. "Chicken salad shouldn't be too long," she said.

In the time he'd been in Bromont, he'd discovered that everyone knew everyone else, and he wondered whether people would notice the strangers in town that were keeping an eye on him from time to time.

He'd just finished his soup when Helene brought him his chicken salad. She laid the salad on the table and said, "Sorry, I didn't mean to interrupt your thoughts. You seemed miles away."

Davis looked up into her eyes, which he noticed were hazel with a burst of gold radiating out of the pupils. Was he flirting with her? Or was she flirting with him? She started to blush.

"I'm sorry, I didn't mean to stare. I don't get out much, and I'm not used to company," said Davis.

"That's okay. I know what it's like to be on your own. Sometimes it's nice to just visit a restaurant to meet people. I'll let you get on with your salad. Is there anything else I can get you?"

"I'm fine, thank you very much. I've taken up enough of your time already."

Not only wasn't he used to female company, he'd also forgotten how to have a conversation with a woman.

Davis was a fast eater, but he wasn't in any hurry and took his time enjoying the salad.

The bistro started filling up and he realized he should make room for other people. He was hoping that Helene would check on him. Unfortunately she was busy looking after other guests. Another waitress came by and asked if there was anything else. Reluctantly he asked for the bill. After he paid, he stood up and headed for the door and was disappointed when he didn't catch sight of Helene as he left.

Inside the bistro two of the younger waitresses were giggling to themselves. Helene noticed and asked what was so funny. "Did you see that guy, the way he was staring into your eyes when you served him? And then the way he looked around to see if you were there when he left?"

"You two get back to work and stop being so childish." The two young women giggled again. "Yes, boss. He was so cute though."

She smiled to herself, wondering who the newcomer was. Yes, he was good looking. She didn't have time for someone in her life right now. What with running the bistro six days a week and raising two young teenagers, she never had time for herself, let alone someone else. It'd been five years since her husband had died and she hadn't even thought of meeting someone else.

Out of habit, Davis checked the rear-view mirror of his pickup truck as he pulled out onto the main road. Half expecting to be tailed by one of the gang, he was pleased to see no one was there. Maybe his luck had changed. As he headed back to his cottage he thought about Helene. He didn't believe in love, but he thought he could learn to care for someone again, spend time with them, and maybe one day… This wasn't the time to get into a relationship. He needed to avoid the bistro from now on.

That evening he sat around the kitchen table going through the files that Dunphy had given him. They didn't seem to have a strategy. Why would the gang look at such different businesses? Some old motels, a mortgage investment company and a construction company. What was their goal? He understood the need to launder drug money, but what was the attraction of these businesses? Was it a test? Were they simply grabbing the first things that came along?

He laid the different files on the table. Each was accompanied by a letter from the same Montreal business broker advertising the business and summarizing the positive features. They each contained a set of financial statements and a three-year history of operating results. Was that it? Some business broker peddling crap businesses on their last legs? Did Dunphy have history with the broker?

He made detailed notes as he went through the material and listed the questions he had for Dunphy. There were six motels located in southern Québec, all within thirty miles of the US border. None had more than fifty rooms. The brochure claimed they were all in small towns, next to restaurants and gas stations. Each property had a different lender. He wondered which were dogs, or were they all dogs? Most were dependent on just room revenue. In all but one of them, the average occupancy for the last three years was trending downward. He couldn't find any details on the age of the motels. The pictures in the colour brochure suggested the buildings were at least thirty years old. Some of them looked like they needed work. And based on the individual debt of each motel, he suspected the asking prices were wishful thinking. Maybe the owners hoped to salvage something out of them after the lenders were paid out.

The financial statements for each motel showed an operating line of credit owing to a rural caisse populaire that he'd never heard of. He wondered if this was an opportunity to pick up a problem loan portfolio at a discount. Maybe that was what Dunphy was looking at.

He opened the file on the mortgage investment company. He knew a bit about the industry. As he scanned through the information, he got the sense that this would be a more profitable operation. The portfolio was split between residential and commercial loans. All were second mortgages. The commercial loan portfolio included a petting zoo, a small motel development under construction, a cross-country ski operation, a trailer park, a five-acre winery, a wilderness park, a ten-unit office building and a summer resort development on a remote lake. Apart from the office building, they were all seasonal businesses, and that meant high risk.

There was no delinquency report, and he wondered how many of the mortgages were current. All the residential mortgages were in Montreal, which was a plus. Yet the fact that almost all the commercial loans were in the hospitality and tourism sector troubled him. The company's historic operating results were good, but the three-year trend was headed down. That made sense. Interest rates were going up, people were having trouble renewing and servicing their mortgages. He'd heard the housing market was slowing down, and he'd frequently seen foreclosure signs on the streets of Montreal since he'd arrived in the city.

He opened the folder on the construction company. It reminded him of the time that his old Vancouver gang had looked at financing a developer. When he started digging, he quickly discovered that the developer was in trouble. He was way behind in the construction of his biggest project. A property search revealed several liens had been filed against the property; most were to unpaid contractors and subcontractors, but there was also a lien for a large amount of unpaid sales tax. It was a tough business at the best of times, developers in trouble often resorting to using money from one project to fund the completion of another. Running a construction company was one of the quickest ways of losing money. It was like musical chairs; only when the music stopped there was never enough cash to pay all the bills.

Davis set the folders aside and headed off to bed to sleep on it. Should he tell the gang what he really thought? Or should he tell them what they wanted to hear? He thought back to his days in Vancouver and the number of business opportunities that came his way. He'd developed a set of rules. Did the business generate positive cash flow? Was it low maintenance, or did it require a lot of management? Was there room to grow? Was there a lot of government regulation?

He knew the construction business was a money pit. Acquiring the motels didn't make sense unless the gang wanted to use them as a means of moving product south of the border. The only business that was remotely viable was the mortgage investment company. It was a good business to launder drug money through.

Davis rolled over. He was so tired he couldn't even think anymore. He needed to clarify his thoughts and make sure the message was simple. He'd draft something in the morning and then set up a meeting.

Chapter 16

Auryse De Riggi was surprised when her husband told her he had to go down to Boston for business. She'd hoped that he would take her along. When he didn't offer, she invited herself.

"That will be lovely, we haven't been away for a long time."

"Auryse, its business, and the guys coming up from Miami aren't bringing their wives. It wouldn't look good; you'd be the only woman there."

"You never take me anywhere. You said we'd go to Miami, you promised."

"I know and we'll go soon … trust me. This is a business meeting and besides, these aren't very nice people."

"They can't be any worse than the people you deal with in Montreal."

"Trust me, you don't want to come. There'll be a lot of drinking, a lot of private meetings—of the type wives don't come to. You understand?"

She understood perfectly what kind of meetings there would be. *Probably taking his bimbo down there.* She started to get angry, then caught herself. This wasn't the time and place to have it out. There'd come a time, she knew. She needed to plan it. She needed to be free of him and everything that he meant, and in a way that he couldn't do anything about it. She couldn't do it all on her own, she'd need help. She knew people.

Did she hate him that much? No, it was worse than that. She despised him. Everything he stood, for, his lies, his cheating, always treating her like a fool with no mind of her own. The little wife that goes to church every Sunday, the wife that cleans his house, cooks his meals, washes his clothes, even lies for him.

"I gotta go, dear, I'll be late for a meeting, you understand."

He barely looked at her as he walked out the door. That's what she'd become, a doormat.

Auryse sat down at the kitchen table and started to cry. Thirty-five long years. She picked up the phone and dialled the number on the card. Yes, she wanted to meet. She had something to tell them.

As Tony De Riggi drove away, he wondered about his wife. She'd always been there for him, always put up with it. They'd had their fights, some of them bad. Who didn't? And at the end of the day, she was still there. He knew he had to take her down to Miami, even if it was only for a few weeks. He'd seen a TV show once, some guy was spinning plates on top of long poles. He started off with one and by the time he'd finished Tony counted more than twenty plates, all spinning at the same time. The guy kept running from one plate to another, shaking each pole in turn ever so gently. Yeah, that's what he felt like. He was looking forward to getting away, and it wasn't just the company. It was a chance to forget who he was and what he did, even if only for a long weekend.

***

Josie's bags were already packed. She never travelled light, whether it was overnight or for three weeks. While she'd been getting ready, she wasn't even sure De Riggi would show up. She wondered what it would be like to spend the whole weekend with him. Would he be able to relax? Would he be on the phone? Could he enjoy himself?

She told the hotel that she was heading home for a long weekend break. No one at the hotel remembered Josie ever going away, even for a few days. No one even knew she had a family. She picked up the taxi outside the hotel, pointed to her bags and quietly gave the driver an address. Ten minutes later she got out of the taxi and told the driver to unload her bags. He was about to say something as he popped the trunk when a swarthy guy about six feet tall jumped out of a black Range Rover, grabbed her bags and put them in the trunk of his vehicle.

Josie paid the cab driver and got into the front of the plush vehicle. De Riggi got back into the driver's seat and pulled out into traffic. He looked over at her.

"I see you've packed light. You know we're only going for the weekend, right?"

"Where are we going?"

"I've booked us into a lodge in eastern Vermont. It's about a three-hour drive, we can stop for lunch on the way."

Josie knew he was unhappy at home and at work. She'd gotten to know a lot of undercover cops through her work, often listening to their troubles. They'd always start talking about problems at work, but it didn't take them long to start complaining about their wives and girlfriends. "They never understand" was a familiar claim. They didn't understand how tough the job was, and how difficult it was to unwind, especially after a long stakeout or weeks of undercover work. She'd become a mother confessor, always there to listen, always there to support and help them. That was part of her job. She remembered a prostitute from years ago telling her that you had to listen and pretend you cared. From experience she knew it was true. A lot of her clients were just trying to escape the stress of their jobs, or their troubled marriages. They needed someone to help them relax and forget, even it was only for an hour or two. Sometimes they didn't even need sex; they just wanted to talk.

Was he really her way out? At first, she thought that getting closer to him would lead to more trouble not less. She wondered if he was trying to escape as well.

As they headed southeast to the Vermont border, De Riggi felt the burden of the city slip away. It reminded him of the times when his parents took him on holiday as a kid. He couldn't remember where it was. There was a sandy beach and a small bay. He kept running in and out of the ocean, chased by his mother. The waves were gentle and so was she. *Where was it?* he thought. So long ago. He was happy back then, not a care in the world, just him, his mother and his father.

Josie was quiet. Maybe she was dreaming of lying curled up by a log fire in a small cabin somewhere in the mountains, the snow falling outside. As they drove through the townships, he thought how beautiful the countryside was and how depressing the busy city of Montreal had become. They were at the border in just over an hour. The border crossing was uneventful; just a few questions about the purpose of the visit and they were gone.

Then it started to snow, and it reminded Josie of her childhood in the Townships, where the winters were always white. She felt like a young girl running away from her parents with her new boyfriend. She too was trying to escape.

He told her that he'd booked three nights at a small remote lodge located in the foothills of the White Mountains. He didn't want to stay at a busy place where he might run into someone he knew.

As he drove the Range Rover along the snowy road, he looked over at her. "I imagine you were expecting something fancier?"

"No. Sounds nice and cozy, and out of the way. I'm sure it'll be lovely."

Chapter 17

Dunphy read Davis's report a second time. It was easy to follow, identified some problems he hadn't thought of and even suggested a strategy in the event the gang wanted to proceed with one of the acquisitions. Dunphy liked his approach. It was as if he'd put himself in the gang's shoes, identifying what would be involved in the event they took on one of the businesses. He must have known they already owned a hotel and some bars in the city. That must have made him wonder why they were even considering motels located out in the boonies.

Dunphy concluded that the gang would benefit by using someone with Davis's brain. But he wondered where he'd acquired all his business knowledge. He sensed this guy was more than just a VP of Logistics at a mid-sized trucking company. He made a note to raise it with De Riggi when they met.

For now, he wanted to talk to Davis. He planned to dig a little deeper. He could be a great asset to the gang. But what if Pigeon was right?

***

When Davis arrived at the Dunphy's office the following day, he slowly walked the lawyer through each business. By the time he'd started on the construction company, Dunphy was tuning him out. He wondered if he should ask for Davis's notes to pass on to De Riggi. He doubted the gang leader would have the patience to sit through all of that. Likely fifteen minutes would be more than enough given his attention span.

As if he was reading his mind, Davis said, "So let's talk about why your client is looking at these businesses. None of them are making any money."

"Let's just say each one offers a unique opportunity."

"Such as?"

"You need to have that discussion with Mr. De Riggi. There's one thing I'd like to know though." Dunphy paused, looked out his office window and then looked directly at Davis. "You've got a lot of business knowledge. You and I know that goes far beyond anything you'd have picked up in the trucking industry. Where did you get all this experience?"

Davis was tempted to tell him that it could wait until he met De Riggi, but something told him that Dunphy could prove to be a useful ally. He recited the background story his handlers had prepared for him, keeping it short but occasionally throwing in a few of his own thoughts that he hoped made it sound more believable.

Davis felt Dunphy's penetrating eyes on him. Did he believe him? Did he have more questions?

"Why did you move into the trucking business?" Dunphy asked.

The handlers had planned for this question. Not only did they develop a background for the time he'd supposedly spent in corporate finance, but they'd also included a story about a three-month stint at a Toronto trucking company as part of a due-diligence review on behalf of a prospective buyer. Davis explained how he got hired at the trucking company. He'd gone over the story so many times in his head, he had almost started to believe the bullshit himself.

"Mr. Davis, you're full of surprises."

Davis decided the time for playing dumb was over. "Assuming your client plans to launder money through one of these businesses and they want to minimize their cash losses, then the mortgage investment company is the best bet."

Dunphy leaned back in his chair and smiled. "Cutting right to the chase, I see."

The two men regarded each other for a few moments. Then Dunphy refilled his glass with scotch and said, "What about the construction company?"

"A mistake. It involves hands-on management, and it's way too tough to monitor, especially given the amount of time your client is likely to spend overseeing it."

"And the motels?"

Davis smiled at Dunphy and said, "Unless there's an advantage to owning properties so close to the US border, I don't see any sense in acquiring them."

Dunphy made some notes, then looked up. "When will Hatfield's be out of the woods?"

"A few months, maybe more. It's headed in the right direction, but you can't rush it and you shouldn't get involved in other businesses till then, or I'll become a firefighter and not a manager."

The lawyer smiled again. This was the sort of language De Riggi would understand.

Long after Davis had left, Dunphy sat in his chair thinking. Toward the end of the meeting Davis had come across more like a gang member than a manager of a trucking company. But he really seemed to know his stuff, and that was good for Dunphy. But if De Riggi invested in one of the businesses and things went sideways, he knew he'd get the blame.

For months now, something had been becoming clear to Dunphy: he couldn't care less about the gang or De Riggi. He was more worried about himself. He wasn't sleeping. He'd always pretended that working for the gang wouldn't last, telling himself it would end one day when he'd made enough money. It never seemed to be enough though. And anyway, it wasn't like he could just walk away. Even his ex-wife knew there was a problem—wife number two. He only had contact with her because he saw his kids on the weekends. And lately she'd been commenting on how stressed he looked.

In desperation he'd gone to his old law college friend, Jean Belliveau, for help. Belliveau listened as Dunphy told him about his so-called problem client, then agreed to make a call on his behalf. Within a half hour, Belliveau was on the phone with the Crown counsel explaining that his client, who was to remain nameless for the time being, had been acting for several years on behalf of a Montreal gang and was looking for a way out. Crown counsel had outlined what would be required of his client. When Belliveau explained this to Dunphy, it sounded too good to be true. He knew that life was never that simple. He hesitated, decided to sleep on it and for two weeks agonized over what he should do.

During that time, whenever he met or spoke to De Riggi he wondered if he knew. But how could he? He realized he was becoming paranoid. It reminded him of something Davis had said. Something about being paranoid in business, and that you could never worry enough. He started to understand what he meant, what he must have felt.

Finally, after several sleepless nights he decided to go ahead and told Belliveau to set up a meeting with the Crown counsel before he changed his mind.

The meeting was arranged for the following morning at the Crown counsel's office.

"I don't want to alarm you, Sean," Belliveau said over the phone. "These guys will need to know what you know. Then they'll decide what they're prepared to do. That's the way it works. It makes sense for you to tell me first. Then I can tell you what I think they'll be prepared to do. Remember, anything you tell me is subject to solicitor-client privilege."

There was silence at the other end. Dunphy was finally at the point of no return.

"Sean, are you still there?"

"Jesus Christ, Jean. I'm just wondering what my options are." Dunphy's suit, usually impeccable, was wrinkled and he had sweat through his shirt. This was a mistake. If De Riggi found out, he was a dead man.

"Come to my office. Let's talk about—"

"There's a bar on Saint Denis," Dunphy said. "The Flamingo. I can be there in forty minutes."

Chapter 18

De Riggi's weekend trip to Vermont with Josie had gone much better than he'd expected. She didn't pressure him about the future or make any demands; she seemed to just want to enjoy the moment. He relaxed for the first time in months. They took a sleigh ride in the snow and had a quiet dinner in a small candlelit restaurant in the village. As they walked back to their hotel through the falling snow, he thought about how simple most people's lives were. He'd never known peace and he'd never stood still, even for a day. Even as a kid growing up in east Montreal, he was always doing something, trying to make some extra money, hanging around with the crowd of young boys in the neighbourhood, each daring the other to steal something or break a window. His dad had told him to smarten up, but he never listened. He got into fights with bigger kids. Whether it was because of his size or the fact that he fought dirty, even as a ten-year-old, most of the kids quickly learned to avoid him. Not that he was looking for trouble, it was just that trouble found him.

He wasn't sure why he'd suddenly thought back to his childhood. Maybe he was trying to figure out how he had ended up where he was today. As he sat down in the cozy hotel room and gazed into the fire, he said to Josie, "Do you ever wonder why your life turned out the way it did?"

"What's wrong, aren't you happy here?"

"You mean right now?"

She nodded.

"Of course. This is relaxing, it gives me time to think. I wish I could do it more often. I just wish … my life was simpler and that I could change who I am and what I am."

"Who'd you rather be?"

"For a start I wouldn't be running around every day wondering how to keep the gang together, how to grow the business, whether we'll get screwed on our next deal."

"Only you can change that."

He was quiet for a few minutes, just staring into the wood-burning fireplace. Then he looked at her and said, "What about you? Don't you ever wonder why your life turned out the way it did?"

"Sure, I do, but there's not much I can do about it. You, on the other hand, have no excuses. You're the boss. You can do whatever you want. If you want to move to Miami, you can. If you want to buy a new house, you can. If you want to slow down and put someone else in charge, you can."

"You make it sound simple."

"It is. Decide what you want out of life and go get it. Isn't that what you've done all your life?"

He couldn't just up and leave. Who'd take over the gang? Where would he go? What would he do? He'd been busy all his life and wasn't sure what doing nothing would be like. He'd never really thought about the future. Maybe it was because he had no one to worry about other than himself. Sure, he cared about the wife, and she never wanted for anything. For as long as he could remember he'd lived his own life, not worrying about anyone else.

"You're different, Josie, you care about people. I know you care about your girls and are always looking out for them. I know you're mad at me for wanting to bring those girls in from the Ukraine. You still care about me too, even though I don't care about anyone."

"That's not true. You just don't like people seeing the real you. It's as if you're scared people will find out who you really are."

"What do you mean?"

"You care about the gang, you care about Pigeon, even though he's a complete loser and hates everyone. You're unhappy. You don't enjoy what you're doing but you're afraid to change."

While he knew she was right, it wasn't as simple as that. He did want to change; to get away from the day-to-day grind of running the gang, making sure things were done right. The business had grown and was getting bigger. That meant he'd be busier than ever. Who would take over when he was gone? Though Pigeon could follow orders and clean up after him, he didn't have the vision to run the gang. He'd even piss off his own guys, and soon they'd turn against him. He was only good for one thing: scaring people. Even his own people feared him.

De Riggi wondered what would happen if he just disappeared or headed off to Miami. He knew the answer. Sooner or later, someone would take over their turf or even the whole gang. Then it wouldn't be long before they came after him. If he were the new leader, the first thing he'd do would be to eliminate any threat. He had to make sure his successor was someone he could trust, someone that wouldn't let the place fall apart.

He looked over at Josie. "What makes you so smart?"

She smiled shyly. "Come on. It's time for bed. We can chat again tomorrow."

They never did talk about it the next day. Still, something had changed in their relationship. He'd developed a new appreciation for her. She knew when to be quiet and leave things alone. He was sure the subject would come up again, and he would listen to her. That's what he was missing. A confidant at work and maybe at home. Could Josie be that person?

Chapter 19

The Flamingo was virtually empty. Dunphy had arrived early and grabbed a table at the far end of the bar. Belliveau was late, and by the time his friend arrived, Dunphy had already drunk half a bottle of the Merlot he'd ordered.

Belliveau slid into his seat and poured himself a glass. "I've thought this through. Assuming you have what they want, and they can use it, they'll offer you a deal. It'll involve witness protection for you and your family, and moving—probably out of province, at least till the trial starts. Assuming the Crown is successful, and your guy goes away, you may have to relocate permanently. A lot depends on what you know, how good it is and how bad they want these guys."

"Marie's going to be pissed," Dunphy said.

Belliveau nodded. "Wives aren't happy in these situations in the best of times. Ex-wives? That's a whole other level of pissed off."

Dunphy played with his wine. "Where would they relocate us?"

"Who knows?"

"And if I do nothing?"

"Have you committed any illegal acts?"

Dunphy emptied the bottle into his glass and drank half of it before answering. "I'm the registered owner of certain properties and businesses owned by the gang, and I know where the money came from."

"Anything else?"

"Like what?"

"Have you benefitted from any illegal acts, witnessed or been a party to murder?"

Dunphy blinked a few times as though trying to centre himself before he answered. "Define illegal."

"You know what I'm talking about, Sean."

"I know what they do for a living, if that's what you mean. And we both know where the money comes from." He looked down at his drink thoughtfully. "Have I actually witnessed anything?" He asked his wine glass. "No." He looked up at his friend. "And my client has been very careful. Keeps his name off everything." Dunphy was nodding along to his own speech. "No paper trail—oh, yeah, he incriminated me so he knows I can't tell on him."

Belliveau picked up his glass of wine and swirled it gently. "Listen, Sean, I don't know exactly who you're in bed with. I suspect the cops know about your relationship already. They may have been watching your office for months. That doesn't mean they can prove anything. But chances are damn good they know who you are and what you do."

Dunphy swore under his breath and took another long drink of wine.

Belliveau leaned forward. "Maybe ease up on the wine so we can talk."

Dunphy looked slightly abashed and set his glass down.

"This is only going to get worse," Belliveau said. "I'm not even sure I should bring this up …"

"Just say it."

"I think you should draft some sort of confidential memorandum about what you've done. Just the areas where you think you've … crossed the line. I'll have someone vet it on a confidential basis, see if there's a case or not."

"Where does that get us?" Dunphy said loudly. Then he lowered his voice, glancing around them before saying in a harsh whisper, "I told you, I'm already incriminated."

"Well, let's pretend for the sake of discussion that you had an understanding with the Crown, and that if you were asked to act in any capacity that you knew was illegal, then you'd run it by them to obtain immunity."

Dunphy loosened his tie and stared glassy eyed at Belliveau. "I do a deal with the Crown, and I'm a rat. And we all know what gangs do with rats." He slammed his fist on the table. "They exterminate them."

"Christ, Sean, I'm saying going undercover on behalf of the Crown is your best option here."

"You want me to just carry on working for these … jackasses … and hope they don't find out I'm whispering all their secrets to the … the Crown?"

Belliveau leaned back with a sigh. "Yes. That's exactly what I want. And I imagine at some point, you'll be required to testify against them."

Chapter 20

De Riggi was in his office trying to get work done, but his mind kept going back to his time with Josie the previous weekend. If only he could slip away with her! He shook his head. Could he really do that to his wife, no matter how miserable he was in his marriage? And he still hadn't found anyone who could take over the gang if he left.

His mind wandered to the call he'd had from Dunphy the day before. The lawyer had met with Davis. Dunphy was impressed with the guy. He liked the way his mind worked, businesslike, methodical. De Riggi had listened to the report and while he didn't understand all the financial jargon, he understood what Davis was saying. He liked the fact that the guy was cautious and understood the challenges of taking on new businesses. And he had brains, something most of the guys around him lacked.

When De Riggi had mentioned expanding the gang's business empire to Pigeon at dinner last night, his second-in-command had just nodded. When he told him Davis was looking at business opportunities for them, he went crazy.

"Why the fuck would you do that, boss? You know I don't trust the guy. Do you trust him?"

"Listen, whatever you think, he has business smarts. Do you know someone else that can do it?"

Pigeon was silent.

"Didn't think so. We've got to look to the future, we can't just sit back. You of all people should know that."

"Maybe. But Davis? We know hardly anything about him."

De Riggi should have kept his mouth shut. Now Pigeon was pissed and would take it out on Davis and anyone else that got in his way. And that was a problem, because for some time now, De Riggi had been toying with an idea. It was a long shot, but maybe, just maybe, Davis had a future with the gang, and not just looking after Hatfield's operation. The last thing he needed was more trouble between Pigeon and Davis. Maybe Davis was his chance to move down to Miami permanently. He was getting ahead of himself. There was no harm in dreaming though.

***

A few weeks later, when De Riggi called Dunphy to set up a meeting with Davis, the lawyer sounded cautious, and he didn't want to attend.

"I think it'd be better if just the two of you met. A one-on-one. You don't need me to decide which businesses to buy."

His lawyer suddenly didn't want to attend such an important meeting?

"What the fuck do you mean, you're not going to be there? Is there something I should know? You getting scared all of a sudden? It's too late to back out now, Dunphy. We're joined at the hip."

Dunphy felt a cold sweat on his brow. Could De Riggi know he was thinking of making a deal with the Crown? "There's … there's something else." Dunphy wracked his brain for a way to distract De Riggi. "It may be nothing, but I think we should check out Davis a bit more. He knows a lot more about finance and business than we thought. Seems … odd … for a trucker…"

His ploy worked. De Riggi immediately reacted. "You found something?"

"Let's just say I'm cautious—"

"Well look into him more," De Riggi said.

"Yeah, and there's another reason the three of us shouldn't meet. I'm pretty sure I'm being followed. I think it's the cops."

De Riggi was silent for a few moments, considering this. "Okay," he said finally. "I'll meet Davis by myself."

When he hung up he started to wonder about Dunphy. Maybe the lawyer was being followed. Maybe he was getting scared—and wanting to put some distance between himself and the gang. He'd have to keep an eye on him.

***

After the phone call with De Riggi, Dunphy poured himself a glass of whisky and pondered his options. He finally fell asleep on the couch in his office. He had a dream that the cops had been following him into the bar on Saint Denis. They'd seen his friend arrive and he was sure they'd taken a photo of the two of them together. He wasn't ready, he just couldn't go through with it. There was too much risk. He was scared, and not just for his family; he knew what the gang would do to him if they found out. When he woke at seven the next morning, he phoned Jean Belliveau and left a message on his office answering machine, saying he wouldn't be coming to the meeting with Crown counsel after all.

Chapter 21

Hatfield's Trucking had finally thrown off some cash. It wasn't much—twenty grand for the month—but it was the first time the company had made any money in as long as Hatfield could remember, and the old owner was still around trying to help in any way he could. So with things shaping up, Davis wasn't surprised when De Riggi called him to talk about acquiring another business. Dunphy had told him the gang boss was impatient to move forward with his plan and might call him directly.

When he heard which business De Riggi was interested in, Davis frowned. Contrary to his advice, De Riggi asked him to look at the motel deal. Davis couldn't understand why the boss would ignore his numbers and the clear explanation of what a money pit these motels would be. What De Riggi didn't tell him was that his plans included one of the motels being used as a transfer point for shipping young Ukrainian women into the US.

At first Lacroix and Primeau were skeptical about him getting involved. Eventually they agreed with him that it was a sign that De Riggi had confidence in him and that it would bring him closer to the gang. No matter how unsavoury it was, it would be a mistake to refuse.

***

For two days, Davis stayed in his cottage and went through the information about the motels again, making his own neat notes. He smiled to himself as he looked at them. His mind was so ordered. He sat back in his chair and pondered some of the challenges they'd be facing by taking over these failing businesses. Replacing management was always a challenge. Who was going to run the business? Did De Riggi have someone in mind? He doubted it.

He stretched in his chair and ran his fingernails along the stubble on the side of his face. He needed to get a new razor, the old one wasn't working so well. He got up and made some more coffee, his third cup of the day and it wasn't even noon yet. He needed a break, some fresh air. Without thinking about it he grabbed his coat and truck keys and headed out the door.

He parked across the street from the bistro. Why was he here? He knew he should stay away from the place, but he was attracted by the thought of seeing Helene. Davis turned off the ignition and got out. Rather than going into the restaurant, he headed for the small park at the edge of town. Though the snow had almost gone—the rain had seen to that—it was still cold.

The park was next to a small school where youngsters were playing in the playground, climbing bars, pushing swings and running around in a fenced-off area. A little boy standing by the fence said "Hello," then smiled and ran off. Two other kids who seemed to be playing a game of tag ran past, both zigzagging as they tried to avoid each other, laughing all the way. He guessed they must have been in kindergarten judging by their size. A bell rang in the distance. Suddenly a group of bigger children came running out onto the field, a few of them chasing each other. One had a ball that he kept kicking; another kept trying to catch him and take the ball off him, but he was too slow.

Davis turned left at the end of the road and decided to explore the neighbourhood. There was a mixture of homes, most were ranch style, although there was the occasional newer two-storey home. There wasn't a lot of traffic. Davis looked up every time he heard a vehicle. He passed several couples, all of them retirement age. The occasional worker, mostly gardeners or contractors doing renovations, gave him a nod as he passed. For a while he followed an avenue lined with trees until he noticed what looked like a treehouse from a distance. He walked over to it and found it wasn't a treehouse but a small, elevated bookstand with a roof and glass doors. He looked inside and saw three rows of paperbacks and a few hardbacks. Almost all of them were used. He opened the door and pulled out a book. He recognized an old Dick Francis book, *Reflex*. There were several romantic novels and a couple of Ken Follett books including *Eye of the Needle* and *The Key to Rebecca*. He realized that it was some sort of local neighbourhood book exchange. Then he noticed the handwritten sign on the side of the bookstand which instructed passersby to "Take one, leave one."

Davis could hear traffic not far away and realized that the line of trees running on the other side of the path must have been planted there years ago to reduce the noise. At the end of the road he came across two tennis courts. It was too wet for anybody to be playing. At the end of the next street there was a small play area and three mothers watching their small children, one of whom was on a swing and two of whom were on a small roundabout that one of the mothers was pushing very slowly.

Yes, he thought, *this would be a like a nice place to live.*

He made his way back to his car and walked into the busy bistro, glancing over the heads of the seated customers. He didn't see the reason he'd come back here. A waitress he didn't recognize told him there'd be a window table if he cared to wait a few minutes. He was in no hurry. He looked at the menu on the board and decided what he'd have, then returned to scanning the small place. She didn't seem to be there.

Lunch seemed to drag once he realized he wouldn't be seeing Helene. He had just decided not to have another coffee when the door opened, and there she was.

Helene didn't notice him at first. She appeared to be apologizing to someone. He overheard her saying that the traffic in the city was getting worse and worse.

Davis stood up just as the waitresses talking to Helene walked away, leaving them facing each other. She immediately smiled.

"So how was the meal?"

"Fine, thank you."

"We haven't seen you in a while."

"I've been busy lately. I should be spending more time around here."

"I hope you do." Her cheeks turned pink. "You know there's a very active community centre here…"

Davis wanted to respond but he didn't want to read more into the conversation than was intended. And besides, his mouth was so dry it felt like he'd swallowed his tongue. After staring at her for what seemed like an age he managed to say, "I'd better be going."

This time it was Davis who blushed.

Chapter 22

To help him assess the motel business, Davis had bought a map of the province of Quebec and the northern US states that bordered it. He then marked the location of the motels De Riggi was interested in. He decided to visit the motels located nearest US border crossings running through New York state and Vermont that were close to major state highways.

As he drove to the first motel, he pondered the situation. Why would anyone buy this business? Could it be fixed? What was working, what wasn't? And most important, what was it worth? The more he thought about the gang investing in small motels in the south of the province, the less it made sense. Hopefully De Riggi would realize it would involve a lot of management with limited upside, and that since the locations were in all small-town Quebec, the gang and their activities would stand out.

He was still frustrated that De Riggi had ignored his advice about going for the mortgage investment company. That might have had some potential. It reminded Davis of what he'd run into when the Vancouver gang had taken over George Koehle's mortgage business a few years back. Like Koehle's company, this business needed refinancing and the financial statements painted a bleak picture. The investors hadn't received a dividend payment in over two years and over ninety investors had served notice that they wanted their money back. The business wouldn't last long. But Davis knew how to fix it.

Surely there were better ways for the gang to ship product south than using some rundown motels close to the border. Also, the township resorts were usually located near a lake and a small rural village, which meant there were a lot of locals, usually in retirement, who would take a keen interest in a new owner. He doubted that the gang taking over a resort would remain a secret for long. No, if De Riggi were interested in a trophy property, then a major city like Montreal would surely be a better place to start. They could even hire professional management to run the hotel rather than getting involved in the day-to-day challenges of running something they knew next to nothing about.

Davis figured that once De Riggi saw some photos of the properties and heard him out, he'd lose interest. And then Davis would be ready with another report on the mortgage company, showing how they could take it over. Better still, the gang would be in a perfect position to use their connections to source new business. It'd even give them a chance to take over some of the properties of some of their more unfortunate borrowers if they got into trouble and couldn't pay their mortgages.

That evening, after a full day visiting motels, Davis enjoyed a fine meal and a spectacular sunset at the bistro at La Cache du Lac Champlain, overlooking the beautiful Lake Champlain. His travels had only confirmed everything he suspected—the motels would be a terrible investment for the gang. Sitting alone in the elegant dining room, Davis's thoughts drifted away from business for the first time in days. He'd just visited two beautiful resort properties in the Townships, both of which he wanted to revisit. Each had year-round activities and was located close to his cottage in Bromont. And suddenly he found himself wondering if Helene had ever stayed at either place. If so, who with? Maybe her husband and kids.

After dinner, Davis focused his mind on business. Why was he even thinking about Helene when there was no chance of a future with her? He argued with himself; he was entitled to a life as well. Just not if it meant jeopardizing the operation. He hadn't told his handlers about her, believing nothing would come of it. He knew that deep down he was looking for something or someone to share his life with. He'd been on his own for too long and he longed to have some company. It was more than just that though.

***

Davis agreed to meet Sean Dunphy in a coffee shop close to the lawyer's office. When he first arrived the place was busy, full of students with red-and-white scarves, but there was no sign of the lawyer. Then he spotted him in the far corner at a table close to the window with his back to the wall, reading a newspaper.

As he sat down, Davis handed Dunphy an envelope that contained a copy of his report on the motels. Dunphy looked at the table next to them and then at the door.

"Are you expecting someone?" asked Davis.

"Uh, no, it's just … Forget it." Dunphy ran a manicured hand along his silk tie and cleared his throat. "So, give me the short form. What did you think of the motels?"

Davis sat back. "I'm not keen on businesses that require a lot of supervision. And it's tough to recommend a course of action when you don't know the client's goals. You wanna tell me why De Riggi's so interested in these?"

Dunphy almost smiled. This guy was sharp. "You should ask him when you see him."

"I'm asking you."

Dunphy stared down at his cold coffee for a moment before draining the last of it. "Let's just say he's in a rush to invest." He looked up. "I think he should take his time." The two men stared at one another for a moment, and the lawyer realized he wasn't going to get much out of Alan Davis without a crowbar to help. Finally he said, "I take it your advice is not to invest in the motels."

Davis nodded toward the report on the table and noticed Dunphy looked around again before he picked it up.

A waitress approached their table and looked at Dunphy. "You want another?"

Dunphy nodded. "And whatever my friend wants."

Davis looked at the young woman, probably a college student making a few extra bucks, and said, "Large Americano, please."

For the next few minutes, the lawyer scanned the reports, taking time to read the summary at the front. Occasionally he looked up at Davis and then checked the room, looking for newcomers.

The fresh coffees arrived. Dunphy kept reading uninterrupted. Eventually he stopped and looked up. "What do you know about mortgage investment companies?"

Though Davis was caught off guard he quickly recovered. "My old man invested in one once, lost some money the hard way." Davis expected more questions, but Dunphy was already preoccupied by the sight of two middle-aged guys who'd just walked in. He closed the report and abruptly stood up, almost spilling his coffee as he grabbed it.

"I need to get back to the office. I'll be in touch." And with that, he left.

***

De Riggi had noticed that his lawyer had become cautious in the last few weeks, convinced he was being followed, so he wasn't surprised when Dunphy insisted that they meet outside the office, preferably somewhere De Riggi wasn't a regular. They'd settled on a small hotel near the Auberge that did a good breakfast.

De Riggi was already waiting for him when the lawyer arrived. He'd never met De Riggi at such an early hour. De Riggi claimed he'd spent the last few days going through Davis's report on the motels, and he'd brought a copy with him. He looked up as Dunphy sat across from him.

"So, what do you think of all this?" De Riggi said, pointing to the file.

Dunphy signalled the waitress, then turned to De Riggi. "I'm pretty sure he figured out the reason for your interest in the motels."

De Riggi didn't answer just watched Dunphy as the waitress filled their mugs with coffee. It occurred to him that he'd never seen his lawyer look so dishevelled.

Dunphy took a sip of black coffee, winced, then sat back like a man who'd had a rough night. "Look, Davis thinks the mortgage company is worth looking at." Dunphy shrugged. "I didn't tell him anything."

"This is going to piss off Walter even more," De Riggi said.

"What is?"

"That I've used Davis to look at the businesses, and if we proceed, we'll be using him to run them. And now he's getting curious. Walter will not like that."

Dunphy touched the white china mug. "What's the alternative? You told me yourself: Pigeon doesn't have the smarts to assess the business, let alone run it."

"Yeah, but you don't have to deal with the guy. He sees himself as the future. This is really gonna get his back up."

"Tony, do you really think Walter Pigeon is the future? Don't get me wrong, he's a good number two. I can't see him changing though; the best you can expect is that things stay the same. And you and I know that's not enough. Forget about growing the business, especially if you plan to slow down and spend time down south."

"Hmm." Dunphy was saying what De Riggi had been thinking for some time. It irked him to hear it out loud.

Breakfast arrived and Dunphy cringed when he saw the bacon, sausages, fried bread and mushrooms. At least there were tomatoes. He didn't want to send it back. He'd have been happy with oatmeal and berries, but he didn't want to piss De Riggi off.

De Riggi shoved half a sausage in his mouth and carried on talking. "So what do you make of Davis?"

"Smart guy, knows his way around a deal. Not sure where he got all his business experience. He knows what he's doing though."

De Riggi chewed thoughtfully as he looked at something in the motel report. He cleared his plate in less than five minutes, barely remembering his lawyer was across from him. When he was done, he glanced up from his reading and eyed Dunphy's plate. The man hadn't touched the sausages, bacon or fried bread. De Riggi resisted the temptation to grab Dunphy's breakfast, touched his large waistline and let out a loud belch. He wiped an egg stain off the side of his mouth with the white napkin.

"Okay, meet with Davis. Tell him to get going with the mortgage company for now." Dunphy nodded and was out of his seat and heading for the door before De Riggi had a chance to say any more. As he left the room he glanced back and saw De Riggi pick one of the greasy sausages from his untouched plate and pop it into his mouth.

Chapter 23

Davis arrived at the bistro a little before noon and the place wasn't busy. He'd been a regular visitor over the past few weeks and had bumped into Helene a few times when he'd had lunch there. Today they sat him by the window next to a poster advertising a play—a crime thriller put on by the local amateur theatre company. He hadn't been to a play in years, and once again he found himself thinking of Helene. He still didn't know if she was single, so why was he even thinking about going out with her?

Davis kept looking, but there was no sign of Helene. He gazed at the poster, wondering what it'd be like to be seated next to her enjoying the play. Lost in a dream, he suddenly heard her voice.

"Thinking of going?"

He looked up. "Sorry, I was miles away."

"I hear it's good, for an amateur production, that is."

He gritted his teeth. In some ways he was more afraid of her than of De Riggi. *Oh well*, he thought, *might as well just get it over with.* "Would you like to go?"

She tilted her head. "Are you asking me on a date?"

Crap. This was getting real. "I guess … both."

She raised an eyebrow and crossed her arms. "I hardly know you."

"You're the only person I know in town."

Davis wanted the ground to open up, and he half expected her to find an excuse to leave the table. She stood her ground, and then there was that smile again. "Why not? It's not as if I've got any plans this weekend. Yes, I'll come. Saturday or Sunday night?"

He caught himself before he sighed in relief. "Whatever's best for you."

"Let's say Saturday. Meet you there?"

"Sure. Maybe we could go for a drink afterward?"

She was silent, staring at him. He felt like a teenager who couldn't believe his luck.

"Sure, a drink would be nice." Her cheeks were a bit pink, he noticed. She coughed and then said, "Now, what would you like to eat?"

He mumbled something and Helene left to put in his order. He couldn't help noticing one of the young waitresses was smiling widely watching them, and she said something to Helene as she walked by.

***

For the next three days, Davis cursed himself, knowing he was headed for trouble. What was he thinking getting involved with a nice woman like Helene? It made no sense whatsoever. He'd not seen anything of Pigeon or anyone else from the gang following him for some time now. That didn't mean they weren't still keeping an eye on him. Who knew where all this would lead.

Now that he'd invited her to the play, he could hardly not show up. He'd just have to make sure it went no further. She'd want to know what he did for a living, where was he from, whether he'd ever been married or had any kids. Everything he said would be a lie. And what if she ever found out the truth? What if he bumped into one of the gang in the village and she saw him?

It would be best for both of them if he didn't show up, and if he never went to the bistro again.

He did go, and the play turned out to be very good. *Dial M for Murder* was adapted for a small stage and a cozy theatre that seated about seventy people and doubled as the local church hall. He immediately wondered if she went to church, then pushed the thought away. They bumped into a few locals who knew Helene, and she was happy to introduce Davis to them, which made him even more uncomfortable. When the play was over, he was going to say he wasn't feeling well and wouldn't be able to go for drinks. And then he'd never go to the bistro again, and that would be the end of it. The next thing he knew, they were walking to a small bar nearby. They found a quiet table in the corner and ordered red wine.

She was just so easy to be with. But Davis was afraid of saying too much and found himself prompting her. "You've lived in the village all your life," he said.

"I've never been farther than college, and that was Montreal. Unless you count the three months travelling through Europe with friends after graduation. What about you?"

He stuck to his script. It was easy to lie when you'd rehearsed the story so many times. This time, his reply *sounded* rehearsed, and he wondered if she could see through him.

He was expecting a question about his personal life eventually, and when it came, he didn't know why, but he told the truth.

"We split up years ago. It just didn't work out. I have a daughter; she'll be almost seventeen now."

"Do you see her much?"

"No."

Perhaps she could tell he was having trouble talking about it, because she changed the subject.

"So how are you enjoying Bromont?"

"I love it. People are friendly, I prefer it to the city. I'd like to see more of it."

"Are you planning on staying here long?"

Could she already be thinking about a long-term relationship? No, she was just being polite.

A few of the cast entered the tavern and one waved to Helene. She smiled back. Word of the newcomer would soon be around town. She didn't seem too bothered.

He thought about mentioning the places he'd stayed at recently, but she seemed comfortable in the silence.

"The acting really was good."

"I agree," she said. "A couple of the cast studied drama at college and have been acting for years."

"Let me guess, the husband and wife?"

"How could you tell?"

"They seemed to know each other."

"Ha! They've been married for twenty years. You're right though, they met at drama school."

"How long have you worked at the bistro?"

"Going on ten years. I own it, actually." She smiled with a quiet pride. "My husband and I ran it together until he passed. It's been a struggle, raising the kids and managing the bistro, and also a godsend."

"I'm sorry about your husband."

"That's life, you carry on."

"How's the business doing?"

"It's tough, but I keep my head above water."

"The kids must have been a great help."

"Sometimes…" They shared a smile. "Oh, they're good kids, and I'm going to miss them when they go off to college. I can't see them sticking around here once they graduate." She looked down at her wine. "There's nothing for young people. I've been here all my life, never seen anything, never been anywhere." She looked up again. "I'm happy."

He stared at her and sensed there was more.

She took a final sip of wine and set her glass down. "I better get going, lots to do tomorrow."

"I'll walk you home."

He helped her on with her coat and noticed a few men looking at her as he followed her to the door.

The ten-minute walk in the cold evening was over too soon. He wondered if he should shake her hand, hug her or do nothing. Before he had time to do anything she kissed him on the cheek. "Thanks again, I enjoyed myself."

He hoped she didn't see him blush as she turned and walked inside.

Chapter 24

There was lots of chatter when De Riggi walked into the clubhouse that evening, but as soon as people looked up and saw him, the place went silent. He saw Pigeon and nodded for him to follow as he headed into his office.

"What's happening? What's all the noise about?"

"We got a mole," said Pigeon.

"What? Don't be stupid. Who says?"

"A few of the guys heard the same story. One was in a bar on Saint Denis and one in Old Montreal."

"Who'd they hear it from?"

"Matisse heard if from one of the Russians. He got it from a crooked cop he knows. Dubois says the same thing, only he heard it from a dealer who got it from some boys out of Toronto."

"Who's the mole?"

"They don't know, boss."

"So how do they know it's our gang?"

"Simple, boss, they mentioned your name."

De Riggi looked as if he was going to explode.

"Who the fuck said—"

"Their words were 'De Riggi's gang.' The very words."

De Riggi sat down in his chair and puffed out his cheeks. "I don't buy it. This is a set up. One of the gangs spreading fucking rumours, you know how it works. Start a war inside our gang."

"But, boss, Henri and Patrice, they're the most cynical bastards going. Next to me, that is. You know that. This isn't just a coincidence. You always said you don't believe in coincidences."

De Riggi turned to his number two. "Who do you think it is?"

Pigeon held his boss's gaze. "Davis, of course. Been with us five minutes and now the cat's out of the bag. Probably working for another gang. I told you he was no good. I can always smell a rat."

"Hmm." De Riggi leaned back. He'd been expecting that answer from Pigeon. "If you're right, that's one smooth fucker, and balls of steel on him. I'm not sure. Too simple. We need to check this out."

"Do you want me and a few of the boys to bring him here, boss? He'll talk, I can promise you that."

De Riggi was deep in thought. "We've got a lot riding on him. There's Hatfield for a start. And he's doing another deal for us too."

"What other deal? You never mentioned another deal, boss."

"We only just decided. A mortgage company. He's arranging for us to invest in it."

"What makes you think he's investing our money, boss? What if he's stealing from us?"

De Riggi looked at him. "It's all going through Dunphy, he won't be touching any of it. I need to make sure Hatfield's solid and that we know enough about the mortgage company, so if anything happens to Davis we can still do the deal. Understand?"

"Yes, boss."

"We need to tread carefully, make sure we don't shoot ourselves in the foot. If it is him, then we'll deal with him. Like we deal with any rat. So don't go off half-cocked."

"What happens when Davis hears about the rumours? He'll disappear, you can bet on it."

"There's only one place he's gonna hear the rumours, so keep your mouth shut and don't go following him—or threatening him. I'll make sure we keep an eye on him. And in the meantime, I'm going to do some checking of my own. If he is the mole, we'll find out. And he'll wish he was never born."

De Riggi had trouble believing the rumour, and he was even more shocked that it could be Davis. What if he did work for a rival gang? Who the hell was that smart? It didn't make sense. If it were true, they'd be in a good position to take over the trucking company and even acquire the mortgage company. He needed to find out for himself. He had some well-placed connections in both the Sûreté and the RCMP. It was time to call in some favours.

First he wanted to hear from his crew.

"Go get me Henri and Patrice," he said.

Fifteen minutes later, with two of his most loyal men sitting across from him, De Riggi's doubts about the rumours were confirmed. Neither Patrice Dubois nor Henri Matisse had gotten their information from a reliable source, even if the relationships were long standing. The Russians had a lot to gain from causing them problems, and a local dealer wasn't the most trustworthy of sources. Were they connected? Matisse had dealt with the Russians before. A deal gone bad. And Matisse had done a good job of sorting out a mess. They were the last guys you wanted to piss off. De Riggi asked him if he'd ever dealt with Dubois's dealer. He was adamant he hadn't and was sure the Russians hadn't either.

"So why do you think the source is telling the truth? What's in it for them?"

"I wondered the same thing, boss," Matisse said. "It's not like he asked for anything in return. Maybe he was looking down the road and hoping a good deed would get repaid sooner or later?"

De Riggi laughed. "You don't believe that, do you?"

"Nah. Can't recall a time when they did us a favour. But there's some real shit going on right now, with the Asians trying to squeeze out the small dealers. Maybe they want to maintain the status quo. Better to know who your enemies are than have to deal with new players."

De Riggi sat back and considered this. "So apart from the Russians you've not heard from anyone else about this, and this is the first time you've heard this rumour?"

"Yeah, boss. It was just that when Patrice had heard the same thing, we got talking."

Dubois had been dealing with the same guy for more than ten years, and he was as solid as any dealer could be. De Riggi wanted to know how it came up in conversation.

"Strange really," Dubois said. "We meet every two weeks, find out what's going on, any bad dope, what other gangs are doing, you know, usual stuff. And it just came out."

"Does your guy have the same conversations with his other suppliers?"

Dubois looked embarrassed.

"What do you mean, boss?"

"Simple question. These chats work both ways. Sharing information like."

Dubois went red in the face. "No, boss, it's strictly one-way."

De Riggi doubted that. He remembered the times when he'd been in the same position. Usually, the information he passed on was part fact, part fiction. Often a test to see how stupid the dealer was and how reliable his intelligence was.

He could see Dubois thinking about his meeting with the dealer. Assessing his reliability and his own stupidity.

"Okay, Patrice, if you hear anything more, or think of something else, let me know as soon as possible. Oh, one other thing. If the rumour is true"—De Riggi leaned forward—"who do you think it is?"

"I was thinking, now we've taken over Hatfield's, I wonder if it's something to do with that. And it could be nothing more than a rumour spread by another gang, people who have something to gain by stirring shit up for us."

De Riggi leaned back. Maybe Dubois wasn't so stupid after all.

***

At ten o'clock that evening, De Riggi pulled into the unlit parking lot of an abandoned building site on the Île Sainte-Hélène. The man he was meeting was already there. Louis Hardin flashed his lights as De Riggi parked. Hardin walked over to his truck and got in.

"You said it was urgent?" Hardin asked.

De Riggi hesitated. The trouble with bad cops on your payroll was that you never really knew whether you could trust them. Who were they really working for? You, the cops, other gangs? *Christ*, he thought, *is there no one you can trust?* Now he didn't have a choice. He had to find out what the hell was going on.

"We have a problem. I need to know if we have a mole in our gang. I need to know what you're hearing on the street."

De Riggi explained where the claims came from.

"That's a serious allegation, and a dealer is likely to know the consequences of spreading such rumours, especially if they can't be proven."

"So how do I find out if we have a mole or not?"

"Start with the suspects, check out the source, maybe set a trap. Have you done any deals recently, or are you about to do a deal? I don't need to know the details, but the two could be related. I assume you have some suspicions?"

"Maybe…"

"Look, sometimes the obvious suspect has been set up and the real culprit is right in front of you. Someone who's pissed off. A deal gone bad, a gang member that's upset and trying to get rid of someone.… I can check around. I've heard nothing on the street. That doesn't mean anything though."

"One of our guys is pretty sure he knows who it is. And I have to say, right now I can't prove him wrong, but it just seems too obvious, too easy."

"Rumours are easy to start. Checking them out is a different matter. Your guy probably wants to beat the crap out of him until he talks and then deal with him."

"Something like that."

"This guy, how important is he?"

"You mean the suspected mole? He's a player."

"I can talk to a few people, but the more you talk the worse the rumours get and then everyone knows. It undermines you and the gang. You need to move quickly—and quietly."

"Tell me, where in the city would I find an honest cop?" De Riggi asked.

"Excuse me? Oh, I see what you mean." Hardin chuckled. "First of all, anyone connected with the gang isn't going to give an honest answer. You need someone legit, someone that can be trusted and a reason why they need to know. Start with a lawyer who's clean and has no contacts with the gang."

"Okay, Hardin, here's the deal. You go find that person and then have him find the mole. There's a lot riding on this. You find him and there's a ten grand in it for you."

"That's a lot of money, Mr. De Riggi." He smiled. "Give me a few days."

Chapter 25

Davis had been busy. He'd met with the board and senior management of the mortgage investment company and was pleased that they understood how bad their situation was. They'd been told by the broker that he represented an investor with deep pockets who was prepared to consider a significant investment. It was evident that their finance director had been given the all-clear to be open. He spent the next half-hour explaining the company's financial problems and the several meetings with shareholders that had failed to reach any sort of compromise. Most just wanted their money back, and it was clear that they'd lost confidence in both the board and management.

When he was finished, the room was silent as the finance director and other three board members looked at Davis. Davis looked down at his notes, then began asking questions. For the next hour he grilled the finance director, who continued to be candid about their precarious situation. At one point, Davis noticed two of the directors cringing. He wasn't sure if it was the realization that things were that desperate or that the finance director was being so open.

"So what sort of plan do you see offering the shareholders?" Davis asked.

At this point the chairman jumped in. "We thought it'd be good to be able to offer some money up front, say thirty per cent of what they're owed. And then if they still want to be paid out in full then over the next six months to a year, we can come up with a final settlement offer, at a discount of course."

Davis wondered if the chairman was one of the shareholders who'd take a discount, and how many friends and family he'd persuaded to invest in the business.

"I presume that all this would be financed by the new investor?" asked Davis.

The chairman smiled. "And I think we need to find a way to entice the remaining shareholders to stay in. Maybe offer to pay them one year's dividend in the next three months."

Davis wondered what would happen to the chairman.

He was starting to get an idea of how to structure a deal using the gang's money. He hadn't decided what sort of settlement offer he'd be prepared to finance, but he knew there'd have to be some money up front. Bottom line: knowing the gang, they wouldn't want other investors involved. And given the infighting amongst the shareholders, if they ended up in liquidation in the next thirty days, any exclusive agreement wouldn't survive the bankruptcy. This deal that had a short fuse; the company would fold in a matter of weeks.

He decided that he could probably get the gang to sign off on an offer in a week or less. He looked around the room and said, "I think I've got everything I need right now. Do you have any questions?"

The chairman just smiled. As if the deal was already done.

***

That afternoon when he got back to his cottage, Davis contacted Dunphy and explained his plan. He asked the lawyer to do a company search and go through the company's corporate records and share structure, and then explained how he proposed to finance the investment and how he expected they could gain control of the company.

When Dunphy complained that things were going too quickly, Davis explained that the company simply wouldn't be around in a few weeks. "And this is what De Riggi wants," Davis said. He heard Dunphy groan.

After he hung up, Davis couldn't help wondering about Dunphy. Recently he'd been acting strangely, was moody and seemed to be looking over his shoulder all the time. Maybe he'd had enough of De Riggi and the gang. *Oh well*, he thought, *not my problem.*

Davis had something else on his mind anyway. Helene had agreed to spend the weekend with him in the Townships, making it clear that he wanted her two kids to join them as well—as soon as she accepted, he knew he'd made a mistake. Still, he couldn't back out.

He was heading to his bedroom to grab a few last-minute items for the trip when a knock on his door caught him by surprise. He was even more surprised when he opened it.

"I happened to be in the neighbourhood," De Riggi said.

Davis regained his composure. "I was just heading out."

De Riggi stuck his foot in the doorway and leaned into the cottage. "This won't take long."

He stepped in past Davis. The place was sparse. There were no dishes lying around, just a book and a few papers on the table, and what looked like an overnight bag. *Son of a bitch. Pigeon was right.* "Going somewhere?" De Riggi could barely contain his fury.

"I'm heading to a resort on Lake Champlain for the weekend … Need a break from all this."

De Riggi stepped forward, his jaw tense, one fat finger pointing at Davis. "I don't believe in coincidences. And you leaving town is a big one."

Davis almost took a step back but held his place. "I don't know what you mean—"

"We have a mole." De Riggi had dropped both hands to his sides, like he was ready to pull a gun. "And all the evidence points to you."

Davis laughed. "Who says? And what am I supposed to have done?"

This bastard's pretty calm. De Riggi curled his hands into fists. "I shoulda listened to Pigeon; he said you were a rat from day one."

"So it's Pigeon's word against mine. I was never going to win that argument, was I? Who am I supposed to be working for?"

"You're cool, I'll give you that."

"Why would I be helping you run Hatfield's, and why would I be helping you buy the mortgage company? Am I part of some big con? And if so, who the hell am I working for? Let me guess, the police, or maybe another gang planning to take over?"

De Riggi stared at him and then sat down. "You're a damn good actor and the biggest con man going. I'll give you that. The fact that you're leaving town tells me you know we're onto you. Who are you going with?"

Davis dropped his chin slightly. "Well, there's this girl … I met in Bromont. And we're going to one of the resorts I looked at for you a few weeks ago. La Cache du Lac Champlain. Look, here's the reservation." He grabbed a paper from the table and handed it to De Riggi. Davis wasn't sure what to do so he decided to push home his advantage. If De Riggi thought he was a rat, he'd have someone follow him and they'd probably never let him out of their sight until they were able to prove he was telling the truth or was, in fact, a rat. He knew the boss was just trying to break him—seeing if he would crack and give something away.

"I thought it might come to this," Davis said. The two men stared at each other for a moment. "I can't work for you anymore."

De Riggi stood up and took a step toward him. "What the fuck are you talking about?"

"You show up out of the blue in my home and accuse me of being a rat with no evidence other than Pigeon's word? There's no way I can carry on."

De Riggi sized him up for a moment. "You got some balls, I'll give you that."

Davis shrugged. "Listen, I don't know what you've been told, but you're the one that's been conned. You know Pigeon's made my life hell these last months. Had me followed everywhere. Been through my home, calling people I know. He doesn't want me around and it's clear you trust him far more than you're ever going trust me."

He waited to see how De Riggi reacted. Was this a chance to discredit Pigeon? It was the first time he'd seen De Riggi lost for words.

"Listen…" De Riggi was trying to figure out what to say, realizing he'd jumped the gun and had maybe made a mistake. "I've gotta be careful, a lot's riding on Hatfield's. And this mortgage deal. I need to be sure."

"So you come to my home, accusing me of being a rat? Maybe you should look closer to home."

"What do you mean?"

"Who has the most to lose from my involvement?"

"You saying it's Walter?"

"I'm not saying anything. Who wants to get rid of me?"

"Nah. Not Walter."

Davis shrugged again. "Well, I can't work like this, always under suspicion. You can find someone else. I'm done. Now if you don't mind, I've got to get going." Davis turned his back on the man and walked toward the kitchen. "And make sure you have your guys follow me to the resort, won't you?"

De Riggi chuckled. *Brass balls, this one.* He left the cottage.

Davis's immediate thought was to call his handlers. Then he had to cancel his trip with Helene. There was no way he'd be taking her anywhere with De Riggi's pit bull Pigeon tracking his every move. Maybe that's what they'd expect him to do. Had he told De Riggi too much? He'd been caught off guard and had tried to act natural. He needed to stop guessing what the gang was doing and figure out what *he* should do. He called Lacroix, who picked up after six agonizing rings.

"We need to meet. Usual place, one hour."

Davis hung up. He then phoned Helene at the bistro. He explained that a problem had come up at work and he'd need to work all weekend and maybe go to Toronto as well. He claimed it couldn't be helped. He could hear the disappointment in her voice. "The kids will be so disappointed; they were looking forward to getting away for the weekend."

"You guys should still go; the rooms are booked. You can even tell your son he can have my room. Look, there's an outside chance I could get there by Sunday morning, but I can't guarantee it. Please say you'll go. I'll make it up to you all, I promise."

She exhaled loudly. "If you're sure."

"I am. Now I've gotta to go. Have a great time."

He knew he wouldn't be going anywhere near the resort, and he had to make sure Helene and her family were safe. As he pulled out onto the main road by his cottage, he saw an old pickup parked nearby. It pulled out as he passed it. He managed to lose the pickup after about two miles, pulling into a side road surrounded by trees on either side. He looked back as the truck sped pass, then he turned around and went in the opposite direction.

Less than twenty minutes later, Davis was walking along the path by the lake. Lacroix was seated at the bench. The leaves were starting to appear on the trees, and it was warm for the time of year, maybe even ten degrees in the late afternoon as the sun still had a few hours before going down.

"Let's go for a walk," said Lacroix, as he stood up and looked back in the direction Davis had come.

"So what's the panic?"

"De Riggi just visited me at the cottage. Accused me of being a mole. I denied it, of course, and asked him what proof he had. He didn't have any." He glanced at Lacroix. "So I take it you started the rumour?"

Lacroix looked sheepish. "We probably should have given you a heads up. We wanted to make sure that your reaction was as natural as possible though."

"Weren't you going to put it out there that Pigeon was the mole?"

"They'll come around to that eventually," Lacroix said. "Vincent thought a more general rumour to start would be less obvious. Don't worry. Our contacts will make sure he thinks it's Pigeon in the end."

"Well I told him I was done with the gang, there was no way I was working for him anymore," Davis said.

"How'd he take it?"

"Said he may have jumped to conclusions, so I told him he had to choose between me and Pigeon."

"And?"

"He left."

Lacroix smiled to himself. The guy had nerves of steel and was quick on his feet.

"So where do we go from here?" Lacroix asked.

"For a start, I think I need to stay close to home. And I need you to watch some friends of mine, the people that I was heading to the Townships with for the weekend."

"You mean Helene?"

Davis stopped walking and faced his handler. "You know?"

"Let's just say we keep an eye on you. So they're still going? Was that wise?"

"I didn't want to let them down."

"Don't worry we've had some people checking on her from time to time. I hear the food's good at the bistro."

"You think these rumours will stick?"

"They're sure gonna slow down De Riggi and make him think twice about Pigeon."

"I'm not sure it's having the desired effect. I'm sure Pigeon's going to be coming for me once De Riggi sits him down."

"Maybe not. We're hoping De Riggi will sideline him for a while. Or maybe deal with him permanently."

"Where does that leave me?"

"You carry on doing what you're doing. Unless you want out. Which'd be a shame now you've persuaded Dunphy that the gang should do the deal. Your star is rising."

"It's all getting a bit…"

"Complicated? Yes, we hadn't anticipated Helene. We have to hang tough. In some ways it'd have been better if you'd gone for the weekend, business as usual. Maybe you let your relationship cool a bit. You're only putting her and her kids at risk."

Davis was irritated. "I didn't plan it, things just happened."

"Yeah, well, maybe slow things down. Pretend to get busier at work…"

Davis knew he'd made a mistake. But he was lonely, and it'd been a long time since he'd felt anything for anyone. His life was on hold, and he wondered how long that would go on for.

As if reading his thoughts, Lacroix said, "Don't worry, she and her kids will be fine, we'll make sure. And this won't be forever. It looks as if we're heading into the home stretch. The next few months will tell."

Chapter 26

Hardin finally called De Riggi and arranged to meet on the Island again. The cop had been busy.

"One of the people I talked to is a retired ex-vice cop. Kicked off the force for being involved in kickbacks. He tells me rumours of a mole in your gang have been around for a while, at least a few years."

"How come I never heard about this?"

"No idea, but the guy gave me three names."

"Jesus Christ. First you tell me the rumours about a mole have been around for a while, and that it could be any one of three people. And I'm the last to know? I only heard about this a few weeks ago. You're telling me I don't know what's going on in my own gang? Next you'll be telling me people think I'm past it."

"I'm just sharing information okay, don't go crazy."

"Get on with it: who?"

"Henri Matisse, Patrice Dubois and Walter Pigeon."

De Riggi felt his muscles twitch. "Guy's full of shit," he sputtered. "All of them have been with me for more than twenty years. Pigeon's my number-one guy. You expect me to pay for this shit? Christ, what bullshit."

"He claims all three were interested in taking over from you at one time or another and he suggested I check them all out."

De Riggi put his hand on his chest and Hardin wondered if he was having a heart attack.

"I arranged for surveillance on all three," the cop said, pulling a file folder from his briefcase. "Don't worry, my guys are pros, they weren't noticed. I also got someone to check out their finances."

"Does this story have an ending? I could be dead before you finish."

"We followed them for almost two weeks," Hardin said as he opened his file. "Got nothing on Matisse or Dubois. Most of the time they were in bars, the clubhouse or at home. Neither have much money. Matisse has four bank accounts totalling two grand and he has a lot of debt, mostly credit cards. Dubois has three accounts and transfers money from one to the other on a regular basis. He owns a cabin up north he visits every two weeks with his piece on the side. He's got even less cash and more credit card debt than Matisse.

"Neither is worth anything, unless you count the bikes and their trucks, and Dubois's shit cabin. There've been no unusual deposits in any of their bank accounts in the last twelve months."

"Is there a punchline to this joke?"

Hardin took a deep breath. He wasn't looking forward to De Riggi's reaction.

"Two things came up on Pigeon. He opened a bank account with a small caisse in Lennoxville about eight months ago. A few months later there was a twenty grand deposit. Then for the last four months there've been monthly deposits of five grand. We've been unable to track down the source of the money." Hardin passed a few papers of banking information to De Riggi.

De Riggi glanced down at them for a moment, then looked up again. "So Walter's making some money on the side. Big deal. That's it, that's all you've got?"

"I said two things. We also got photos of him going in and out of the same bar on the East Side. Three times in the last two weeks."

"Yeah? Well, we do a lot of business in bars."

Hardin reached into his pocket and pulled out an envelope. "Each time he goes into the bar, the same two guys follow him out and then they go their separate ways."

"Probably dealers."

"They're not dealers." Hardin handed him the envelope containing some grainy photos. "They're cops."

De Riggi reached up to turn on the interior truck light to get a better look. Really he just needed more time to digest what he'd just heard.

"How do you know they're cops?" he said finally.

"My guys recognized them."

"Your guys?"

"Ex-cops."

He looked at the photos again. They weren't any of the cops on the gang's payroll.

"One other thing."

De Riggi wondered how it could get any worse.

"The bar, it's a gay bar."

De Riggi didn't move for a moment. Then he threw the pictures at Hardin. "Now I know this is all bullshit. I've known Walter for twenty years. Christ, I've even spent time with him inside. There's no goddam way."

Hardin was leaning away from the angry boss. "You asked me to see what I could dig up. That's what I did. None of it points to Davis." He opened the door and got out of car, leaving the pictures scattered on the seat and floor. "I'm sorry, Mr. De Riggi, but the only dirt I could find was on Walter Pigeon."

Chapter 27

De Riggi needed to be sure about Pigeon. He'd already screwed up with Davis; the last thing he wanted to do was be wrong again. He wasn't sure what was worse, Pigeon being a rat or being gay. How could you work with a guy for all that time and have no idea who he really was? He needed proof—proof beyond a few photos. As he sat in his armchair at home staring at the photos again he phoned Dunphy.

"We need to meet," he said when the lawyer answered.

There was a moment of silence on the other end. De Riggi could picture the weasel smoothing his tie. "I have meetings all day—"

"Then we'll meet tonight," De Riggi said. "Your office—"

"No."

"Excuse me?"

"I mean … look, Tony. I'm not sure it's safe. I-I'm being watched."

Jesus Christ. De Riggi wanted to reach through the phone and strangle the little shit. "Why is everyone so goddamn paranoid lately?" Before Dunphy could answer, De Riggi gave him the name of a bar on Saint Denis and told him to be there at eight o'clock. Before Dunphy could argue, De Riggi hung up.

Dunphy sat in his office gazing out the window and wondered what would happen if he didn't show up. He finally decided he'd better go to the meeting. At seven-thirty, he hailed a cab from just outside his office. He told the driver to head to Old Montreal. After about fifteen minutes of continually looking behind him he was satisfied he wasn't being followed. He told the driver he'd changed his mind and gave him the name of the bar on Saint Denis.

When he arrived, De Riggi was already seated at the back of the bar with his back to the wall. Dunphy recognized the place; it was a biker hangout. He headed to the back and sat down.

The gang boss was glaring at him. "What kept you?"

"I needed to make sure I wasn't being followed."

"You're paranoid."

"What's so urgent?"

De Riggi was about to smack him across the face. Who did this jumped-up little lawyer think he was talking to? Something wasn't right—Dunphy's attitude had changed in the last few months. He needed to find out what was going on with him. But now wasn't the time. He needed him, at least for the time being. He stared at him with his penetrating eyes. Dunphy looked away, realizing he needed to show more respect, pretend nothing had happened.

Finally De Riggi said in a low voice, "We have a mole in the gang."

Dunphy tensed up. What did he know? Was it him De Riggi was talking about? He started to sweat. He'd been so preoccupied with his own problems, he hadn't been paying attention to what De Riggi wanted.

De Riggi didn't seem to notice anything as he relayed the story and his chat with the crooked cop Hardin, scattering the pictures across the table between them.

"What makes you so sure? How do you know it's not a set up?" Dunphy asked.

"Why the fuck would it be a set up?"

"It hasn't crossed your mind?"

"Yeah, it's crossed my mind. That's why I'm dealing with this. I need to be sure. That's your job. That's why you're here." The boss's eyes were bulging, and his face was red.

Dunphy shrank back slightly. His hand was damp as he stroked his silk tie. "Photos can be faked," he offered, not quite able to look De Riggi in the eye.

"What about the bank accounts?" De Riggi passed a file folder to Dunphy, who took a few minutes to peruse the bank statements inside.

"These look real."

"You're not certain?"

Dunphy sighed. Suddenly he felt exhausted. "Look, we all go back a long way. Walter's the last person I'd think of. He knows he's taking over soon enough. It doesn't make sense. And anyway, who could he be working for?"

De Riggi settled back slightly, slowly regaining his composure.

"So, Tony, do you know the cops in the photo?"

"No."

"Maybe that's a start," said Dunphy. "It only makes sense if they're bent."

De Riggi leaned forward again. "And if they're bent then maybe he's working for another gang." The boss was getting worked up again. "And why meet in a gay bar? Walter … who'd have thought?"

"If it is another gang, that could have been their idea. Maybe they own the club," Dunphy offered. "And you know he doesn't trust Davis. You've been using the new guy more and more. Maybe he thinks Davis is getting in his way, or worse, maybe he thinks Davis is taking over."

De Riggi was back to glaring. "This isn't helping. How do I find out if it's Walter?"

Dunphy loosened his tie and signalled the waiter. "You set a trap."

"What kind of trap?"

"I don't know." He was suddenly very hot. He needed a drink. "You know Walter better than I do. Who else have you told about this?"

"Just you."

"How well do you know any of your guys?"

De Riggi exhaled. "When you put it like that, it could be any of them."

"You don't have proof that it's anyone else. You need to talk to someone that's not bent, someone you know will tell the truth."

The waiter had made his way over to them, and De Riggi waited impatiently as his lawyer ordered a drink. As soon as the young man was gone, De Riggi hissed, "And who'd that be? Who am I supposed to talk to for Christ's sake?"

"Someone that knows the criminal underworld."

"So I just pick up the phone and ask? Is that what you're saying?"

Dunphy removed his suit jacket and let it drop to the seat beside him. "Someone in law enforcement. Maybe a cop, maybe someone in the ODCP, that's the Office of the Director of Criminal and Penal Prosecutions."

"Great, yeah, I can see it know, I'll just pick up the phone and say, 'This is Tony De Riggi, I need to know if my number two is a mole.'"

The waiter returned with a large mug of beer. Dunphy snatched it from him before he had set it on the table and took a long swallow. He wiped his mouth with the back of his hand. "I know some guys. Lawyers who've acted for the ODCP. If they don't know, then chances are they know who does. And if he is a mole, he's more likely to be working for another gang than the cops." He took another long drink, then reached across the table. "I need the photos. We need to know if the guys he met are crooked cops or not."

"If Walter betrayed me after all these years…"

Dunphy finished his last gulp and pushed the mug away. "Just leave this with me. In the meantime, don't say or do anything with Walter. Where is he, by the way?"

"He's around. I told him to lay off Davis but knowing him he's probably been tracking his every move."

Dunphy got up and left the bar. De Riggi had given him an idea.

Chapter 28

Something made Dunphy decide to call Jean Belliveau and meet up with Crown counsel after all. Whether it was the knowledge that De Riggi trusted him to check out Pigeon, the fact he was sure someone was following him or just the continuous lack of sleep, he didn't know. He'd reached the point of no return.

Dunphy met Belliveau the next day at Belliveau's office near the Quebec criminal courts in Ville-Marie. He didn't care if he was being followed anymore. When he walked into the conference room, there were four people he didn't recognize: two from the Security Service, including its Quebec head, an Inspector Yves Vincent; a Marc Tremblay, one of the city's head prosecutors; and a representative of the Quebec RCMP.

Belliveau leaned back in his chair. "My client wants to help in any way he can. But before we give you anything, we need some guarantees. We're looking for release from prosecution and witness protection for himself and his family."

"My kids," Dunphy interjected.

"Sean, it's possible they'll go after your ex too."

Dunphy shrugged. Then, seeing the looks on the other men's faces, he added, "Yeah, fine. Whatever."

The prosecutor cleared his throat and leaned forward. "Once your client tells us what he knows, we'll be able to advise on what we're prepared to offer."

Belliveau turned to Dunphy, his eyebrows raised. It was now or never, Dunphy realized. He was tired of looking over his shoulder. And this seemed to be the only way out. Finally, he looked over at the men, waiting eagerly across from him, and began to speak. For the next hour, he walked the group through the history of his involvement with the gang and what he did for them. He explained how they were heavily involved in drug trafficking through the Port of Montreal, how they recently acquired Hatfield's Trucking to continue to use the port for trafficking, how they were using an Old Montreal hotel as a high-end brothel and their plan to acquire other motel properties outside the city, which might be used to expand their human trafficking business. He mentioned the name Alan Davis. De Riggi once believed he was the mole, but now believed that the real mole was the long-time gang number two, Walter Pigeon.

When Dunphy was done, Vincent finished making a note and passed it to Tremblay, who turned to Belliveau. "Your client's assistance could be of value to the Crown and, subject to his ongoing cooperation, we'd be prepared to offer a deal. We'd like a fifteen-minute recess while I caucus with my colleagues."

Belliveau and Dunphy were escorted to a private room on a different floor of the building. About a minute after they left, the door opened again, and a short bespectacled man walked in. Bernie Lacroix nodded to his boss, Vincent, and the other Security Service member and shook hands with the RCMP corporal.

The Crown counsel said, "Inspector, maybe you and Corporal Lacroix can bring us up to speed and suggest a strategy."

Vincent looked at Lacroix and said, "This is a rather fluid situation."

Lacroix wondered what he meant by fluid, and what Davis might make of the comment.

"Rather than repeat the story, I'll have Corporal Lacroix give you the rundown."

Lacroix took a deep breath, then started giving them the background to the operation. "For almost a year now, under the direction of Inspector Vincent, my colleague Corporal Primeau and I have been involved in an undercover operation known as Long Way Back. It involves Alan Davis, a former gangster from Vancouver. Davis agreed to leave witness protection and go undercover to help penetrate De Riggi's gang. He started by working for Hatfield's Trucking, a Montreal-based trucker that ships drugs on the gang's behalf out of the port. The gang now owns the trucking company and Davis has taken over day-to-day management. Recently the gang hired him to acquire and manage other businesses on their behalf to launder drug money. Through Davis's efforts, they're about to acquire a mortgage investment corporation."

Lacroix looked at his boss, who nodded for him to continue.

"Our initial goal was to get him close to De Riggi, his gang, port officials and others who've been aiding the gang in developing and maintaining their stranglehold on the port. De Riggi successfully took over the longshoreman's union several years ago and uses the container ports as his own private playground. He imports drugs through the port on a regular basis with impunity. We suspect that several port officials, as well as members of the Sûreté, City police and Customs, are under his influence. There's now a prospect of Davis becoming a full-time member of the gang. De Riggi recently indicated that he wanted to step down and spend more time in Miami. His logical successor up until recently was Walter Pigeon."

Lacroix poured himself a glass of water. "Pigeon has never accepted Davis. Always believed he was a mole and still does. We recently leaked a story that the gang had a mole, and that Pigeon was the mole."

Tremblay looked around the room. "What do we do with Dunphy?"

Vincent looked at Lacroix and said, "Corporal, what options do we have at this point?"

"Davis knows he's at even greater risk after being accused of being the mole. He still wants to continue. Leaving Dunphy in place is our best option. If he suddenly disappears, De Riggi will know something's up."

Tremblay looked at him and said, "Sounds like Dunphy's at the end of his rope. It must have taken a lot for him to come here. Asking him to go undercover puts him more at risk, along with the entire operation."

Vincent looked up and said, "We'll tell him we want him to carry on as usual. We can keep an eye on him. That'll reinforce his claim that he's being watched. He could also help convince De Riggi that Pigeon is a mole."

Lacroix looked at his boss. "I agree, sir. We have Dunphy feed De Riggi information that reinforces the idea of Pigeon being the mole—which means Dunphy will have to carry on for a few more months and act like it's business as usual."

Ten minutes later, Dunphy and Belliveau were called back into the room. They met Lacroix, and Tremblay told them that while they were prepared to do a deal, they wanted Dunphy to remain in place and carry on as if nothing had happened.

It took a bit of persuading on Belliveau's part. Eventually his client nodded.

Tremblay wanted to know exactly what information they would have Dunphy leak about Pigeon, and how they were going to stop De Riggi digging further.

"With respect," said Lacroix said, turning toward the prosecutor, "you don't really need to know that."

Vincent stared at Tremblay and then smiled at Lacroix. "Quite right, Corporal." He looked around the table. "Unless there's anything else…" He turned to Dunphy. "Then we'll leave Corporal Lacroix to discuss the details." One side of the table stood up and departed, leaving Lacroix, Dunphy and Belliveau alone in the room.

For the next half-hour, Lacroix walked his new asset through the plan in more detail. "When the time comes to drop the information on De Riggi, keep it simple," he said. "Don't embellish the story, say that's all you were told and that you can't name the source because all you know is it's a senior criminal lawyer in the Quebec bar who's represented gangsters. Say it's rumoured this lawyer has protection from the gangsters he represents."

Belliveau leaned forward. "If I may?"

Lacroix nodded and Belliveau said, "I suggest you add just a few details to give De Riggi the sense that this source is legit. Say the other cops and prosecutors don't like him, and he'd once been shot at when leaving the courthouse after defending a gang member charged with murder."

Dunphy had heard of such lawyers and suspected that De Riggi had too. What De Riggi made of the message was up to him.

Lacroix smiled. "It's not going to be easy for De Riggi to find out the truth without admitting he has a mole. That makes the gang look weak. And that'll make De Riggi want to deal with Pigeon sooner rather than later."

As they walked to their cars, Belliveau explained to Dunphy that it was the best deal that they could have hoped for. Dunphy wasn't convinced, but he knew there was nothing he could do about it. And he took strange comfort that he'd be under surveillance by the cops, albeit for different reasons than De Riggi might have expected.

After Dunphy and Belliveau left the room, Lacroix sat alone for a while, his mind whirling. Finally, he decided he would not tell Davis about the deal with Dunphy. The less he knew the better, and the more likely he'd act naturally. Pretty soon Dunphy would be telling De Riggi what he'd "discovered" about Pigeon. At that point he expected that Pigeon would disappear. Sooner or later, De Riggi would have to promote someone else to take over. The guys controlling the port would be calling De Riggi, wanting to know what the hell was going on. He'd likely be summoned to New York. He could also expect trouble from other gangs. Any sign of weakness was usually a reason for gang turf wars to escalate. Davis was still a long shot to replace Pigeon, but Lacroix doubted the alternative candidates would be any more attractive to the gang boss.

Chapter 29

De Riggi had been preoccupied ever since Hardin had shown him the pictures of Pigeon coming out of a gay bar. He'd barely spoken to anyone for a week, and his business was suffering for it. He knew that sooner or later the rumours would spread to the people who controlled the port, the crooked cops and crooked Sûreté officers that were a part of his organization. The people who controlled the port would force him to deal with Pigeon. The call he'd received earlier that morning from his lawyer, suggesting that there might be even more evidence against Pigeon, made him realize that he might never find out the truth, but proof or not, Pigeon could no longer act as a member of the gang.

Once De Riggi decided he had to deal with Pigeon, he took Dubois along to meet Pigeon in an abandoned cottage near the Vermont border. There was always the prospect that Pigeon would have backup too, especially if he thought De Riggi believed there was any truth to the rumours. When they arrived at the lane to the cottage, De Riggi could see Pigeon's truck parked outside. He parked his truck out of sight.

"What do you want me to do boss?" asked Dubois.

"You stay here, keep an eye on the place. If you hear shots and I don't come out, wait. When he comes out, kill him."

"What do you plan on doing boss?"

"I'm gonna deal with him once and for all."

"Boss, why don't I go in first?"

"Not this time. This is my job."

He walked slowly to the cottage. If Pigeon had company, he'd soon know.

De Riggi banged loudly on the door. There was no sound inside. Suddenly Pigeon appeared from around the back of the cottage. He was unarmed. "Boss, I didn't hear you arrive. Where are you parked?"

"Up the lane. You on your own?"

"Who else were you expecting?"

De Riggi grunted. "Let's go inside."

Pigeon led the way. As De Riggi walked behind his second-in-command, he felt the rigid steel butt of his gun in his back pocket.

Once inside, De Riggi glanced around uncomfortably. There was a bottle of cheap bourbon next to a half-filled glass on the table. Pigeon had clearly been here for some time.

"You come on your own boss?" Pigeon asked.

"What do you think?"

"I'd have brought company, if I believed the rumours."

The two men stared at each other for a moment. "Is that what they are, Walter?"

Pigeon turned and poured a second glass of bourbon. "If you've come to kill me, get on with it. If it's not you, it'll be someone else. Before you do, whether you believe it or not, I'm telling you I'm not a mole." He offered the glass to his boss, who shook his head. Pigeon shrugged and took a sip. "I can't prove it right now. Someone's done a good job of stitching me up. Real professional job." Pigeon set the glass down and looked his boss in the eye. "You know the gang's my life. Boss, you know I'd never do anything to cross you or the gang."

"Save it, Walter." He pulled out his Glock. "You're going to disappear, permanently."

De Riggi pointed the Glock at Pigeon's head and neither man moved. Then De Riggi swung his weapon downward and fired into the floor six inches from Pigeon's feet.

Pigeon jumped. "What the fuck?"

De Riggi slipped his Glock into this back pocket. "Listen: in thirty seconds, I'm out of here. Dubois is in my truck parked up the lane. I'm gonna tell him I've dealt with you and I'm gonna bury your body myself, since we go way back and all."

Pigeon looked like he wanted to say something. De Riggi put up his hand. "You gotta disappear until I've figured this all out. And I mean *disappear*. You contact no one. As far as the rest of the world is concerned, you're dead. Capeesh?"

"Boss, what are you doing?"

"Walter, you gotta trust me. I know that don't come easy for you, this is the time, otherwise someone else is gonna make sure you really are dead."

When De Riggi got back to his truck, Dubois was standing behind it with his gun out.

"I've dealt with him," De Riggi said. "Take my truck back to the clubhouse and park it."

"We gotta clean things up here, boss."

"No. This is my mess. I'll clean it up."

"Boss—"

"You have your orders, Patrice."

He watched Dubois drive out and then headed back to the cottage. He'd already decided where he was taking Pigeon. He'd wouldn't like the place, but he'd be safe and out of the way. The guy he was staying with would make sure he stayed put.

Arvida was almost three hundred miles northeast of Montreal. Even with good traffic it was a tough five-hour drive. Ever since he'd retired from the nearby aluminum smelter, De Riggi's older brother had lived on small farm outside of town. De Riggi hadn't been there in years, but whenever he wanted to hide, that was the place to go. His brother knew what De Riggi did, and he never asked any questions.

He didn't seem surprised when he got the call, but he had expected it to be his brother who wanted to hide and not one of his gang.

When he dropped Pigeon off at the farm, De Riggi made it clear to him that he had to stay put and that if he disappeared from the place, his brother would call him.

And if Pigeon showed his face in Montreal in the next three months, De Riggi really would shoot him.

***

The long drive back to Montreal gave De Riggi plenty of time to think things through. He knew that by now the guys at the port would have heard the rumours about the mole and would be worried for their own sorry lives. And they wouldn't be satisfied that Pigeon was gone. They'd want to know who was replacing him; they'd want to meet his new number two. They'd always told him that Pigeon was a lightweight and that he'd better make sure he had the right guy lined up to take over, otherwise they might have to deal with another gang. Chances were that they might already be thinking of getting into bed with someone else. And with Pigeon dead, the gang would be expecting him to make either Matisse or Dubois his number two. Neither of them had what it took to take over.

Davis was the better business brain. De Riggi shook his head. *It always seems to come back to this guy.* The closer he got to Montreal, the more convinced he was that Davis would be the right choice.

There was something bothering him even more. What if the mole wasn't Pigeon? Or was he being paranoid, not knowing who to trust?

Chapter 30

When De Riggi called Davis and told him he wanted to meet at the gang's clubhouse, he wasn't surprised the man refused.

"Listen," De Riggi said, "if I wanted to deal with you, I'da done it a long time ago. Walter Pigeon was the rat and I've dealt with him. Let's move on. I want you to close the deal on the mortgage company."

"We don't have to meet to close the deal. Dunphy and I can sort that out."

"There's something else…" The boss' voice had an edge, and Davis wasn't sure how far he could push the man. He was silent, making De Riggi wait. The boss had patience, and after a minute, Davis said, "Meet me at the lake. You know, the place where Pigeon blew someone's head off a few months back?"

"That's out in the bloody Townships, for Christ's sake."

"You want to meet or not?"

De Riggi laughed. "Okay. Four p.m." He hung up.

Davis was worried. De Riggi might have dealt with Pigeon, or maybe he'd decided to clean up a few other loose ends. Dunphy could close the mortgage deal by himself, they didn't need him. Then who'd run things? *No,* he thought, *he's not getting rid of me just yet.*

***

De Riggi arrived at the park early and there was no sign of Davis. He didn't have time for this, especially after the call he'd had the night before. He'd been summoned to New York. The boys had heard the rumours, and the big boss wanted a face to face. He wanted to know about the mole and whether De Riggi was still in control. And these guys didn't mess around.

De Riggi told them everything was fine, that he was about to close a deal. They gave him two weeks to get down to New York.

Davis saw De Riggi from a distance, seated on a bench. He was pleased that De Riggi was alone. He'd told his handlers about the call, and they'd arranged for some people to be close by. When he'd called Lacroix, he said he was convinced that the purpose of the meeting wasn't to get rid of him.

"You're right," Lacroix said, "De Riggi would've arranged for someone else to do that. And he wouldn't have chosen the lake, more likely your cottage. Besides, you chose the location, right?"

"Yeah," Davis said.

"He has plans for you," said Lacroix. "Rumour has it that he's got problems south of the border and needs to convince those guys he's still in control."

As Davis walked toward the bench, he passed a young couple pushing a stroller. De Riggi stood up and nodded.

"Let's go for a walk." As Davis turned to walk with him, he heard someone coming from behind him. He looked back and saw two joggers about twenty yards away running toward them. He was worried that Lacroix had overdone things. De Riggi didn't seem concerned though. He waited till the joggers had passed them, not even bothering to look at them.

De Riggi said, "You seem a little nervous. Expecting company?"

"I could say the same thing about you."

De Riggi laughed. They walked in silence for a few moments. Then De Riggi stopped and said, "I want you to join the gang. Official like. You're good with numbers and managing things. We could use your help to grow our business."

"You don't need me in the gang to advise you on business."

"True. We're working more and more together and this'd make it more of a business partnership."

"More like it'll be easier for you to keep an eye on me. Next thing you'll be telling me where to live and who I should associate with."

"Nah, we don't do things like that. No, I see a real future for you. Who knows, one day maybe you'll be running things."

"What makes you think I'd be interested? Besides, how are the rest of the boys gonna feel? Up until recently you all thought I was a mole. Some of them probably still do. I don't see it. I'd always be looking over my shoulder. You and I both know I'll never be treated like one of the boys."

De Riggi stopped walking and the two men faced each other. "I need you to be on the team, one of us."

"I've already done more than I planned to. I helped you with Hatfield. You wanted some business advice, I gave you that. That's it, I'm done."

"That's one thing I like about you: you're your own man."

"Is there another way?"

"Thing is, there's a gap in our organization and I want you to fill it. I want you in for the long haul." De Riggi touched the scar over his right eye. "Not too many people say no to me." He stared at him and then started to walk again. Davis could see the joggers coming back toward them.

De Riggi turned around and faced him again. "Maybe Dunphy was right, maybe that's the future, lawyers and businessmen running things. But I need to answer to some people. They've got plans for us and want to know I've fixed my problems and got some brains behind the muscle."

"Then you call me your business adviser, your accountant, whatever."

De Riggi chewed his lip as he considered things.

"I'll be in touch," he said finally. "In the meantime, get the mortgage deal done."

Davis watched as the boss headed back. Had he pushed too hard? No. There was no way he was going to join the gang. He'd agreed with Lacroix that if it came up the answer was no. Continuing his role as adviser was safer. Besides, there was no way other gang members would be happy with him taking over Pigeon's position, if that's what the boss had in mind. He couldn't tell if De Riggi was angry with him or not used to people not doing as they were told. Whatever De Riggi thought, he knew Davis wasn't a pushover. Far from it. He had balls and maybe he could take over after all. What was in it for Davis? Surely De Riggi must have wondered about that?

***

De Riggi met Matisse and Dubois at the clubhouse that evening. Word had spread already that Pigeon had been dealt with. He needed to deal with the rumours going around. Were they still dealing with Davis? Who would take over? And what about the rumours that another gang was taking over? While he didn't have time for gossip, he knew that both the men carried a lot of weight in the clubhouse. They needed to calm things down. He needed to take them into his confidence, get a sense of what guys were thinking and what everyone thought of Davis.

As he looked at the two of them, he knew neither would take over the business. They both had spent nearly thirty years taking orders; he doubted they'd change. He still wanted to hear what they had to say. He started with Matisse.

"Who do you see running this place five years from now?"

Matisse looked at the floor, then he looked at Dubois.

De Riggi grimaced. "Well, Patrice? What do you think?"

"Boss, I uh … hadn't really thought about it. I guess I'd always assumed it'd be Walter."

"Come on, you guys, I'm not gonna be here forever. There was a time when I thought one of you'd take over."

Matisse looked at him. "That may have been true ten years ago boss. But … I've seen what you do. You work twenty-four seven. You're not afraid to make decisions. You deal with some powerful people. They'd intimidate me, I don't think I could handle it. You're always looking for new business. That's not me. I'm not a leader, never was. I figured Walter would take over. I know that was his hope one day."

"I guess I'm the same," Dubois piped up. "I couldn't handle it. I still can't believe it … about Walter."

They both looked at the ground, as if they were embarrassed. And De Riggi knew his instincts about them had been right. "Well, what do you think of Davis?"

Matisse looked up, startled. "Boss?"

"I'm serious," De Riggi said. "The guy's got a good head on his shoulders."

Matisse shrugged. "I never had anything to do with him—Walter never had a good word to say about him. I guess now we know why."

"And you, Patrice?"

Dubois glanced up at his boss. "Once I heard the rumours, everything Walter said, I thought Davis was the mole. He was the only new guy we've dealt with in the last few years. Walter's been around as long as we have … I guess we were all wrong." Dubois sounded steadier when he asked, "What do *you* think of him boss?"

De Riggi shifted in his seat. "He claimed he could fix Hatfield's and I didn't believe him. He's turned it around though. He's identified a few businesses we should look at. He's smart, not scared of anyone, and if he has something to say, he says it. And he listens." The two men nodded along as their boss listed all Davis's assets. "There's a problem."

"What's that?" Said Dubois.

"He doesn't want to join the gang."

"Why not?"

"Claims he never set out to join the gang, just wanted to help Hatfield sort out his mess. He wants to stay as a business adviser, that's all."

"What's wrong with that, boss?"

"Maybe nothing."

Dubois looked up. "Boss, remember that time you took me to the meeting with Dunphy?"

"What about it?"

"Didn't he tell us we should be hiring professionals to manage our business? He's the one that told us to get an office downtown."

"You're right, Patrice, he did. So neither of you'd have a problem with us using Davis more?"

They both looked at each other and nodded.

"Why not, if it's good business?" said Matisse.

"What about if he took over one day?"

"You mean run the gang?"

De Riggi looked at them both. "That's what I'm saying. Maybe not today, but down the road. In the meantime, he'd become more familiar with our business."

Matisse said, "So what would he be doing that's different from what he's doing today?"

"He'd get to meet some of the senior people in the city. Like the guys who run the port, and maybe some of the senior cops on our payroll."

Dubois jumped in. "Doesn't it come down to whether you trust him?"

"Yeah, it sure does."

"You and Walter checked him out good, I remember Walter telling us," Dubois said, then turned slightly red as he realized what he was saying. "I guess what Walter said doesn't really matter now…"

De Riggi grunted. "Walter was afraid. He thought Davis would become the number-two guy in the gang and eventually take over from him."

Dubois said, "Or maybe he was afraid he'd get found out."

Chapter 31

The next day, De Riggi told Davis that he was prepared to continue their relationship with Davis as a business adviser. Davis felt a huge relief that he would no longer be pressured to join the gang. Instead, he'd be privy to all the underground dealings the boss had planned without having to be formally initiated.

Over the next few months, De Riggi began taking Davis to meetings where he met senior executives from large construction companies; the presidents of powerful Montreal unions, including the construction workers and the municipal government employees' union; and a private equity firm that managed some of the big union pension funds. When Davis asked De Riggi how he knew all these people, he simply said, "Some of them I've known for thirty years, when they were just starting out. Many of them I helped when they had problems. I've worked at it for years; my network is important."

De Riggi told Davis he'd been invited to a dinner with port officials, and he wanted Davis there. He introduced Davis to the four individuals seated around the table in a big boardroom at the port's offices. They explained that they were looking at a new vision for the port that involved moving to a new location. Everything was hush-

hush, but De Riggi had a chance to get in on the ground floor. The land they'd identified was worthless right now, some sort of industrial wasteland. If they had their way, down the road it could be of real value. In addition, the old port lands would eventually be offered for sale and there would be opportunities to control the bidding process. They told De Riggi they couldn't be involved in buying the properties and were quick to remind him that they were confident he'd take care of his friends.

Davis assumed that any major construction project at the docks would involve high-level political decisions. Contacts at the City would be critical. Relationships with the big construction unions and developers known to support the current City administration would also prove useful. Davis realized De Riggi would have been one of several parties that were getting the heads up, as the slimy politicians started to jockey for position and make sure that their friends benefitted from the opportunities and eventually shared in the wealth. He wondered what other connections the gang boss had.

Over the next several weeks, the gang acquired a few parcels of land at the site where the proposed container port was to be located. Davis hired a surveyor and a planner to rezone the site to light industrial and spent money having engineers perform geotechnical studies. Then he brought in a contractor to prepare an estimate of the costs involved in having the buildings demolished and the site cleaned up. De Riggi and Davis attended several meetings with Port officials. De Riggi was impressed by Davis's questions and the way he conducted himself. Davis was making a good impression with the port officials.

There was a time when De Riggi couldn't make one of the meetings and told Davis to go on his own. Davis was surprised when he showed up and no one asked where his boss was. Later, he told De Riggi they should consider optioning the remaining five lots that made up the rest of the proposed new site. He also cautioned him that nothing was guaranteed and the port might still end up going with a different site. Davis told him it was time to spread the risk and take on a few partners.

De Riggi disagreed. Was it greed, or overconfidence? *Whatever it is,* thought Davis, *De Riggi is thinking like a greedy gangster and not like a businessman.*

Davis was overseeing the mortgage company, which was providing a safe vehicle for the gang to shelter some of its drug money. He'd set up a new investment fund that was owned just by gang members. When he tried to explain what he was proposing to De Riggi, the gang boss just waved him away, telling him to just do it and not bother him with the details.

While Davis had become more involved in the investment side of the gang, he was no closer to the drug business. Maybe De Riggi wanted to keep that private, or maybe Matisse and Dubois were more involved than he realized.

Lacroix and Primeau kept asking if De Riggi ever talked about the drug business and whether Davis should raise it. He told them to be patient and let things happen. At some point De Riggi would share his connections with the drug trade. Davis sensed that someone inside the port as well as someone inside the Montreal police was part of the operation; but he had no idea who. What Davis didn't say was that he might never hear about the drug side of the business if he kept refusing to join the gang.

Chapter 32

De Riggi's New York contacts were coming north for a visit. De Riggi knew the reason. They'd heard about the mole and wanted to make sure he'd dealt with it. They'd also been telling him for months that they had big plans for Montreal but that he needed to hire some businesspeople to run the organization. He'd been stalling them, telling them about the trucking company and some real estate they'd been looking at near the port. And about a new guy they'd hired and how he'd done a good job with the trucking company and was helping expand their business.

De Riggi had told Dubois and Matisse that for the purposes of the visit Davis would act like a member of the gang. De Riggi thought he knew how his New York counterparts would handle the trip. They'd start with dinner at a nice Italian restaurant and then arrange a few visits to some of the clubs and hotels that the gang owned. He'd put them up at the Auberge and make sure they were taken care of. He wanted them to spend time with Davis and have a look at some of their businesses. In the past, such visits would end up with everybody drunk, with everyone telling stories and lies that got bigger as the night wore on.

The three New Yorkers who came up this time weren't the usual ones. Jimmy Canfusco, the number-two guy, came with a couple of his lieutenants. Jimmy rarely set foot outside of New York, and never came north. Known as the Jimmy the Finisher, the number-two guy got his nickname because of how people's careers in the mob seemed to end after he paid them a visit. Everyone feared Jimmy, even his close associates. He clearly had his eye on the top job.

Most of the time, Jimmy's job was to deal with problems. Ruffle a few feathers, mix things up, give guys a wake-up call, remind them they needed to pick up their game or else they'd be out. He was good at it, but he didn't have a smooth touch, and his way of motivating people was by threat. Unsurprisingly, given the organization he worked for, it didn't always encourage loyalty; in fact, quite the opposite. He'd been told to be careful with the guys in Montreal. There'd been some problems. His job was to find out what was going on and report back. While the New York boys saw big things in Montreal's future, it would always be a branch operation. Given its proximity to New York, the boys felt there was lots of untapped potential and great upside for expansion of the drug business. They'd toyed with the idea of putting one of their own into the branch's leadership, but experience had taught them that was usually divisive and resented by the locals. Better to make a fuss of the big fish in the small pond and make them feel part of a major organization.

So this time the reasons for the visit would be different. The New York bosses would not only check out the rumours about a mole, they'd also take a close look at De Riggi's organization and decide if he had the right people at the top. He knew they'd be talking to their contacts, which included some of the other gangs they used in the past for the smaller jobs, as well as some of their police contacts.

The more time Davis spent with Matisse and Dubois, the more he realized they were just order-takers. They showed little initiative, drank too much and weren't very discreet. When they went to dinner with the New York guys, their casual dress and poor manners at the dining room table shocked their guests, who were dressed smartly, knew their wines and enjoyed proper Italian food. Both drank beer after beer, ate too much and leered at the waitresses. Even De Riggi was embarrassed.

Jimmy Canfusco was seated between De Riggi and Davis at dinner. Davis figured his Italian suit must have cost over a thousand bucks. He noticed his nails were manicured and his hair recently coiffured. He probably spent more on his personal appearance in a week than De Riggi did in a year.

Canfusco declined the offer of accommodation and transportation while in Montreal. It was as if he couldn't get out of the place fast enough. Davis wasn't sure what impression Jimmy took away with him, but he doubted it was of a sophisticated team of gangsters dominating the Montreal crime scene. He would've described the evening as dinner with a biker gang who preferred pizza and beer to fine Italian cuisine and Barolo wines.

Canfusco peppered Davis with questions about their real estate investments and their operating companies. He asked where he thought organized crime was headed. "So you think we need to be surrounding ourselves with professionals, businessmen, accountants, lawyers and bankers?"

"I do," said Davis. "Things are becoming more complicated; a lot of the leg work can be contracted out. We need new ways to move money around: trust accounts, nominee bank accounts, offshore bank accounts, real estate, investment funds. Business is changing and we need to change, or we'll be left behind."

Canfusco looked at De Riggi and pointed at Davis. "Where did you find this guy, Tony?"

De Riggi chuckled. "Long story. Let's just say, he's good at finding new business opportunities."

Canfusco looked over at his two associates, who were trying hard not to look bored. They appeared to have run out of things to say to Matisse and Dubois.

After only three days, Canfusco cut his visit short and headed home. De Riggi wasn't happy, and he half expected he'd be summoned to New York before too long.

***

Over the next three weeks, De Riggi went down to New York and then made trips to Boston and Miami. He never told Davis the purpose of the meetings. Davis assumed they'd involved some future drug deals coming through Montreal and a directive from New York about beefing up the ranks. De Riggi told him New York expected some big wins soon and were always looking for ways to invest.

Davis realized they'd have to start taking more risks. Real estate was a safe bet if you were a long-term investor. He didn't know what De Riggi did with all the money the gang made. He started to think about his own compensation and decided that he couldn't work for peanuts forever. De Riggi would soon smell a rat. Why would a smart businessmen work for nothing? He told his handlers that it was time for him to tell De Riggi he wanted part of the action and that he needed a better idea of the sort of cash the gang was generating to better advise them on how they should invest their money. The handlers were hesitant, but he persisted, telling them that that's what he'd expect if he were De Riggi. Why else would he be working there?

A month after the New York boys had visited, Davis and De Riggi met in one of the hotel rooms on the top floor of the Auberge. De Riggi insisted on eating breakfast before they started. After about twenty minutes he was ready to chat. "What took so long?"

"What do you mean?"

"I didn't expect you to work for nothing."

Davis set his coffee cup down. "What did you have in mind?"

"The boys get five per cent of the profits. They never see the books, and they never complain about what they get paid. Probably for good reason."

"That may be fine if they don't bring in any business." Davis said.

"What did you have in mind?"

"Forty per cent."

De Riggi laughed. "Let's start at twenty and review it in six months."

"Thirty per cent and we review it in three months?"

De Riggi scowled at him and said, "I was right about you. Okay, you got a deal."

De Riggi had been putting off the discussion, unsure how to handle Davis. New York had made it clear that Davis or someone like him had to become more involved if the gang were to continue to represent their interests. They had no time for the old guard. He'd pleaded for more time, and they told him he'd had enough.

Relieved that Davis wanted in, he had to take him into his confidence now. The risks were high, but so was doing nothing. New York would use another gang, and they'd soon start to take over the port and all his drug contacts. Things were happening too quickly. Though he knew he needed to talk to someone, he wasn't sure who he could turn to.

He looked Davis in the eye, wondering what was going through his mind. As always Davis's face gave nothing away.

"The boys in New York want to import more product through Montreal, and they want us to handle it. We need to change. I think I've calmed them down about the mole. The thing is … they weren't impressed with our operation or our people. They want to focus more on acquiring legitimate businesses to launder money and bring in the right people to run them."

De Riggi gazed out the window, then looked back at him.

"We need to hire professionals. It seems you made quite an impression on New York. Unfortunately, so did Matisse and Dubois, and not in a good way." He finished his coffee and wiped his lips with a napkin. "New York sees a different future. They see guys like Matisse and Dubois as hired hands. They want more guys like you, people that can run businesses, make business decisions, manage money and protect their investments."

"So what does this mean for me?"

"It means we become business partners. You become one of us. They even went as far as saying that they could see you taking over down the road."

Davis leaned back in his chair. This was everything he'd feared. It was also the logical next step. And there was no turning back now.

De Riggi had a half smile on his face. "It's funny, I thought I'd be pissed," he said, "but I'm not. Things were growing too fast; I was losing control and there wasn't anyone I could pass things on to. I was all over the place, chasing deals, organizing shipments, kissing ass, putting out fires..." He looked out the window for a few moments before continuing.

"Anyway, if I don't ... Well, let's just say New York will bring in someone else and take over the docks." De Riggi turned back to Davis. "I'm kinda relieved, tell you the truth. Someone's forcing me to decide. I was planning to slow down a bit, spend some time down south. There's no way I could do that and run the gang. I know that now."

"You're getting deeper into bed with the guys from New York. You sure that's what you want?"

De Riggi shrugged. "Yes and no. They have worldwide contacts. They can ship more product through the port for us than we could ever imagine. And they can source much bigger deals—and we get a piece of the action. We'll probably make three or four times more than we would if we stick with our own suppliers. They don't care about Montreal real estate. They just want a secure pipeline into the city, and they need our network. It'd take them years if they started from scratch. That means I have some value for the time being." He leaned an elbow on the table and stuck his finger at Davis. "A lot depends on you."

"Me?"

"They figure I got two years, maybe three if I'm lucky. Sooner or later someone's gonna take over our turf. That's the way of the world. They claim they've seen it many times before in cities much bigger than Montreal. Whatever way you wanna look at it, we're being taken over by the big boys. We're becoming part of a big franchise. They see the world differently. They're looking at the big picture, not just North America, the whole world. And they want me to groom someone to take over. Someone like you."

Chapter 33

Davis met some of the gang's suppliers and heard more about the crooked cops on the gang's payroll. De Riggi never used the cops' names, so he didn't have much to report to his handlers. One senior cop seemed to be in the know whenever there was a big shipment of drugs arriving into the port. De Riggi claimed he never knew how the guy did it, but all too often he would call De Riggi and tip him off that one of their shipments had been identified and would be picked up at the docks. On a few occasions De Riggi had arranged for the longshoremen at the port to delay unloading containers or even change the schedule so that by the time the ship docked, that container was relocated on board or hidden on the dock, buried under five other containers all stacked one on the other.

On a few occasions over the years, when his contact hadn't tipped him off about a search, De Riggi ended up losing the cargo. Usually, the container would have a small quantity of drugs and the gang's losses were minimal. Only once did they suffer a significant loss. He accepted it as part of the cost of doing business.

Slowly Davis got a better sense of the size of the gang's drug business. He wondered what De Riggi did with all his money. He must have been sitting on millions, especially since he shared so little with the other gang members.

***

Davis had been busy and hadn't noticed the change of season. It was June, and he wondered where the time had gone. He had trouble changing his outlook. He was constantly focused on the gang's business, meaning he'd had little time for Helene and had reverted to the gangster he used to be when he lived in Vancouver. He'd become a full-time gangster and had difficulty being a normal person. His minders had told him that to be successful, he had to think and live like a crook 24/7. In a strange way he enjoyed what he was doing and had to keep reminding himself that he was still playing a part in a very dangerous game.

Davis was headed to Dunphy's office to discuss expanding the size of the mortgage company's portfolio of loans. As he crossed the park near his office there were several couples in shorts enjoying the summer weather, young men kicking a soccer ball around and children chasing each other as their parents tried to keep up.

Dunphy was relaxed as they talked about the mortgage deal. He'd made the decision to leave the gang and hoped that by talking to the Crown, his troubles would soon be over.

"Looks like you and De Riggi are working well together," the lawyer said.

"Tell me, Sean, how well do you know De Riggi?"

"What do you mean?"

"You've worked with him for years. Does he listen to you, does he follow your advice?"

Dunphy set his coffee cup down and pulled open one of his desk drawers. "Why do you ask?" He took out a mickey of whisky and opened it.

"He's changed. He's more open, seems to listen more, less suspicious."

Dunphy shrugged as he poured a generous amount of whisky into his coffee.

"Maybe he's just getting comfortable with you—and finding that he enjoys working with businessmen. Maybe he's finally accepting it's the way of the future."

Dunphy took a sip of coffee and leaned back in his chair. "He knows he needs to delegate more. He won't always be around and needs to bring someone on. Letting go isn't easy for him. He's been used to doing things his way."

Davis wondered how much Dunphy knew of the gang's affairs and their financial resources.

"What about you, what are your plans?"

"I just do what I'm told."

"If De Riggi spends more time down south then you'll have to deal with someone else."

Dunphy raised his coffee in a toast. "You learn to adapt," he said, smiling.

"Well, how would you feel about working with me?"

Dunphy was surprised by the question. Davis was worried this was coming out of the blue and might have made him suspicious. He was trying to get Dunphy to open up, but the lawyer continued to be guarded.

"I think we'll be fine, don't you?"

"His visits to the States, do they worry you?"

"Why would you ask that?"

"The gang's been through a lot recently, what with Pigeon, acquiring the mortgage company and these real estate deals we're doing. There's a lot going on. Maybe it's time to slow down a bit, let things calm down."

"I don't disagree. That's just not Tony's way. He wants to be part of a bigger organization, and he figures the guys in New York are the answer."

Davis was hoping Dunphy would carry on talking, but he was done.

"If there's nothing more, I've got some other things to do this morning. I'll check with John Smith and get back to you. I'm sure he won't have a problem with what you're proposing. I'm not even sure De Riggi needs me to sign off on things anymore, but it's not a bad idea."

After Davis left, Dunphy wondered what was behind Davis's questions about De Riggi and the gang. Was he having second thoughts, or was there something else? He liked Davis, respected his business judgment and thought he'd make a good leader. Taking over the gang, if that's what he wanted and that's what De Riggi decided to do, was another thing. Dunphy felt sorry for Davis. He'd fallen into the gang almost by accident. And now it seemed that he was close to taking over operations in Montreal. There'd be no going back.

Chapter 34

The only thing she had to do was tell them ahead of time when De Riggi was heading to the States. That's all, they'd do the rest. The fact that the pair of them were flying down to Boston together was a complication, but they said they'd handle it.

Josie Chouinard had her moments. In some ways she thought she might love De Riggi, in other ways he reminded her of the life she'd fallen into. She lived in fear for days, wondering whether he knew what she'd done, how she'd betrayed him. The final straw had been the trafficking of the Ukrainian women.

For months she'd been waffling—should she leave things alone or do something about it? She knew that someone else in the gang was running the day-to-day operations and the chances of him getting caught were small. She hoped that if he became aware he was under surveillance, he'd end his trafficking scheme. She doubted that her testimony alone would be enough to tie De Riggi to the crime. The police would need something more than the testimony of the Ukrainian women and an unhappy girlfriend. That wasn't her problem.

Then a chance meeting with an old flame, an undercover cop, changed everything. The guy was since happily remarried and at first wanted nothing to do with her; that was, until she started to cry. Then he put her in touch with an officer in the RCMP's people smuggling unit. At first he didn't believe what she told them. After some initial surveillance the RCMP were able to piece things together. They obtained a missing-persons report from Interpol, matching the photographs of a few of the women included in the report with those taken by their undercover surveillance team. Their contact in Paris had told them of a Russian gang with contacts in the eastern US who regularly transported young women who'd been promised a new life in the States. Landing in Boston by freighter from Ukraine, they'd then be shipped to New York and other US cities. Some had even been shipped across the border by truck into Canada and ended up in Montreal.

Josie was worried. The surveillance team had a van parked just down the street from the Auberge. Every time she met De Riggi for their weekly rendezvous at the hotel she was convinced he'd find out, even though she'd been acting since she was sixteen, pretending she enjoyed it when men used her for sex. She didn't give a lot of thought to what would happen to her after the trap was sprung; she just wanted to put an end to it, and she hoped that De Riggi and the others would be put away for a long time. She doubted she'd stay in Montreal after that. She wasn't sure what she'd do, but if she were given a second chance, she'd make the most of it. Maybe set up some sort of halfway home for young girls that needed a roof over their heads and someone to look out for them.

The RCMP officer handling the case in Montreal told her they were working with the FBI, and once the Americans had all the evidence to support a prosecution, they'd arrest De Riggi the first time he set foot on US soil. Unbeknownst to her, Vincent and Lacroix had already visited Boston in the hopes that the FBI would clear any action with Montreal before arresting De Riggi. They shared some photos of De Riggi's New York contacts. The photos were a complete surprise to the FBI. The RCMP Security Service quickly realized the mistake of assuming information sharing was a two-way street, and they worried that Davis's days of penetrating deep into the Montreal gang's network might be numbered. A new layer of outside involvement increased the chances of leaks in the investigation, further exposing him. At some point they'd need to bring Davis up to speed. For the time being they decided the fewer distractions he had, the more likely he'd be able to continue making progress.

The other thing that Josie wasn't aware of was what De Riggi's wife, Auryse, had done. Whether it was knowledge of the human trafficking, her hatred of her husband, his many affairs or spending a lifetime being treated as a doormat, only she knew what drove her to making the call in the first place. Once the first contact was made, the Quebec Sûreté officer was smart enough to realize the nature and value of the information she'd shared with him. Quickly his superiors passed the information on to the Security Service.

When Lacroix and Vincent became aware of the human trafficking ring that De Riggi was involved in, they moved quickly to try and obtain evidence of her husband's involvement. At first they couldn't believe it when she said her husband had visas and Ukrainian passports in his safe at home. She could provide them with the original documents, but they had to be returned to the safe as soon as possible, since her husband was in the habit of checking his safe every day.

The RCMP officers remarked on how calm De Riggi's wife appeared. The whole operation was over in less than two hours, on a Sunday morning when De Riggi was paying his weekly visit to his mistress at the Auberge. Auryse had complained of a headache and told him she wouldn't be going to church that day.

They knew De Riggi's wife's testimony would be needed and that the information they had would only connect him to the Russians based in Ukraine and not to his friends in New York. The more they strategized, the more they realized that they couldn't control the outcome. The Russians were a bargaining chip they might be able to use to turn De Riggi against his New York contacts and those at the port.

Vincent had had some bad experiences dealing with his friends in the US and wasn't confident. They'd see a small undercover operation in Montreal as chicken feed compared to the human trafficking ring and

New York mob connections. He concluded that they had to plan for the worst. That meant not standing in the way of De Riggi's arrest in the US and being prepared to have Davis pulled at a moment's notice.

De Riggi told Josie he'd meet her at the airport. He had a bit of business to take care of on Saturday morning, then they'd spend the whole weekend together. Late September was a wonderful time to visit Boston, he said. And they'd be staying at the finest hotel in the city, The Langham. They had a jacuzzi spa in the room, he said.

Josie wanted to feign some last-minute sickness. Her handler told her that this would be suspicious and De Riggi might cancel the trip. She should go. By the time she got to the airport she was barely holding it together. When she met him, she kissed him on the lips and gave him a big hug. She marvelled at how easily she could pretend.

He seemed preoccupied on the plane, and if she showed any signs of nerves, he was too busy to notice. She didn't drink on the eighty-minute flight but noticed he had two whiskies. After they landed, they picked up their bags from the conveyor belt at Logan Airport and walked toward security. There were three lines of passengers queuing to go through passport control and De Riggi chose the middle one. As the passport officer looked at their passports, he asked if they were travelling together. De Riggi nodded. The officer lingered on Josie's passport for a few moments. The line behind them started to get longer and then suddenly two officers appeared at their side.

The larger of the two looked at De Riggi and then Josie and said, "Sir, madam, would you mind coming with us, please? Just a routine check. It won't take long."

De Riggi stared at the man and then noticed the other security guard scanning what looked like a list of passengers.

"What's this all about?"

"Just routine, sir, I assure you. Please come this way. Madam too."

De Riggi was tired, and the alcohol wasn't helping.

"What's the problem, something wrong with our passports?"

"No, sir, nothing like that. As I said, it's just routine, won't take five minutes. If you'll follow me. Please bring your bags."

Chapter 35

Late that weekend Davis had a call from Dunphy telling him De Riggi had been arrested at Logan Airport in Boston and shipped to Ray Brook Federal Correctional Institution in upstate New York. The medium-security prison was where most federal inmates in the region were held pending trial. Dunphy was to arrange for US counsel to be hired and do whatever he could to get De Riggi released as soon as possible.

When he hung up with Dunphy, Davis dialled the emergency number his handlers had given him and left a message. Primeau called him back about twenty minutes later. Davis shared his news, and he heard his handler's loud sigh over the phone.

"Sorry, we only just found out ourselves. I was about to call you. We were worried that the bastards might do something like this." Primeau and Lacroix had been caught off guard.

"What do you mean? You knew this would happen?"

"Not exactly. We brought the FBI up to speed at our end and shared some information that we hoped they'd sit on—De Riggi's involvement in human trafficking—"

"Human trafficking?"

"Yeah. Girls from Ukraine. They arrive by cargo ship to the US then get shipped across the border in container trucks."

"That's not possible, I'd have known."

"He doesn't use Hatfield's for everything."

Davis wondered what else De Riggi, and his handlers, hadn't told him. "That's why he wanted the motel properties," Davis said, shaking his head. "It makes a lot more sense now."

"They literally called me an hour ago."

"How safe am I?"

"Look, I doubt De Riggi is gonna point the finger at you. However—"

"What does the FBI know about my involvement?"

"Nothing as far as we know. Just that we've been targeting De Riggi and his gang for over a year and a half. They've no idea of your involvement, and it's gonna stay that way." Primeau paused. "There's something else you should know."

"What's that?"

"The information about the trafficking operation came from De Riggi's wife and a woman named Josie Chouinard, De Riggi's lover. We don't know how much either of them knows about your involvement—or even whether they mentioned your name to the authorities."

"His wife turned on him?"

"Yeah. As far as we know, he doesn't know it was her. Came out of the blue. Seems she was fed up. Guess she wasn't as stupid as he thought. From what Dunphy said, we think De Riggi believes all the info came from Chouinard. She's now under FBI protection somewhere outside Boston."

Davis frowned. "This whole thing is starting to fall apart. If the FBI decides to investigate De Riggi's activities in Montreal—"

"If they do, they'll do it through us."

"Yeah, but the minute they find out about me, who knows who they're gonna tell. Christ, now I gotta worry about Dunphy finding out, the FBI, and oh, I almost forgot, the gang too."

"There's something else we got to think about too."

"You mean this gets worse?"

"Pigeon's body still hasn't shown up."

"So? These guys are pros at covering their tracks."

"Maybe. We think De Riggi would've wanted to send a message about how he deals with rats. So it might mean Pigeon's still alive. De Riggi and Pigeon go way back—hold on … Listen, Bernie's just walked in…" After a moment of silence, Primeau came back on the phone. "We need to meet. Remember the old motel we met at a few months back, just outside Granby? Ten a.m. tomorrow. Look for a red Camaro parked outside the unit."

Davis hung up and poured himself a drink. He couldn't imagine what his handlers' latest plan was, and he didn't care. There were too many things going wrong, and there was nothing that he could do about it. He couldn't believe Pigeon was still alive. The handlers were right, if the gang had dealt with him, they'd have wanted to send a message. So where was the body?

Chapter 36

By morning, Davis had made up his mind: he was done with the gang. He pulled into the parking lot of the motel at 9:55 and shut off the engine. No matter what they said, he was out. They couldn't say he hadn't given it his best shot. He knew neither of his handlers would try and talk him out of it. They'd all come a long way, but at the end of the day the gang would likely disappear. The RCMP might recover some of the gang's money and real estate. The land the gang acquired at the new port site would end up being worthless and the man pulling the strings at the port would remain a mystery.

Lacroix was nervous when he opened the motel door. He knew Davis would want to pull the plug on the whole operation, and who could blame him? They'd come all this way, but they'd lied to him, or at the very least omitted critical information. He'd read somewhere in the Bible about sins of omission, and he felt guilty. He avoided eye contact as Davis walked in.

Davis saw Vincent and Primeau seated at a table. Both stood and greeted him. Vincent told him to have a seat.

"Mr. Davis, I can't imagine what must be going through your mind right now. We wanted you to at least hear us out."

Slowly Vincent told him what they knew. The chances of De Riggi being released anytime soon were remote. Based on the evidence that the FBI had put together, he'd end up being found guilty and would likely spend fifteen to twenty years in a federal penitentiary.

"Without you, the gang may fall apart," Vincent said. "We can lay charges based on the evidence we have to date; we may even be able to get some convictions, including Pigeon, if indeed he's alive and shows up. The case against the port officials is questionable at best. It'll come down to a misunderstanding; the new port location will remain a dream. We'll be no further ahead in getting the big boys. De Riggi's top contacts at the port, City Hall, the Sûreté and the Montreal Police will remain a secret. The gang's assets will be seized by the Crown, another gang will take over the gang's turf, along with their stranglehold on the docks and the longshoremen and checkers who work there."

"That is, of course, if we do nothing, sir," said Lacroix.

"Quite right, Corporal. We still have one or two cards to play, you see, Mr. Davis. Lacroix and Primeau have come up with a plan, but it all depends on you."

Lacroix jumped in, "Sir, if I may, I'd like to tell him what we've come up with."

"Of course, Bernie, go ahead."

Lacroix looked at his notes as he started to walk Davis through the plan. He reminded everyone that the original goal of the operation was to identify and uncover evidence against those individuals who had enabled De Riggi to continue to operate at the port for as long as he had. He listed the different organizations they suspected were involved. Then he listed some assumptions that they'd made. De Riggi had been arrested on claims that he and his gang were involved in the human trafficking scheme. Even though he had no knowledge of the scheme, the RCMP could arrest Davis on the basis that he was part of that scheme. This would help reinforce the belief within the gang that he was not the mole and allow him to take over the day-to-day running of the gang in De Riggi's absence—a good lawyer would be able to get Davis released pending trial. Once things died down, hopefully the people the RCMP were targeting would be forced to take Davis into their confidence.

Their plan was simple: arrest Davis and charge him. He'd be able to continue running operations while out on bail and Davis's immediate arrest would be needed to ensure his creditability with the gang, the port and the New York contacts.

Reading his expression, Lacroix said, "Don't worry, your arrest is just for show. You'll have to trust us on that."

"So now I go to prison. How long? A week, a month, three months? How certain are you that I'll be released before the trial?"

"We're confident it'll be a week max," said Lacroix.

"Where does Pigeon fit in to all this?"

"We haven't found him yet. The prospect of Pigeon suddenly appearing on the scene is remote, but we have to plan for that possibility. Even if he does show up, the fact that you've been arrested will make it that much tougher for him to persuade anyone that you're the mole. Don't worry, we're looking for him. If he's alive, we'll find him."

Davis no longer believed they cared what happened to him. He was more paranoid than ever and realized he could trust no one. He doubted Pigeon would show up out of the blue. If he was still alive, he'd probably try and contact someone inside the gang. The chances were good that another gang member would make public Pigeon's sudden reappearance. In the event he did appear, they'd arrest him and charge him with the murder of Harry Parker.

"What about De Riggi? I have to speak to him if he we're to have any chance of penetrating the inner circle."

"We'll arrange for him to be brought back to Montreal to stand trial. We'll probably time your arrest for when he returns to Canada. Once the dust settles, you two will be able to talk, maybe even while you're both in prison. In the meantime, the best we can do is to see if we can find a way for you and Dunphy to visit him while he's down in detention in New York. It might be safer if it's just Dunphy, I don't want to risk you getting arrested in the States."

"How can you be so sure they'll send him back to Canada? Is there something you're not telling me?"

"What do you mean?" asked Lacroix.

Davis saw him looking at Vincent, who nodded ever so slightly. Lacroix looked at Davis and said, "Okay, we have a deal with the States. We can bring De Riggi back anytime we want."

Davis rolled his eyes, wondering what else they'd not told him and whether he'd ever get a straight answer from his handlers.

Lacroix held up his hands. "Listen, our only hope is you being accepted as the new leader. The less you knew the better. You had to be seen as knowing nothing about the trafficking, the arrangement with the States and your planned arrest. If there's any chance the gang find out what's really going on, you're done."

Davis wasn't convinced. "Where does Dunphy fit in to all this?"

Lacroix looked at Vincent, who nodded again. "Dunphy wants out. De Riggi's incarceration is probably the opportunity he's been waiting for, but we're confident he will help us."

"Why?"

"We have an arrangement with him. He's committed to help us in any way he can. We're confident he'll act in our best interests and follow directions."

Davis looked puzzled. Vincent smiled at him and said, "Mr. Davis, we appreciate that you're the one taking all the risks here. There are some things you're better off not knowing. If you're able to accept the fact that Dunphy will cooperate, then surely that's all you need to know."

"How long have you had this … arrangement, as you call it?"

"As I said, the less you know…" Vincent cleared his throat. "At least think about it—just don't take too long."

He had a lot of questions and doubted they'd completely thought the scheme through. Davis had to admit that his immediate arrest in Montreal along with a few other senior gang members would help remove suspicion within the gang that he was somehow involved. Then De Riggi would realize that if he wanted to keep the gang together, his only hope was Davis.

Davis was still on his own. The RCMP was still pulling all the strings and had kept things from him. What else hadn't they shared?

As these thoughts were running through his mind, he reached a decision. Then he thought of Helene. He'd already put her at risk, and once she heard the news that he'd been arrested along with other gang members, that'd be the end of whatever relationship they had. He might even have to move. He wondered if, just for the sake of appearances, Lacroix would visit her at her home in Bromont, asking her if she knew that her boyfriend Alan Davis was a gangster.

***

Back at his cottage, Davis had just finished dinner and was considering his options. He never liked to walk away from an unfinished job, but he'd been involved in this one for over eighteen months and there was no end in sight. He'd always known the risks. He'd let himself be talked into it at first and then things had just snowballed. He never thought that he'd be taking over the gang. Clearly it was something the Security Service had considered at some point. Maybe even from day one.

He thought back to his time at the fishing lodge. Life had been so simple then. He almost laughed when he considered how different his life was now, though there was nothing funny about his situation. Taking over the gang was high risk, especially when he didn't know who was on his side. Whatever his handlers said, he was alone. He needed to talk to someone, but who? The only person he could think of was Helene. And that wasn't an option. He should never have gotten involved with her.

If he went ahead with the plan, he'd be even lonelier. It made him think of his daughter. Where was she now, what was she doing? Probably had a part-time job, even a boyfriend. He didn't even know what she looked like now. All he had was a photo of her as a little girl. He walked over to the bookshelf and pulled out the book that contained his returned letters. He'd written one about a year ago and the other at Christmastime. Both had come back to his PO box in Montreal marked "No longer at this address."

He'd tried to track her down, hoping that she and his ex were still in Vancouver. He was told by the private detective he'd paid to do some leg work that they'd moved away. Someone said to the Prairies, another said the BC interior. The guy had run out his retainer and asked for more money. Davis told him to close the file. Once this was over, if he was still alive, he'd track his daughter down himself. Maybe the RCMP could help.

If he stayed in the gang, he'd need to meet up with De Riggi. Transferring him to Montreal made sense. Davis could visit him there. What would De Riggi do next? Primeau seemed to think De Riggi only knew about Josie ratting him out, her and those girls from Ukraine. Could he be convicted only on their testimony? Unless they had some other evidence they weren't telling him about. No, De Riggi wouldn't be worried about them. He'd still make sure they were silenced, just in case. What he didn't know about was what his wife had done. Her testimony would also be needed.

There was no guarantee that De Riggi would share his contacts with Davis. He might even try to run things from inside. The Security Service must have thought of that. There were endless possibilities, and it could take months for a clear picture to emerge.

Then there was Dunphy. Davis wondered what they'd told Dunphy about him. Probably nothing. Davis frowned. He'd been in the dark long enough. It was time he knew everything. They had to come clean about Dunphy, Pigeon and all the other things they'd failed to share with him. The trouble was, how would he know if they'd told him everything?

Davis realized he was already thinking like a gang leader. He spent the next hour considering how to proceed. If De Riggi didn't spill his secrets, then Davis would force him to share them. And he thought he knew how. He'd get the RCMP to leak rumours that there were two different gangs attempting to take over the docks, that De Riggi was done and was going away for a long time. The rival gangs were moving in on his turf, scaring dealers, stealing hookers from his clubs. Gangs were even approaching some of De Riggi's own gang members telling them he was finished. The list was endless. He'd make De Riggi realize that unless he took immediate action, everything he'd helped build over the last fifteen years would disappear. The boss had to hear the message from someone he trusted. Davis could reinforce the message, and so could Dunphy, but it had to start somewhere else. And there had to be some hard evidence.

Some things were easier to arrange than others. If it were him, he'd start by firebombing one or two of the gang's clubs. Maybe arrange to have a few of the gang members beaten up. Soon things would snowball the way rumours always do, and eventually De Riggi's key contacts would tell him he had to do something.

Davis poured himself a whisky. He was enjoying this, and he thought the irony of his plan wouldn't be lost on the Security Service and the RCMP—he was creating a fake gang war to force De Riggi to hand over control of the gang, along with his best-kept secrets. Despite going back and forth, he always came back to his initial idea. He headed off to bed thinking that it wasn't a bad plan. They might have a problem with it, since they'd be the guys starting the gang war. That wasn't his problem though. For the first time in a long time he thought that maybe he could be in control, telling them what the plan was going to be rather than the other way around.

Chapter 37

Before he met with the Security Service, Davis called Dunphy. From what Dunphy told him, it appeared De Riggi's arrest had been coordinated by RCMP in Montreal and that all the evidence to support the charges and the arrest had been supplied by Canadian authorities. The RCMP was pushing for De Riggi to be returned to Montreal to face charges. He said De Riggi's New York attorney was unclear when that was likely to happen and suspected that the RCMP and the FBI had been planning the arrest for some time, but that the FBI might have jumped the gun. Dunphy questioned what evidence existed to tie De Riggi to the trafficking scheme. The FBI stonewalled the US lawyer and cited some statute that gave them the right to arrest and hold an alien without evidence for up to thirty days.

Dunphy said he'd already contacted a few criminal lawyers in Montreal to see if they would act for him. Once he mentioned De Riggi's name, the lawyers went quiet. Davis wondered whether the RCMP had been pulling the strings from the start. What he couldn't figure out was why they'd had De Riggi arrested in the US. That didn't make any sense.

Davis headed out to meet with his handlers. The group met in a drab office in an old building in downtown Montreal. In addition to

Vincent, Lacroix and Primeau, there was a Crown counsel by the name of Carroll in attendance. The lanky man only nodded in Davis's direction when he was introduced. Vincent explained that in the interest of time they'd decided to have counsel present to ensure Davis's rights were being protected. They also indicated that if he was unhappy with their choice, he was free to choose other counsel.

Davis was surprised by their approach, since for all they knew, he was coming to tell them that the game was over, that he was no longer prepared to risk his neck.

Vincent asked Davis if he was ready to discuss his position. He said he was, but first he wanted answers to a few questions that had been worrying him since their last meeting. He listed them off one by one. What role did the Security Service play in De Riggi's arrest? Why did it happen in the US? What deal did they have with Dunphy, and who was he really acting for? What did they know about Pigeon and his whereabouts? Was De Riggi's arrest really related to human trafficking as opposed to drugs? Was their plan all along to sideline him to allow Davis to take over as gang leader?

Vincent put his hands together as he looked at him and said, "Mr. Davis, I made the mistake of underestimating you. I should have taken you into our confidence from the beginning. For some time, I have vetoed both Corporal Lacroix and Primeau's recommendations. I decided not to share all our plans with you. I was wrong and should have listened to them. That said, we are where we are, and the future of this operation, whether it's over today or whether we carry on, is entirely up to you. Corporal Lacroix will now bring you up to speed on certain events I decided not to share with you, much to my regret."

Lacroix cleared his throat and looked at the Crown counsel and then Davis.

"First of all, some time ago Dunphy came to us looking for a deal. He wanted out but knew he had too much knowledge to just walk away. He wanted protection; he was afraid of De Riggi and scared for his life. We decided to leave him in play. We believed another pipeline into the gang's activities would be helpful. Dunphy disappearing would warn De Riggi something was up, force him to close ranks, and who knows what that would've meant for you. He does not and has never had any idea of your real identity and that was always the way it was going to be. Since our arrangement he's kept us informed of De Riggi and the gang's activities, including the acquisition of the mortgage company.

"We coordinated De Riggi's arrest with the FBI. Ever since the girls from Ukraine started to complain and Josie Chouinard put the finger on De Riggi, we've had the Auberge hotel under surveillance. It wasn't until De Riggis's wife provided us documentary evidence from his safe, including the girls' Ukrainian passports, false work visas and then paperwork showing payments from one of his Montreal companies to a New York-based company listing various charges for shipment of merchandise, that we were able to implicate him.

"We needed to get him out of the way while we planned the final act of the operation, which was to facilitate your taking over the gang. We decided to have him arrested in the US to ensure he wouldn't think you were in any way responsible for his arrest. You had no knowledge of the human trafficking operation and we felt that was the easier route to go.

"As for Walter Pigeon, initial reports suggested that De Riggi personally attended to his execution. Given the absence of a body and the gang's need to send a message, we've decided De Riggi may have faked his murder and instead relocated him somewhere. He was probably hedging his bets and decided that his long-standing number two may not in fact have been the mole. This is only a theory, but we need to plan for such an outcome."

Vincent looked at Davis. "Does that answer all your questions?"

"What makes you so sure De Riggi will be returned to Montreal?"

"We have an arrangement with the FBI. We try him first and then they can have what's left of him. They accept that in the grand scheme of things they have what they want."

"What's that?"

"His connections with the New York mob."

"Where does that leave me?"

"Good question. Right now, you're a person of interest to the FBI. Their information suggests you're De Riggi's number two and are viewed quite favourably by the New York gang. They know the New York gang believes that De Riggi is done, there needs to be a new guy running the show, the rest of his senior people are lightweights—and they've been looking at you as someone who can change things in Montreal. We don't want you heading south anytime soon: they'd be likely to arrest you. And it would muddy the waters if we had to secure your release."

Until now the Crown counsel had been quiet. Carroll cleared his throat and they all looked at him. "I think this would be a good time for Mr. Davis and me to speak privately," he said, absentmindedly twirling one side of his dark mustache.

Davis had been deep in thought. At the suggestion, he stood up and took his time pouring a coffee. The meeting reminded him of the time back in Vancouver when he'd sat in a room of Mounties and a Crown prosecutor, slowly walking them through the inner workings of the Vancouver gang that he was betraying. Did he feel any different this time? His life was still at risk, maybe more than ever. He had felt alone then, although he did have the one-eyed lawyer Richard Peek helping him wade through the mess he'd gotten himself into back then.

He sipped his coffee as everyone except Carroll left the room. When the door closed behind them, he stayed quiet for a few moments. Finally, he decided to bounce his plan off Carroll, see if the lawyer really was on his side. This time it was the RCMP who'd be taking the risk, and he'd be the one with an idea of what was coming down the line and what to expect. There was something else he wanted Carroll to do too; he wasn't sure they'd go for it, but he thought he'd ask. He had nothing to lose and at least it'd be something in case things didn't work out.

Carroll listened in silence as he explained his plan. The counsel nodded when he told him he'd have to create some urgency when trying to force De Riggi to give up his innermost secrets. When he mentioned that the RCMP would have to incite a gang war, Carroll uncrossed his long legs and pushed back from the table. Davis hadn't pulled any punches describing what he had in mind. Firebombing a few of the gang's clubs, roughing up some gang members, maybe threatening a few of the strippers, approaching some gang members and telling them that De Riggi's days were numbered, that the sooner they joined their gang, the better, and spreading the rumour amongst the gangs in town that De Riggi was finished and that other gangs were moving in on their turf. This was sure to add to the gang's problems.

When Davis was finished, Carroll calmly told him it wouldn't work. "You're asking the RCMP to go to war. People could get killed."

Davis was incensed. "Can you think of a better way? De Riggi needs to know the gang's under siege, otherwise he'll just sit there trying to pull the strings from inside. Other gangs will start muscling in once word gets out anyway. All we'd be doing is lighting the match and making sure we're careful that it's viewed as a gang war."

"They simply won't go for it."

Davis was ready to punch this guy. "Look, I was hired eighteen months ago for who I am. A gangster, plain and simple. I know how De Riggi thinks and this is how he's gonna react. This isn't the time to play by the rules. You need to think like a gangster. Act like one. The RCMP knew that going into this. Nothing's changed. Up until now it was only my life that was at risk. It's about time these guys took some risks. Fight fire with fire."

Carroll cleared his throat again and sat up even straighter. "If this ever got out, there'd be hell to pay. They'd all be out of a job, maybe even go to prison. It's against the law."

Davis leaned forward and set his elbows on the table. "Do you think De Riggi cares about the law? First thing he's gonna do is order me to get rid of Josie Chouinard and the Ukrainians. Doesn't matter if you have enough evidence without them: he'll want revenge. And if it's not me, it's going to be one of his gang. And if by some remote chance we uncover De Riggi's top contacts by the end of this, he'll know it was me and he'll have someone come after me. Remember, he'll be in the relative safety of Bordeaux Prison, where he'll be bribing guards to get access to people, money, protection, phones, the works. It won't take him five minutes to organize, and he won't think twice. You and I know he's got plenty of contacts inside."

Carroll stared at Davis thoughtfully for a few moments. "This is the plan you're proposing to the Crown?"

Davis bit his lip. He really didn't like this guy. "Yes. There's something else."

"What is it?"

"I want my daughter taken care of."

Carroll was caught off guard. "Your daughter?"

"I want a trust fund set up in her name."

Carroll was back to twirling his mustache, a habit Davis was already starting to hate.

"Well. Let's see if they go for your plan first."

"They'll go for the deal," Davis said. "They want it bad."

***

Ten minutes later, as Davis walked them through his plan, the reactions were mixed. Primeau nodded after each step, Lacroix was hesitant and Vincent downright indignant.

"What makes you so sure De Riggi will take the bait?" Lacroix asked.

Davis shrugged. "You know him better than I do. He's not gonna sit by seeing the gang being attacked and do nothing. He'll view it as personal. He's got a lot invested in this city, he's hardly gonna let another gang take it all. Besides, he needs money, even in prison. He's thinking he'll be out soon."

Vincent looked at Carroll. "Counselor, I'm sure you've explained to Mr. Davis that even we are not above the law."

Carroll only nodded, much to Vincent's annoyance. He was hoping the man would support his position.

Davis stood up and walked to the window. He was agitated and couldn't stay in his seat for another minute. "Look," he began, turning to face the table. "De Riggi's had nothing but time to think. He'll want to reassure the gang and his key contacts that he'll be out soon, and the minute he's back in Montreal he'll be giving orders. He'll have to trust someone. And that's where I come in."

"What makes you think he'll confide in you?" Vincent asked.

"Who else is he gonna confide in? He's either killed Pigeon or hidden him somewhere far away. Matisse and Dubois are errand boys. He's got no choice."

"You're pretty sure of yourself," Vincent said.

Davis took a breath. It was like trying to explain something to a child. "He's two steps ahead of you, maybe three. He's been inside before. He's already figured it out. One thing he can't count on is returning to Montreal." He looked directly at Vincent. "You control that."

"It's not without risk," Primeau said.

Davis laughed. "It's been nothing but risks from day one. And I've been the one taking all of them." Davis glared at Vincent. "Well, now it's payback time."

"Excuse me?"

Carroll cleared his throat and waited until they were all looking at him. "Mr. Davis would like you to set up a trust fund for his daughter. One hundred thousand dollars. No strings."

Vincent was the first to react. "Out of the question. The whole thing is preposterous."

Davis looked around the room. "Do you guys not get it? I'll be the target of every gang in town. Once De Riggi finds out he's been conned, he'll find a way to get me, prison or no prison. Don't tell me I'm wrong. Remember, I've been there; I know what I'm talking about. If you don't know the story, ask the guy that introduced me to you in the first place."

Vincent and Primeau looked confused.

Lacroix said, "Corporal Lossan, sir."

"Oh, yes, I remember now," Vincent said darkly. "Well, I don't like it."

Davis was squeezing the back of a chair as he glared at the man. "If we don't try something now, the whole operation's over. The last eighteen months down the drain." He pushed the chair suddenly, almost knocking it over, and turned from them. "You figure it out. I'm going for a walk."

When Davis was gone, Lacroix turned toward Vincent and began telling him how up until now Davis had done all they'd asked of him and then some. Even Primeau had to admit that Davis had accomplished far more than he'd expected. Vincent put up his hands and demanded they be quiet. He looked at Carroll. "You mind giving us a few minutes?"

As soon as the lawyer left the room, Primeau looked at Vincent. "Boss, remember, Pigeon pointed a gun at Davis a while back. The guy's psychotic. There's no telling what he's likely to do. And now Davis has that to worry about as well."

Lacroix stood up, walked to the window and looked out for a moment before facing them. "We knew we were hiring a gangster when we hired Davis. That's why we did it. What he proposes is extreme, but he's right, we haven't got much time and the rules don't apply anymore. In fact, they never did."

Vincent frowned. "Firebombing buildings. How does that make us any different from them? What if someone gets killed? There's too much risk, too much can go wrong."

"So that's it," said Primeau, "the end of the line. We just roll it up and never discover who's cooperating with the gang?"

Lacroix looked between them and stepped forward. "We can control the fires, even make sure no one's around when they start. None of this will come back to us. We can minimize the chances that anyone's hur—"

"Listen, gentlemen, much as I appreciate your enthusiasm, this is a nonstarter, I can't sanction it." Vincent's voice had a hard edge to it. One that told them this was his final answer.

Still, Lacroix persisted. "What if Davis arranges it?"

Vincent smiled. "I'll pretend I didn't hear that, Corporal."

"Maybe you didn't hear it," Lacroix said.

Vincent raised his eyebrows.

"Look, sir, we owe it to Davis. He's the one taking all the risks, and as for the trust fund, well, that's peanuts. Think of all the money we've blown on the operation with almost nothing to show for it— way more money than what Davis is asking for his daughter, ten times that amount, maybe more—what if he delivers? Won't that be worth all this time and money?"

Vincent was silent. Lacroix sensed the man was wavering. "I know how to handle this so there are no questions asked. Remember the LaPierre case four years ago?"

Vincent narrowed his eyes. "How did you hear about that?"

"Let's just say I hear things."

Vincent continued glaring at Lacroix, then turned and paced to the window. After a few tense moments, he faced them again. "I can't be part of it. Understand?" The men nodded. "This conversation never happened."

Despite almost hopped with excitement, Lacroix only said, "Yes, sir."

Vincent headed for the door, and stopped before leaving. "And Bernie…"

"Yes, sir?"

"Make sure I don't regret this."

Chapter 38

Over the next several days the handlers' plan unfolded. Davis was arrested and charged in connection with the gang's human trafficking ring. He was held in Bordeaux Prison. Three days later, at nine in the morning, the RCMP conducted coordinated raids on the gang's two most popular nightclubs, their clubhouse, the Auberge hotel and De Riggi's residence. They'd toyed with the idea of arresting some of the girls employed at the clubs but decided that might scare off some of the witnesses who had filed statements against De Riggi. The police found nothing at the clubs or the hotel except cash in the overnight safes. There were two gang members at the clubhouse when the police arrived; they had offered little resistance since they were both sleeping off a hangover. Apart from a sophisticated surveillance system that had been turned off, all they found was a safe, a small amount of cash and a limited amount of drugs. They made no arrests. De Riggi's wife was out when the police arrived at her home, and they were forced to break down the door. When she came back, she found that they'd seized his computer, emptied the contents of his safe and taken away two boxes of records. Primeau gave her a copy of the search warrant and a list of items that they'd seized.

Two days later, two of the gang's nightclubs were torched and a fire broke out at the clubhouse. Nearby residents assumed the firebombings were the start of a gang war. All the fires broke out early in the morning, shortly after the clubs had closed for business. Whoever torched the clubs used a simple accelerant. Bar staff at each location told the police they'd received an anonymous phone call around 3:00 a.m. claiming there was a bomb on the premises. The staff called the police and then quickly cleared the premises. The fires started shortly thereafter, before police had arrived. The damage to the night clubs was moderate and fortunately no one was injured. The fire marshal reported that the fires appeared to have started in the washrooms, since those were the areas where most of the damage occurred and where the heat had been the most intense. The fire in the clubhouse caused only minor damage because of the sprinkler system.

At the end of his first week in prison, Davis had had a visit from Matisse. The gangster told Davis about the firebombings and the police searches. He'd heard rumours that De Riggi was done and would remain in a New York federal penitentiary. He said they could expect more trouble from rival gangs. Davis told him to arrange for additional security at all the clubs and the hotel and do whatever he could to keep the gang together. Davis said the timing of the fire bombings was suspicious and he was surprised that so many people knew about De Riggi's arrest. When he told Matisse too many things were happening at once, almost as if someone was orchestrating the whole thing, Matisse just shrugged.

Meanwhile, De Riggi had spent the last seven nights in a New York cell with a drug dealer. The guy snored, but what was worse, he started having nightmares and found himself waking up screaming at the top of his voice every night. The guards ignored his complaints. Once De Riggi woke up in the middle of the night and found his cellmate standing by his bunk staring down at him. De Riggi had complained again. They just laughed at him. De Riggi had met his lawyer twice, some expensive suit Dunphy had gotten him. The guy was useless. What really bothered De Riggi was the fact he had been arrested in the US. All his offences had taken place in Canada, and all the witnesses were based at the hotel he operated in Montreal. The suit said it was likely he'd be returned to Montreal in a few weeks, but for now he wasn't allowed contact with anyone other than his US lawyer. De Riggi desperately needed to talk to someone in Canada. "Contact Dunphy," he told the suit. "Tell him to contact the trucker. He'll understand."

De Riggi was moved to Bordeaux Prison the following week and was shocked to see Davis there. They had a chance to talk in the prison yard, and Davis told him what he'd heard from Matisse about the firebombings and the police raids and how he'd been arrested and charged for being part of the gang's human trafficking network.

They started to walk to the corner of the yard, all the time watching for guards. When they reached the wall, Davis told him that he expected to be bailed out any day.

"Listen, the first thing you do when you get out is find that bitch Josie. Her and those hookers that swore statements. Understand?"

"I hear you. I know they're going be watching my every move. It isn't going to be easy."

De Riggi looked over his shoulder, then back at Davis. "I have contacts. They'll know where they are. There's another thing. I need you to contact some people. They'll be wondering what the fuck's been going on. They'll need to be calmed down, reassured like. Tell them that you're taking over in my absence. Tell them I expect to be out in a month, two tops. In the meantime, you're running things."

Davis noticed a prison guard heading toward them and took a step back. The guard ignored him as he leaned in and said something quietly to De Riggi. Di Riggi nodded and waited for the guard to walk past them. "Listen, I don't have much time right now. Here's the names of three guys you need to talk to. The first is a senior inspector in the Sûreté. He'll know how to find you, and he'll be able to track down Chouinard, and the hookers too. The second guy's a big cheese at the port. He controls things. He knows about you already. You need to meet him and tell him what's happened, and that you'll be running the show till I get out. Tell him you and I are talking regular. I'll get word to him; he'll contact you. That's the way it works. Now the third guy is our contact with New York. He'll be in touch with you too."

De Riggi whispered something to Davis and then shook his hand. Davis walked away across the yard, tightly holding the small piece of paper he'd just been given.

Back in his cell, Davis looked at the piece of paper. The names didn't mean anything to him. He wondered who they were and how they'd contact him. The inspector in the Sûreté would be easy. The other two ... He wondered what the handlers would do. How would the Sûreté inspector know where Chouinard and the other witnesses were? He must have a contact somewhere in the Security Service who handled witness protection. Or maybe it was someone within the Crown counsel's office.

***

Davis was released on bail on the Friday. No one came to pick him up, so he had to get a cab to take him home to Bromont. On his release, his first thought was of Helene. He wondered if she'd heard about his arrest. He needed to avoid her. And he needed to contact Lacroix and Primeau and tell them about De Riggi's message.

He just wanted to get home, have a shower and change his clothes, maybe go for walk. The sudden freedom was strange even after only two weeks inside. De Riggi must have found it tough as well; he'd been only twenty-five when he was last in prison, and that was just for a week. He was no longer a young man. Davis wondered how long he'd last.

As he sat in the back of the cab, he went over his plan again. He wasn't sure what he should tell Matisse and Dubois. He knew De Riggi would have called them by now and told them he'd put Davis in charge and that they were to help him. He might have told them about the Sûreté inspector, but Davis doubted he'd mentioned the names of the other two guys.

Davis decided to keep a low profile knowing that he'd be watched by the cops. Or at least that's what everyone expected would happen. He'd meet up with Matisse and Dubois and explain what he wanted them to do, and how they could help find Chouinard and the four Ukrainian women. He knew it'd be a wild goose chase. He needed to keep them busy though. He'd let them believe a gang war was about to break out at any minute and that it was important for them to keep up their guard. They could help by spreading the word that Davis had taken over while De Riggi was still inside. He wondered if De Riggi would have him watched now he was out of prison. He knew he was being paranoid and that even De Riggi would have a hard time figuring out what had really happened. Pigeon was another problem—if he was still alive. Davis couldn't afford to worry about that right now.

When he arrived back at his cottage, he knew someone had been there while he was away. The place was still neat and tidy, though some of his books had been moved and some files in his desk had been put back in a different place. He checked all the rooms a second time and nothing was missing. He took a shower and changed into clean clothes. It was nice to be home.

Suddenly the phone rang. "The lake, one hour." The caller hung up.

***

Davis kept checking his rear-view mirror until he was sure he wasn't being followed. When he arrived at the park there was no one around. He walked past the bench and carried on glancing behind him. He saw Primeau walking toward him. He waited for him, and they both continued around the lake. Davis recounted his meeting with De Riggi in prison. He then read out the names that De Riggi had given him.

"Do you believe him?" Primeau asked.

"Why wouldn't I? He's desperate. He doesn't have any options. The gang's under attack. He has to do something. Why would he give me fake names?"

Primeau nodded.

"Do you know René Gamache, the inspector from the Sûreté?" Davis asked.

"No. It won't take long for me to find out who he is, though."

"De Riggi's pretty sure he can track down Chouinard."

"We'll check him out."

"The other two should be in touch with me soon. I'm supposed to calm them down, tell them he'll be out in a month, then things will be back to normal. And I'm in charge until then."

Primeau was quiet for a while, deep in thought.

"What's your plan?" he asked finally.

"I guess I need to be seen around town, play the part. And wait for them to contact me," Davis said. "One other thing: have you been to my cottage?"

"No, why?"

"I'm pretty sure someone's been there while I was inside. Nothing's gone, but a few things have been rearranged."

"I'll check around, maybe someone from the Montreal police. Though I doubt it." Primeau turned around and said, "I'll get back to you on the Sûreté inspector. Let me know when you hear from the other guys. And another thing, we've put a tail on you, just in case." He headed back in the direction he had come from.

Davis carried on walking. It was nice to be free. As he walked around the lake, he remembered the letter he'd thought of writing while in prison. It was to his daughter. He decided to write to her again. Maybe for the last time. He'd planned to give it to one of his handlers and ask them to deliver it. Hopefully they'd have a better chance of tracking her down. He'd given it a lot of thought. This might be the only memory she'd have of him, and he wanted to set the record straight. Whether he survived or not, he needed her to know what kind of man he really was. Sure, he'd made some bad mistakes. He'd tried to put it right, to make amends. Maybe the guy who delivered the letter would tell her what her old man had done. It might not make any difference, he just wanted her to know that he still thought of her after all these years. He still loved her and cared for her. She was the reason he'd tried to change. She'd have the trust fund, but that was just money. The letter she'd keep forever. Maybe when this was all over and if he survived, he'd spend the time tracking her down himself. He'd take the chance that she might not want to see him.

Chapter 39

The call came early the next morning. "Your boss called," the voice said.

"Who is this?" asked Davis.

"He wants me to track down some people."

The Sûreté inspector, thought Davis.

"Meet me at Café Saint-Jacques on Saint Denis. Two-thirty this afternoon. Make sure you're not followed."

Before Davis could say anything else, the caller hung up. Davis wanted Matisse at the meeting so he could do the legwork. He knew if he showed up with someone else it might spook the guy, so he went alone.

There were quite a few people in the bar when Davis arrived. He was early. How would Gamache recognize him? Davis sat at a corner table and ordered a beer. By the time he'd finished his beer it was 2:45 p.m. The guy wasn't showing. Davis took a long look around and didn't recognize any newcomers. He'd give it five more minutes.

A guy walked past him and headed for the washroom. He returned a few minutes later and sat down across from Davis. "Your photo doesn't do you justice." He smirked.

Gamache was in his late fifties, wore glasses and had a large dark moustache peppered with grey. Davis guessed he was about five feet ten. Even though he was wearing a raincoat, Davis could tell he was in shape.

The waiter came by and left a beer in front of Davis. Gamache nodded and the waiter came back with another a moment later.

Gamache stared at Davis. "So, how can I help?"

"Didn't my boss explain?" said Davis.

"He said very little, just that he needed to find some people quickly."

Davis explained the situation. The man nodded. "This won't be easy. They could be anywhere."

"Can you help or not?"

"Yeah, but it'll cost."

"We figured that."

"Twenty grand, ten up front and ten once I've found them."

"I'll get Dubois to arrange payment. He'll contact you."

"No. I'll contact him."

Three days went by, and Davis had heard nothing. The Sûreté inspector hadn't been in touch, and neither had De Riggi's other contacts. He was beginning to wonder if it was all a hoax. He'd called Dubois and told him about the inspector. Dubois said he'd arrange for the payment. He claimed that things had been quiet and there were no signs of other gangs casing their clubs or the hotel. The two clubs that had been firebombed were closed, and the insurance company was playing hardball and had hired an investigator. The investigator said the claim would take time to assess since there were "suspicious circumstances."

"What? They think we torched the place while me and the boss were in prison?" said Davis.

"Claimed it looked like arson," said Dubois. "The investigator's an asshole. Said the whole thing looked planned."

"Listen," said Davis, "finding Chouinard is the number-one priority. The boss has given me a few other things that need doing. Give me a few days. And be careful, the cops are everywhere."

***

That Sunday morning around 9:00 a.m. there was a knock on the door. Davis looked through his curtains and saw a black sedan in his driveway. He opened the door and a guy dressed in a black suit introduced himself. "Mr. Landry wondered if you might care to go for a drive?"

"I don't know any Landry."

"I understand that you and Mr. Landry have a mutual acquaintance. A Mr. De Riggi."

"Where are we going?"

"Mr. Landry just wants a few words. It shouldn't take too long."

Davis grabbed his coat and followed the black suit. The driver opened the rear door of the sedan. Even though the windows were tinted black he could see there was no one inside.

Davis looked at the driver, who said, "Mr. Landry has asked me to apologize. He wants to make sure we're not being followed." Davis climbed into the back seat and the driver pulled out. After about half a mile the driver said, "As I suspected, we're being followed. This may take a bit longer than planned. I hope you're not in a hurry."

The sedan took about fifteen minutes to lose the blue Ford that had been following them. The driver was obviously used to losing tails. He slowed down at an intersection, waited for the lights to turn amber, then put his foot down. The Ford was left at the lights as the sedan took the first left and the second right. He carried on driving for another thirty minutes, checking his mirror to make sure the Ford was gone. Eventually he pulled into an abandoned warehouse near the old docks.

They sat in the vehicle and after about ten minutes, another vehicle pulled up alongside them. The driver of the sedan got out, walked around to Davis's side of the car and opened the door. "Mr. Landry will see you now."

Davis got out and followed the driver, who opened the door of the other car for him. Davis climbed in the back seat next to a man in his seventies who was extremely well dressed, wearing a suit and overcoat. Davis thought he looked like a politician.

"Mr. Davis, please forgive all the cloak-and-dagger business." The man had a soft voice with a British accent. "Unfortunately, I've found this is often the best way to conduct business. The rear of the car is soundproofed, and my driver, Marcel, is the model of discretion. He's been with me for twenty years."

The driver pulled out of the warehouse and out of the docks. They were headed north.

"I understand Mr. De Riggi is in a spot of bother, and he's asked you to step in and represent him?"

Davis wasn't sure what he was expecting, but this well-dressed old guy wasn't it. It took a few seconds for Davis to respond. "Sorry, it's just that..."

"I'm not what you expected? Is that it? Completely understandable. People are often surprised. Anyway, let's talk business. Tony has spoken a lot about you. Says you have a good financial mind. Even the gentlemen at the port are impressed. The thing is we need to determine whether Mr. De Riggi's absence will be short term or long term. We believe it's the latter, in which case we need to decide whether we can still do business. We've had a successful relationship for many years, and it would be unfortunate if that were to end. Our sources tell us the charges are serious and the chances of him leaving Bordeaux Prison any time soon are ... remote."

Davis decided against pleading his case. Something told him the old man was not used to being interrupted.

"Since we can't deal with a business partner who's locked up in a prison, we must consider alternatives. Now, before you attempt to placate me with assurances of his imminent release, please be aware that we have well-connected friends. Our information is from the most reliable sources. Our decision on whether to maintain this relationship will depend largely on who we are dealing with and on ensuring that Mr. De Riggi won't be tempted to, shall we say, 'share our little secret.'"

He looked over at Davis.

Davis didn't need any explanation. The soft-spoken Brit had left no room for doubt. If he wasn't released soon, De Riggi would be dealt with. The same thing would happen to Davis in the event they decided they weren't going to use the gang. He wondered if De Riggi knew that meeting this old man might result in both their deaths. He suspected he'd have figured that out.

Davis had questions. Who was this guy? What gave him so much power? Why had nobody been able to touch him? No one even knew who he was.

"Mr. Davis, no questions? Didn't he tell you who I was?"

"No, he didn't."

"Surely he must have told you something?"

"There wasn't time. They kept us apart in prison. All he could do was pass on a name."

"Then let me tell you what's so special about our relationship."

He spent the next fifteen minutes explaining how he'd first met De Riggi. He was a senior official in the provincial government's Department of Justice. De Riggi had been prosecuted for some criminal offence and Landry had identified a mistake in the evidence. The case was abandoned, but somehow De Riggi found out that it was Landry who had had the case dismissed.

At one time Landry was tipped for great things. Unfortunately for the powerful bureaucrat, there had been some nasty rumours going around that several government officials linked to the City of Montreal had received kickbacks as part of a quid pro quo scheme whereby large contracts were awarded to various building contractors involved in bidding for the 1976 Montreal Summer Olympics. The contracts were awarded without a legitimate bidding process and went to contractors with strong union ties. While Landry never received any payment, he got caught up in the witch-hunt. After that, he was passed over for promotion and vowed to get even. An old friend helped him join the board of the Port of Montreal as a government appointee. After a while he saw an opportunity to benefit financially from his position and he took it.

Davis didn't understand how this man helped the gang financially. Landry sensed his confusion.

"It's simple. Because of me, De Riggi and his gang have the run of the port. One day that will end, but as the chairman of the board I'm able to influence a lot of people. Not just at the board and management level, in Ottawa as well. Who do you think deals with all the people that want to investigate crime at the port, change the security systems, outsource labour and get rid of the longshoremen?" Davis was impressed. He didn't want Landry to know so he just nodded as Landry continued. "And for my trouble, I get a percentage of everything the gang brings in through the port. My fee is based on a fixed percentage of tonnage coming through the port every year. No matter how much the gang ships through the port, my fee is guaranteed. The funds are paid into a lawyer's trust account and then transferred overseas."

The old guy was smooth. There'd be nothing to tie him to the money. The account was probably held in some offshore trust that was subject to privacy laws.

He stared into the old man's eyes.

"What do you want from me?" asked Davis.

"I need to be satisfied that the gang is going to survive. If there's any likelihood that's not going to happen, I need a contingency plan."

"That contingency plan would involve another gang?"

Landry smiled. "We understand each other."

Davis hadn't been paying attention to where they were going, and when he looked up, he realized they were heading back to Bromont. Landry seemed to be finished talking and was staring out the window, so Davis let his mind wander. He knew little of the inner financial workings of the gang. That was probably the way De Riggi preferred things. He hadn't given much thought to who was handling De Riggi's banking. He'd be surprised if it were Dunphy. That was something he needed to find out. In the limited time he'd spent with Landry he got the sense that he was used to being in control. Davis resisted the urge tell Landry that everything would be fine, that the gang would survive De Riggi's incarceration. He knew he couldn't ensure De Riggi's silence while he was in prison. He'd concluded that Landry might be the brains behind the gang, possibly even their banker. He also decided that words weren't as important to Landry as actions.

They arrived back at the cottage and Davis got out.

"I'm glad we met, Mr. Davis," Landry said.

"What happens now?"

"We'll be in touch. Please say hi to Tony when you get the chance."

De Riggi had underestimated this man. Landry was already considering his options. Davis was sure he wouldn't want to change gangs, but he was a survivor, and if that's what it took, he wouldn't think twice about getting rid of De Riggi.

Chapter 40

Lacroix and Primeau had decided that the lakeside near Davis's home was no longer a safe place to meet and arranged for him to meet them at another lake in the Townships about ten miles away. When Davis first went there, he thought it was a bad choice. It was busier and heavily wooded: lots of places to hide without being seen. He knew it didn't matter. If someone wanted to get to him, they'd have plenty of chances. And it was unlikely the gang would be following him: he had realized he was more likely to be attacked by a rival gang wanting to put De Riggi's organization out of business permanently. He was glad he'd given Primeau the letter he'd written to his daughter. He didn't know if she'd ever get it, but somehow he believed his handler when he said he'd make sure she got it one way or another, once the operation was over.

Lacroix had come on his own and as soon as he saw Davis, he sensed something was wrong. Davis quickly brought him up to speed on his meetings with the Sûreté inspector Gamache and Landry.

"What do you think Landry's gonna do?"

Davis shrugged. "I'm sure he's given a lot of thought to bringing in a new gang to run the port. That'd take time and it's a lot of disruption. It's easier for him to leave us in place. He needs to know we're still in control, and that I can handle things. My guess is he'll give us some time, but he'll want to see that we've made some changes and that the gang's no longer under threat."

"What about De Riggi? Would he arrange to have someone deal with him inside?"

"Possibly. I don't think he'll do it though."

"Why do you say that?"

"He'll tell me to do it."

"What?"

"Think about it," Davis said. "This guy's got a lot riding on this. Who knows what else he's invested in? Land deals, port expansion, construction contracts. He's gonna want to keep control. That means his own guy running the gang. What better way to prove I'm his guy?"

"Christ."

"That's what I'd do if I were him."

Lacroix sighed and ran a hand over his face. "Where does New York fit into all this?"

"I don't know. Either they're trying to expand their network here, or they're a source of the drugs. I don't think they have anything to do with Landry. If they had, you'd have heard something by now," said Davis.

Lacroix was silent for a few moments, running things through his mind, considering the options.

"So what do you propose we do?" asked Davis.

"You need to sit tight and wait. Pretty soon Landry's gonna make his decision. We'll check out the management team at the port, see if there are any connections to him. Gamache isn't gonna find Chouinard or the girls. And sooner or later you'll hear from New York."

"Should I tell De Riggi that Landry doesn't think he's coming out and wants him quiet?"

"De Riggi will know what that means."

Davis nodded. "At least I'll have told him."

"That may be right, but for the wrong reasons. If De Riggi knows Landry is going to get rid of him inside prison, he might think more about his own sorry skin."

"You mean he'll squeal on Landry?"

"Why not? Especially if he figures his own gang has been told to deal with him."

Davis was quiet for a few moments. "One of the things that troubles me," he said finally, "is I have no idea how the gang really works. Apart from two names and a New York contact, I've got nothing."

"Okay, you visit De Riggi and tell him what you heard from Landry. And maybe we raise the heat on him in other ways."

"Let me guess, another firebombing?"

"The longer he's inside, the more he's at risk. When he hears what Landry told you he'll be forced to make a deal with us or die in prison. Which would you choose?"

Chapter 41

When Davis arrived at the jail the next morning, De Riggi was in a good mood. He was starting to make some contacts inside, was given a wide berth by most of the cons who clearly knew who he was, and even the guards kept their distance. He smiled when he saw Davis walk in the room and sit down across from him.

De Riggi looked at the three guards who were in the room. One was standing by the door casting his eye over the dozen prisoners who were seated at the tables across from their visitors. Another was walking between the aisles that separated the prisoners, and the third was scanning the room, checking that the guests weren't trying to pass anything to the cons.

He looked at Davis and in a quiet voice said, "Tell me about your visitors."

Davis told him about Landry and the trouble he had taken to ensure they weren't being followed. De Riggi smiled and said, "Landry always was careful. I don't know how he's managed for so long. I can't understand how the port hasn't figured things out."

Davis needed to spit it out. "There's a problem, a big problem. He wants your silence. He's convinced you're not coming out anytime soon."

"He knows I won't squeal."

"It's not that. He says he wants to keep working with us. If he has to though, he will find another gang. Says there's too much at stake to leave things to chance."

"What are you saying?"

"He's gonna take you out." Davis let that sink in for a moment. De Riggi looked surprised. Had this really not occurred to him? "Didn't say it in so many words," Davis continued. "He implied it'd be nice if we did it. And if not, that he'd make it happen."

De Riggi's face grew purple with rage. The veins in his forehead bulged and he started to shake as he stood up and raised his voice. "I don't believe it. That fucker's going take me out?"

Cons started to look at him, visitors were alarmed. One of the guards walked over. "Is there a problem here?"

De Riggi stared at him and mouthed the words "Fuck off." The guard walked back to the door but kept looking at them. He then nodded to another guard, tapped his watch and stuck up two fingers. The other guard disappeared.

"What about that bitch Chouinard?"

"I met Gamache and he's on it."

"Tell Matisse to come see me. He'll know what to do. Landry's gonna act right away. I'm not safe even in here. Bastard has friends everywhere." De Riggi was looking around them as he spoke. Suddenly he looked much smaller, nothing like the boss Davis had met months ago. "Tell Matisse to get on it right away."

"What do you want me to do?"

Three guards were coming toward De Riggi.

De Riggi looked from them to Davis. "Get me the fuck out of here," he said. Then De Riggi stood up, still holding eye contact. "And for now, I'm just gonna have to find another way to protect myself."

Suddenly he turned on the guard nearest him and punched him in the face. He was about to swing another punch when he was grabbed from behind. Two guards wrestled him to the ground. One of them pulled his hands behind his back and handcuffed him. As he stood up, De Riggi looked over at Davis and smiled. He was headed for solitary.

That evening Davis met Matisse and Dubois in a bar in Old Montreal. He told them about his meeting with De Riggi and how the boss wanted Matisse to arrange for his escape as soon as possible. Matisse nodded, as if he'd done it before. Davis had told them about his meeting with Landry and the warning about De Riggi's silence; neither was surprised at De Riggi's response. Even though Bordeaux had a reputation for being an easy place to escape from because of the corruption among the guards, they expected the police would be keeping a special watch on their boss and it might take up to a week to arrange an escape.

As Davis listened to the two gang members discuss strategy, he thought about what his handlers would make of his visit to De Riggi and the likelihood of the gang being able to arrange his escape. De Riggi's death inside prison would mean the failure of the operation. They'd never be able to go after the New York gang, nor prove anything against Landry. They needed his cooperation and all the information inside his head.

Davis heard his name called twice and looked up. Both gangsters were staring at him.

"I'm trying to figure out how we make sure the boss is protected while he's inside," he said as an excuse.

"Well I need more time," Matisse said. "I think you should meet with Landry again. Tell him we'll take out the boss."

Davis nodded. But the more he thought about his meeting with Landry, the more he realized he wouldn't leave things to chance. He had too much at stake to wait for someone else to take care of De Riggi. No, he had to take care of De Riggi before Landry dealt with the problem.

Chapter 42

Primeau arranged for them to meet at the same law office he'd met them in several weeks before. It didn't take Davis long to bring Primeau and Lacroix up to speed.

"Landry's threat hit him hard. He's like a rat in a cage."

Primeau smiled. "Once the gang bust him out, how does he deal with Landry while he's on the run?"

"It doesn't solve his problems, it just gives him time," Davis said. "How easy is it to break out of Bordeaux?"

"It's been done," replied Lacroix.

"So it comes down to how much time we have before either they spring him or Landry gets to him," said Primeau.

"I have a few ideas," said Davis. "Is Inspector Vincent coming?"

"No, he can't make it. We'll debrief him later today."

"You may need to make a decision pretty quickly," said Davis.

"Not a problem," said Lacroix.

Davis stood up, walked over to the table and poured himself a coffee. "Here's what we think we know. And jump in at any time if I've missed something or you disagree." Davis looked over at them and they both nodded.

"De Riggi's not getting out of prison anytime soon. Landry is likely to have someone take him out. He's probably planning it as we speak. We need him alive, and we need him to testify against Landry and the New York gang. Without him, it's over."

"Tell us something we don't know," Primeau said. Lacroix scowled at him.

Davis tilted his head. "How about this: we go after De Riggi in prison. Make it look like an inside job."

"We're taking out De Riggi?" said Primeau, rolling his eyes. "Great, I can definitely see Vincent signing off on this."

"Let him finish," Lacroix said.

Davis sipped his coffee, then set it down. "We make it look like an attack, make sure De Riggi thinks he's been targeted by someone, Landry, another gang, it doesn't matter. He's taken to hospital and then relocated. Somewhere where we can keep an eye on him and see if he wants to talk."

"You really think he'll talk?" Lacroix asked.

Davis smiled. "Maybe, but as far as Landry is concerned, he's been dealt with. I'll still be running the gang, and we still have a chance at getting Landry and the New York connection."

They were both silent. Finally Lacroix said, "So when you say 'we' take out De Riggi, you mean the RCMP?"

Davis nodded.

Primeau threw his hands up. "Do you know how hard it was for us to arrange the firebombing of the clubs? Do you understand what you're asking?"

"I'm not asking for anything. I'm just telling you what you need to do if you want Landry and the New York connection. Don't blame me if a week from now De Riggi's dead and everything we've worked for over the last two years has been a waste of time."

Davis walked to the window and looked down onto the street. Life was carrying on. Summer was on the way. He turned around. "I guess I better get back to work. I'm sure you'll let me know what you decide to do before too long." He headed for the door, not knowing what they were going to do, and for the first time he didn't care anymore. It was up to them.

Chapter 43

De Riggi had been stuck in solitary for four days. He was only allowed out for one hour a day to walk in the prison yard escorted by three guards. He wondered if the prison authorities knew something was going on, whether it was a breakout or a possible attack, and whether Matisse had been able to organize anything yet. What the fuck was taking them so long?

What the guards didn't know was that he'd managed to obtain a shiv from one of the prisoners before he was placed in solitary. It wasn't much, but it was something. That evening, after he'd had his short walk in the yard, he returned to his cell and found a note on his bed. It simply said, "Tonight."

What did it mean? At first he thought it was a message telling him to get ready for a breakout. Then he decided it could just as easily be a warning. Why would they warn him? *No*, he thought, *tonight is the night. But how? Some of the guards must be in on it. One of them must have left the message. There's no way a prisoner would be allowed anywhere near solitary.* He ran through several more scenarios, knowing it was hopeless. He just had to wait.

At 9:00 p.m., the lights went out, as they did every night. They normally woke him at 6:00 a.m. when they'd slide a tray with his breakfast through the bottom of his cell door. He was determined to stay awake and start to figure out what he'd do once he was out. Where would he hide? What had Matisse planned? He wondered how he'd be able to run the gang and came to the realization that those days were over. At first he thought the cops would want to talk to him, see if he had anything to say, maybe even discuss a plea arrangement. Something didn't seem right. He'd been left alone. What did the police know that he didn't? Why had Josie given him up? Was it just the Ukrainians? He clenched his teeth. No. He would not think of her. She had betrayed him. And if he ever got the chance, he'd slit her throat himself.

De Riggi took a breath and forced himself to focus. He thought about different hiding places and remembered Pigeon. He hadn't spoken to his brother since he'd dropped Pigeon off at the farm. The fact that he hadn't heard from Pigeon was a good thing. Going to his brother's place even for a week or two until he was able to plan something longer term made sense. He wasn't sure where he'd go after that.

He must have drifted off, because the next thing he heard was the cell door being opened. The room flooded with light. It was barely daylight outside, and he had trouble focusing. He had no idea what time it was. As he lay on his bunk he felt inside his pocket and put his hand around the shiv.

"Stand away from the door," the guard said.

Two guards walked in. "Stand up!" De Riggi was slow to move, and one guard lifted a baton and said, "Do as I say."

Slowly he swung his legs off the bunk and stood up.

"Hands on the wall. Now!"

He moved two paces to the wall and placed his hands against it. The guard used his baton to search him.

"What's in your pocket?"

"My toothbrush," said De Riggi.

The guard swung his baton hard across the back of De Riggi's head and he slumped to the ground.

When he woke up he found himself in the back of a speeding ambulance, sirens blaring. He tried to move his arms and legs but couldn't. He looked down and discovered he was in a straitjacket strapped onto the stretcher. He felt groggy and his head throbbed. There was no one else in the back of the ambulance and he couldn't turn his head to see who was driving. He had no idea who had taken him or where he was going. Was it Landry? It didn't make sense. It'd be far easier to have killed him inside prison. If it were the gang, there'd be someone inside the ambulance with him.

The ambulance started to slow down, and the siren was turned off. It was light outside now. Where were they heading? De Riggi was used to being in control; he didn't know what it was like to be on the other side. He didn't like it.

After another thirty minutes the ambulance slowed down even more, and the road felt different. The smell was different too. What was it? Where was he? He guessed they were headed east, toward the Townships, certainly away from Montreal. Ah, that was it: manure. He was in the countryside.

The ambulance came to a stop, and he heard the front door open. Then the back doors opened and a man dressed as a nurse climbed in and started to undo the straps of the stretcher and then undid the straitjacket.

"Take your time getting up. Rub your arms and legs, let the blood start circulating before you stand up or you'll fall flat on your face."

"Who the fuck are you?"

"All in good time."

The man left the ambulance.

He could hear voices outside and slowly stood up, holding onto the side of the ambulance to keep his balance. He reached the back door and saw two RCMP cruisers and four Mounties standing by their vehicles. Two plainclothes men walked toward him and introduced themselves.

"What the fuck…? Why am I here?"

"Let's go inside."

One of them pointed to the door of a nearby farmhouse. He started to follow him and was about to fall when the bigger cop grabbed his arm. De Riggi stared at him and said, "Let me get this straight. You guys kidnapped me from prison?"

The big cop smiled. "Let's get inside, shall we?" De Riggi gingerly walked across the farmyard, up the three steps and through the front door.

Inside the farmhouse, seated at the head of the table was a grey-haired guy who looked to be in his sixties. He sat in one of the chairs and two other men sat opposite him.

The old guy cleared his throat. "Mr. De Riggi, my name is Yves Vincent. I'm an inspector in the RCMP and the head of its Security Service for Quebec. These two gentlemen are Corporals Lacroix and Primeau. We've been tracking you and your gang's movements for the last twenty-four months."

"That's nice, but why am I here?"

"I was getting to that. After your arrest on charges of illegal smuggling of immigrants into Canada, we became aware of a plot to kill you while you were inside Bordeaux."

De Riggi was silent.

"Does the name Landry mean anything to you?"

"Never heard of him."

"He's the individual behind the attempt to kill you."

"What attempt?"

"The attempt that was to be made on your life later today. Fortunately for you, we found out about it just in time."

"This is all bullshit, and you know it."

"In that case, you won't have a problem going back to Bordeaux, will you?" Vincent looked at Lacroix and Primeau. "I guess you were wrong, gentlemen. It seems Mr. De Riggi thinks he's safe. We might as well send him back."

He nodded to Primeau, who got up and walked over to De Riggi.

"Come on, let's go. You might just get back in time for breakfast."

Lacroix noticed that De Riggi touched the scar over his right eye and exhaled.

Lacroix looked at him and said, "We heard you wanted to head south and spend time in the sun. You won't be seeing any sunshine for a long time. That's if you survive in prison, of course. If it's not Landry, it'll be someone else. Maybe the gang that Landry brings in to run the docks. It's just a matter of time. A few days, maybe a week if you're lucky."

De Riggi looked at Lacroix and said, "You've got it all figured out, haven't you? Think you know everything."

"Not everything, Mr. De Riggi," said Vincent. "What I do know is that yours and the gang's days are numbered."

They all stared at De Riggi. His face gave nothing away. Vincent waited a full minute, looked his watch and then said, "Okay, have it your way. Just remember, rumours are easy to start but hard to kill. When you head back to prison, people will know where you've been and who you've talked to."

"What the fuck's that mean?"

"It means that you don't have much time. Goodbye, Mr. De Riggi."

Primeau escorted De Riggi outside, handcuffed him and put him in one of the police cruisers. He nodded to the cop and then headed back inside, where Vincent and Lacroix were deep in conversation.

So that's the end of the operation, thought Lacroix. *He isn't falling for it. Or has he just decided that he isn't a rat?*

Lacroix was telling Vincent they could only keep him in solitary for so long, and even there he wasn't safe.

"I know, Corporal. What else can we do? If he wants to take his secrets to the grave, that's his call."

Chapter 44

The drive back to Bordeaux Prison was uneventful. Neither cop said anything to De Riggi. He noticed a cruiser ahead and another behind them. As if they were expecting someone to rescue him. Where did they get their information? How did they know about Landry, and how did they know about the attempt to kill him in prison? Or did they know? Was he being paranoid? No, they'd been one step ahead. He began to think about the bombings at the club. Who was really behind that? He knew the cops didn't care about the club being firebombed, but innocent people could have been hurt or even killed. Would they risk that?

That bastard Landry must've been plotting this all along. He started to realize that maybe he'd been trusting the wrong people. Maybe Pigeon wasn't the mole after all. What he didn't understand was who the hell would go to all that trouble to make it look like he was?

He'd underestimated the cops. Maybe he should have listened to what they had to say. He'd known that they'd wanted him to rat out Landry and the guys in New York. Christ, that'd be another group that would be going after him inside. Davis had yet to hear from New

York. Maybe that was why? Who could he trust? He thought about Dunphy. He'd been unhappy for a while. Did he want out? Was he helping the police? Then there was Davis.

De Riggi closed his eyes. His wrists were getting sore from the handcuffs. He was going around in circles, not knowing who to trust or what to do. He needed to speak to Davis and Matisse. In solitary, he couldn't speak to anyone. Maybe that was the best place for him? But there was no truly safe place in Bordeaux.

By the time he saw the sign for the prison he'd made up his mind. They were just entering the city, and he knew he had to make a deal to save his life. And to do that, he had to become a rat. *Better a live rat than a dead gangster*, he thought.

Primeau and Lacroix were also heading back to the prison. By the time they arrived, De Riggi was already in a holding cell. They met the warden, who wasn't happy. Their little stunt hadn't gone unnoticed by some of the guards. Pretty soon word would spread to the prison population. De Riggi wasn't popular with either group and the warden wanted to know how long they'd be playing their game. They explained that they wanted to increase the pressure on De Riggi by moving him into the main building and exposing him to other prisoners. They thanked the warden for his cooperation and explained that there was likely going to be an attempt on De Riggi's life in the next forty-eight hours and it would almost certainly involve one or more of the prison guards.

The warden told them to get a court order. He didn't want to be blamed for facilitating the murder of an inmate, and they could make it easier for everyone if they found another place to put the prisoner. In the meantime, he'd be kept in solitary.

Lacroix knew their request was extreme, but he also figured De Riggi would be at risk even in solitary. One or two days wouldn't make much difference, and maybe he'd see the light and change his mind. The cops headed back to headquarters to see if they could get their boss to fast-track the order.

***

On his way back to solitary, De Riggi demanded to see the warden.

The guard laughed. "What, do you miss your friends?"

"I got information for the warden. It's urgent," De Riggi told him.

The guard told him he'd pass on the message.

The guard had almost finished his shift for the day and was heading off on a two-day break. He was looking forward to spending some time with his son, who'd just started kindergarten. By the time he'd completed his paperwork and signed off for the day he'd completely forgotten about the request. It was only when he was driving home that he remembered. He'd pass on the message when he got back.

***

The next morning, De Riggi's cell door was found open. De Riggi was lying on the floor unconscious, a pool of blood beneath him. The shiv lying near him was covered in blood. The guard checked his pulse. He couldn't feel anything at first, then he felt a slow faint beat. He called for backup and the prison doctor.

Thirty minutes later De Riggi was in Sacre Coeur Hospital undergoing surgery. He'd lost a lot of blood and the surgeon was worried some major organs had been damaged. It wasn't clear how long he'd been unconscious.

The warden called Vincent and gave him the news, saying he had no idea how anyone had gained access to the cell. Initial indications suggested a guard must have been involved, since the solitary wing was only accessible through two gates, both of which were monitored by guards.

"You don't say," Vincent muttered.

When Lacroix and Primeau arrived at the hospital, the surgeon had just finished operating. A nurse explained he was just cleaning up and would be available in a few minutes. The prisoner had been taken back to intensive care, but it would be several hours before he'd regain consciousness. The young surgeon walked into the waiting room and greeted the two cops.

"Mr. De Riggi survived the operation. He received almost two pints of blood. There was no damage to major organs, which was a minor miracle since he was stabbed twice in the stomach. If it had been in the back, it would have proved fatal."

"What are his chances?" asked Primeau.

"As long as there isn't an infection, there's every chance he'll recover."

"Is there anything more you can tell us?"

"He has a damaged liver. There are large fat deposits and accumulations of scar tissue. This can often result in cirrhosis, kidney failure, liver failure and cancer."

The fact that De Riggi's liver was shot didn't surprise them. Primeau made a mental note to remind De Riggi, when he woke up, that he should take better care of his health. He knew he'd appreciate the concern. As long as he was around to testify, that was all that mattered. He was getting ahead of himself; De Riggi had to agree to testify. The doctor left the waiting room and the two cops headed off to meet the warden at Bordeaux Prison.

When they arrived, the warden was just finishing a meeting with the officers who were investigating the attack. At their request, the prison guards overseeing security were going through the camera footage. The camera was located at the entrance to the secure doors between the main prison building and the secure wing that contained inmates held in solitary. The guards had gone through all the footage between the hours of midnight and 7:00 a.m. on the morning of the attack. The colour video was grainy, but when it was played back on the monitor it showed that four officers had walked through the secure corridor between those hours. All the officers on camera had been scheduled to be on duty that night, and all were authorized to have access to the wing.

The video footage also picked up an individual in prison clothes and a baseball cap entering the corridor at 2:30 a.m. and going into the secured wing at 2:31. The same individual was seen re-entering the corridor at 2:38 a.m. and exiting to the main prison one minute later.

"Male, Caucasian. Looks about six feet tall," Primeau said as they watched the video.

"And there's a tattoo on his right arm," said the guard in charge of prison security. The man was clearly proud of the equipment, telling the officers it was a 1982 RCA monitor that was one of the latest surveillance cameras on the market. He claimed few Canadian prisons were equipped with such state-of-the-art technology.

When Lacroix had the guard replay the footage, they noticed the individual was nursing his right arm when he passed back through the corridor. Six inmates matched the picture on the monitor. Four of them didn't have tattoos. The fifth had a faded tattoo on his left arm. When they arrived at the final prisoner's cell, his roommate said the prisoner was in the hospital wing being treated for a burn he'd suffered a few days before. The guard told them the prisoner was a lifer.

Lacroix and Primeau accompanied the guard to the hospital wing and spoke to the prison doctor. He'd treated only one patient in the last three days, and it wasn't for a burn. The doctor pointed to a prisoner who'd come in with a nasty wound on his right arm early that morning. The nurse was wrapping the dressing on the prisoner's forearm and part of the tattoo could be still seen between his wrist and the bottom of the dressing.

When he saw them coming over, the prisoner made no attempt to escape. Where would he go?

When questioned, the prisoner claimed he'd never heard of Landry. His record showed that he was a former member of a rival Montreal gang that had had several run-ins with De Riggi's gang. He smiled and admitted that when he'd been approached with the chance to set the record straight and earn some money for his family, it was simple. Without knowing it, he had done the police a favour. When pressed to name the guard that helped him gain access to the secure wing, he refused.

***

That afternoon when Lacroix and Primeau visited De Riggi, he was ready to talk. He was convinced that Landry was behind the murder attempt. When they told him the name of his attacker, he claimed not to know him. Primeau explained what his attacker told them and a light seemed to go on in De Riggi's eyes. His past was catching up with him; he had too many enemies. His attacker could've been anyone. He knew the next time he was attacked in prison would be the last. It was time to make a deal.

Over the next few days, De Riggi gave them names of the gangs' connections with the Sûreté, drug suppliers and corrupt politicians deeply embedded in provincial and municipal politics in Quebec and Montreal, including Landry. He even named a former federal cabinet minister who'd had responsibility for Montreal's port. Then there were the union leaders and senior executives of big construction companies that he'd dealt with and who'd invested in his drug empire.

He was hesitant to give them details of his business empire until he had a deal worked out, saying that giving up the names should've been enough for the time being. He teased them, claiming they had no idea how big the gang's business interests were. When pressed he refused to give up more information until he had a lawyer present. When they listed the gang's activities that they were aware of, including the extensive drug business, the prostitution and the human trafficking business, he just smiled.

Primeau and Lacroix knew there was more, and it was just a matter of time. They wanted the names of all of his contacts in New York, his contacts in Europe and the big dealers that controlled a large part of the East Coast drug trade. They knew their friends in the States would be very keen to start going after the New York drug business. It wouldn't knock out the New York dealers, but it would be a setback. And they'd have to start up their Canadian network from scratch.

Eventually De Riggi gave them the details they were looking for. The cops marvelled at the extensive and complicated network of investors, suppliers and business contacts that he'd accumulated over the years, as well as the value of the assets that he'd accumulated.

Lacroix, Primeau, Vincent and a representative of Crown counsel met with Davis in the lawyer's offices. They shared what they'd learned from the confession and wanted to know if he knew any of the names De Riggi had mentioned. He said he knew of some of the New York contacts that he'd met a few months before. The only thing that troubled him was how one man could have kept it all together. Who kept score? Who was the bookkeeper?

Davis had his theories. He didn't believe that De Riggi took care of this himself; it would've required a professional. Someone close, someone De Riggi respected, not hired help like Dunphy or any professional that he might have recommended. No, he thought, maybe it wasn't just a bookkeeper. Maybe it was one of his partners. Likely someone who had as much to lose as he did if things unravelled.

Chapter 45

The Security Service and the Crown expected that there was more to come from De Riggi and that maybe Dunphy could fill in the gaps. For the time being they'd been busy arranging for the arrest of gang members. They needed to make it look like a major gang bust. So along with the arrest of Matisse, Dubois and other gang members, they arrested Davis.

When they went to arrest Landry at his home in Westmount, officers discovered that no one was at home. They checked his office and were told by a secretary that Mr. Landry had taken a short vacation and had left for Germany a few days before. She wasn't sure when he'd be returning.

Matisse and Dubois quickly went for plea deals and, after spilling their guts and sharing their limited knowledge of the drugs business, were shipped off to out-of-town holding cells pending finalization of relocation arrangements to the Prairies. With De Riggi's help, the Security Service was able to locate various bank accounts and other assets, such as real estate in Montreal, and, of course, the company's investments in Hatfield's Trucking, the mortgage corporation, as well as various bars and small hotels, including the Auberge.

De Riggi's lawyer negotiated a plea bargain that included witness protection and relocation to a small town in Alberta. They were surprised that De Riggi didn't have any questions for them. When they asked about Pigeon, he just smiled.

"I don't expect you to believe this, and I don't care. Walter and I go back a long way. The more things pointed to Walter being the mole, the more things I discovered about the guy that I never knew. I was going to kill him, but I owed him big time. I let him go. I don't know where he is—he may still be alive—I never killed him."

The clubhouse was seized. Other Montreal gangs were quick to act on the news of the gang's demise and the rumours that De Riggi had become a witness for the prosecution. There was a lot of conflict between rival gangs to take over the gang's dealers, distribution network and their stranglehold on the port.

Davis was released from prison and taken to a safe house. The RCMP offered to get someone to go to his cottage and pack up his belongings. Davis insisted on doing that himself.

"I'll come with you," said Lacroix. He'd taken a liking to the man and was worried that Pigeon might still be around.

As he packed up, Davis thought about where he might go, and he toyed with the idea of going to BC to find his daughter. He wanted to say goodbye to Helene. He wished he could explain to her who he really was. The relationship was over though, and whatever they had was long gone. Too many lies. He hoped that one day she might find out the truth, not that it would make any difference.

When he was finished packing, Davis drove with Lacroix to his safe house on the outskirts of Montreal to meet with Primeau and Vincent one last time. They confirmed that the trust fund had been set up for his daughter, and that someone in BC had been tracking her down. They wanted to know his plans. They insisted he not contact Helene. Lacroix even offered to meet her and tell her how he'd helped them. Davis knew he couldn't tell her everything, but at least she wouldn't feel as bad about falling for a gangster.

Davis assured them he was leaving immediately. They told him to let them know where he was headed since they may have some news for him about his daughter. Davis promised he would once he settled. As they got up to leave Vincent shook his hand and thanked him for all his work. Primeau went to shake his hand and at the last minute gave him a bear hug. Lacroix did the same, and as he let go Davis noticed a tear in his eye as he said, "Thanks for all your help."

***

Davis decided to drive into the village one last time. He was heading back to the Maritimes to check up on his old boss at the fishing lodge. His mind kept returning to Helene. He took the turnoff for the village and there on the street he saw a few of her friends. Instantly he realized this would be a terrible mistake and drove past the bistro without stopping. As he headed back to the cottage, he recognized the road to the lake. On a whim he decided to stop there for ten minutes and go for a short walk.

He pulled the truck into the parking lot and got out. He looked back down the street and saw a car he thought he recognized. It must have been Lacroix or Primeau keeping an eye on him, making sure he left without seeing Helene.

He walked around the lake and reflected on his time in the Townships, how he'd met Helene and the time they'd spent together. What would it have been like to live with her, here in this quiet little town? He was just dreaming. He couldn't live here, and she'd never move. Maybe he would visit her one day when they were both old and talk about things that might have been. He was kidding himself. He would never see her again.

He turned around and headed back to his truck. He was about fifty yards from the parking lot when he noticed a man wearing a hoodie pulled down over his head walking toward him. As he got closer, he sensed something familiar about the guy, but he kept on toward his car, his mind still on Helene. Suddenly the guy stopped, pulled down his hood and called out, "Recognize me now?"

Davis froze. Pigeon had three days' growth of beard and bags under his eyes, and he was holding a gun. "You've been busy, haven't you? And to think I was the only one who figured it out. You fooled everyone." He waved his gun. "You're the mole."

"What are you talking about?"

"Still trying to con people, huh?"

Davis backed up a step and Pigeon raised the gun and pointed it at his head. "Don't move or I'll do it right now."

Pigeon looked over Davis's shoulder and noticed a woman with a dog in the distance. He nodded toward some trees a few metres away. "Over there. Move."

Davis looked to where he'd pointed and saw a path between the trees that bordered the park.

"Come on, move. We don't want anyone else getting hurt now, do we?"

They reached a clearing in the trees and stopped.

"I'll ask again. Are you the mole?"

"De Riggi told me you were the mole, said he had evidence. Even claimed he'd dealt with you."

"You're still denying it."

"I don't know what you think you know. I was arrested along with everyone else."

"So how come you're out? Let you go for good behaviour?"

"Does it matter what I say? You're gonna kill me anyway. De Riggi said you were a psycho."

He'd hit a nerve. Pigeon's eyes bulged. He was still holding the gun out in front of him, and it was still pointed at Davis's head.

"He said you were supposed to take over, but the guys in New York had other ideas. Didn't think you had the brains for the job. And then when the evidence pointed to you being a mole, well, that was the end of it."

Pigeon was red-faced and shaking with anger. "I was set up and you know it." His gun hand faltered slightly, and he lowered the muzzle. Davis wondered if he should charge him. Instead he held back and said, "All I know is De Riggi was arrested and you were nowhere around. The clubs got bombed, the clubhouse—"

"You coulda set the whole thing up."

In the distance a dog barked. Pigeon turned in the direction of the sound, trying to figure out what to believe and how much time he had. He turned back to Davis. "Where's De Riggi, and where's Matisse and Dubois?"

"Rumour has it De Riggi did a deal with the cops. Once he was attacked inside Bordeaux it was only a matter of time. For all I know Matisse and Dubois did a deal too."

"You're saying they're rats?"

"All I'm telling you is the word on the street."

Even though Pigeon looked confused he was still pointing the gun at Davis.

The dog barked again, louder this time. It was getting nearer. Pigeon glanced over his shoulder and Davis made his move. He was only ten feet away when he lunged, but Pigeon was too quick.

The bullet hit Davis's right temple and he dropped to the ground. Pigeon walked over, gun cocked, ready for another shot to the head. Just then, a small terrier came barking through the trees, its owner not far behind, calling its name.

Pigeon ignored the dog and kept the gun pointed at Davis until the terrier lunged and started tearing his pant leg.

"Why you little fucker!" He shook the dog off and pointed his gun at it. At that moment, the woman came into the clearing, calling the dog's name again. Pigeon glanced at her, kicked the dog and ran in the opposite direction further into the forest.

Chapter 46

Lacroix was first to receive the news: Davis had been shot in the head at close range and was unconscious when found. He'd been shipped to Sacre Coeur Hospital in Montreal. As Lacroix walked down the corridor from Vincent's office, he thought of the irony. Davis was now in the same hospital that De Riggi had been in not long ago. Over his career Lacroix had witnessed several shootings in the Montreal area. He'd learned more about gunshot wounds and their impact on the victims than most people would in a lifetime. He'd also spoken to several neurosurgeons and probably knew more about traumatic brain injury than most doctors.

He knew that gunshot wounds to the head were fatal ninety per cent of the time. Of the small number that survived, many would suffer from seizures and other impairments that would require rehabilitation and medication for the rest of their lives.

The nurse had told him over the phone that Davis would likely be in surgery for another three to four hours. *A good sign*, he thought. *At least he's survived this far.* In the meantime, he would head out to Bromont and speak to the investigating officer.

When Lacroix reached the lake, crime-scene investigators were everywhere. They had yet to find the bullet. The middle-aged woman who had found Davis was still there, sitting on a bench. She'd been able to explain to the investigating officer what she saw, but she was clearly distressed. Even though she hadn't gotten a good look at the assailant, she remembered he was of medium height, dressed in dark clothes and looked as if he hadn't shaved for several days. When asked how many cars were in the parking lot, she indicated that there were several but had trouble identifying them, saying that she wasn't in the habit of looking at vehicles when taking her dog for a walk.

Based on the woman's statement, the attack occurred around 10:30 a.m. That meant that it had happened almost ninety minutes before the surgeon operated on Davis. Lacroix knew that that was too long and that Davis's chances of recovery were negligible.

He wasn't sure there was much more he could learn, at the site or from the witness. He called Primeau and brought him up to speed. The two men agreed to meet at the hospital.

When Lacroix arrived at Sacre Coeur Hospital, he checked in at the front desk. Davis was out of surgery and had been moved to intensive care. The fourth-floor nurse told him the surgeon should be able to meet with them within the hour. Lacroix grabbed a coffee from the cafeteria on the ground floor and headed to the waiting room. There were two couples nervously waiting for news of someone. A middle-aged man was biting his nails; his partner was staring at the ceiling. The other couple looked as if they'd been crying and were trying to keep it together.

Lacroix had spent many hours in similar waiting rooms, asking questions of loved ones, trying to piece together the last hours of a close relative caught in the crossfire of some gangland murder, or questioning a relative of a gang member desperately trying to keep it together and not blab to the authorities about what might have happened and who might have been responsible.

After about thirty minutes, Primeau arrived.

Finally Lacroix's name was called over the intercom, telling him to report to the ground-floor reception area. By the time they got to the reception the nurse was waiting for them. Lacroix and Primeau introduced themselves and showed their IDs. She took them to the doctor's office.

The neurosurgeon's name was Turnbull. He was a tall, middle-aged man with a friendly smile. He directed them to two empty chairs, looked down at the opened file on his desk and said, "Mr. Davis suffered a perforating wound to the upper right frontal lobe. The exit point was approximately one inch lower, at the side of the right temple. The good news is the bullet avoided any major vascular structures and blood vessels. However, the bullet caused pressure on the brain, so we were forced to do a partial craniotomy to relieve the pressure."

"What are his chances, doc?" Primeau interrupted.

"I was getting to that." The doctor adjusted his glasses. "A lot depends on the next twenty-four to forty-eight hours. There was significant blood loss. He was in a coma when he was admitted, and we don't know how long he was without oxygen before the paramedics arrived. We can't rule out brain damage. In fact, it's likely, if he survives. He's not a young man."

"When can we see him?" asked Primeau.

The doctor frowned. "I'm sure you've both seen the effects of close-range gunshot wounds to the head. It's a miracle he's still with us. He probably won't ever regain consciousness. If he has close relatives, I'd be contacting them."

"Cheerful, and so full of good news," Primeau said as they left the doctor's office.

"What do you expect? He's telling it the way it is."

"Think it was Pigeon?"

"Maybe," Lacroix said. "It could be another gang. We need to find Pigeon. In the meantime, I'm gonna contact Helene and let her know what happened."

"Do you think she's at risk?"

"No. She needs to know the real story though, not what's in the papers."

"Think that's a good idea?"

"No. but I'm going to tell her anyway. We owe Davis that."

Chapter 47

There was no answer at Helene's door, so Lacroix decided to visit her at the bistro. It was early, so he hoped he'd catch her on her own, getting ready for the lunch crowd. When he arrived, the place was closed, so he banged on the door. An attractive, dark-haired woman in her forties opened it. Before he could say anything, she told him they weren't open for another half-hour.

"I'm looking for Helene."

"That's me."

He showed her his ID. "I'm Corporal Lacroix with the RCMP. I'm here about Alan Davis. I wonder if we could have a few words?"

"I don't have anything to say. As far as I'm concerned, I wish he'd never existed."

"Look, I promise this won't take long."

"I want you to know I had no idea who he was until I read about him in the newspaper, and I know nothing about the people he dealt with or what he did. I'm sure I can't be of any help to you. As I said, I wish I'd never met him."

"There are some things you need to know. Can we talk inside?"

She looked angry as she stepped aside. "You might as well come in. Though I can't imagine I'd be interested in anything you have to say, Corporal." She walked over to a table by the wall. Lacroix followed her.

"Alan is not what he appears to be," said Lacroix.

"You won't get any argument from me on that. He fooled a lot of people."

"He was shot yesterday. He's in critical condition."

She was shocked but regained her composure quickly. "Well that's terrible. It sounds like his past caught up with him."

"You need to know the whole story. And while I'm not authorized to give you all the facts, I know he was very fond of you and never wanted to put you or your family in harm's way. Alan had been working as an undercover agent for the RCMP. He was part of a team that was tackling gang crime in the Port of Montreal. He'd successfully infiltrated one of the gangs that have been running drugs through the port. He was largely responsible for the conviction of several gangsters and the seizure of millions of dollars of assets, as well as the identification of various individuals with gang connections who were involved in facilitating drug trafficking."

Helene's mouth had dropped open slightly. She closed it and stared past Lacroix for a moment. "I don't believe it," she said softly. "He told me he ran a trucking company on the outskirts of Montreal."

"That was his cover."

Helene glared at Lacroix, walked over to the window and looked out onto the street. Then she turned and said, "So you're saying, contrary to what the papers say, he's not a member of the gang, he wasn't involved in drugs and trafficking of young women from Ukraine."

"That's correct."

"So why was he arrested then, along with the other gang members?"

"To make it look like he was one of the gang."

Helene came back to the table. The fire in her eyes had disappeared and she was a bit pale now. She looked up at Lacroix. "Who shot him?"

"We don't know," the corporal answered kindly. She sat down. He pulled out a chair across from her and took a seat. "Maybe a rival gang member, possibly a former gang member that thought he might be a mole. Look, I've already said more than I should."

"Where is he now?"

"Sacre Coeur in Montreal."

"What are his chances?"

"Not good." He grimaced. Helene's eyes were watery, and he felt a surge of guilt. "Anyway, I thought you deserved to know what kind of man he really was. He did have a past, but he made up for it."

"What do you mean?"

"I've already said too much." He stood up and turned to leave.

"Corporal!" she called. He turned to face her again. She was standing now, and some of the colour was back in her cheeks. "I'm glad you came. Thank you for telling me all this."

Lacroix nodded and was going to turn again when she stopped him with an outstretched hand.

"What about his daughter? Can you find her?"

"I don't know. We'll try." He was going to leave then, but he decided Davis wouldn't mind if he filled things in a bit more. After all, wouldn't he want Helene to know the kind of man he really was?

"A few weeks ago, Alan knew he may have been exposed, knew he was risking his life for the operation. He told me that if anything happened to him, he wanted us to find his daughter and let her know what he did and that underneath it all he was a good person. He had his lawyer set up a trust fund for her in the event of his death. When we find her, she'll know the truth. And she'll be well taken care of."

Chapter 48

The following morning Helene called Corporal Lacroix and told him she would like to visit Alan in the hospital. They met at the hospital reception and Lacroix took her to the Intensive Care Unit and led her to Davis's room.

The last time Helene had been in a hospital was when her husband had died almost ten years ago, and it was starting to bring back painful memories. As she entered the room, she held her breath for a few seconds and then exhaled. Alan's head was propped up by several pillows, and he was hooked up to a noisy respirator while another machine kept pinging every second, measuring his vital signs. The top half of his head was completely bandaged. He looked peaceful, as if in a deep sleep.

Lacroix looked at her and said, "Why don't I leave the two of you alone? I'll be in the waiting room."

She approached his bed and looked down at his face. The right side was swollen and there was yellow bruising above the cheekbone. She touched his hand, avoiding the bandage that held the saline drip in place. She sat in the chair next to him and tried to block out the noise of the respirator and the monitor, thinking about the times they spent together.

"Oh, Alan, why didn't you tell me? I couldn't believe it when I read the newspaper." She started to think about him recovering and what his life would be like. Would he be permanently disabled? Would he be able to live a normal life? Was there any way, even if he recovered, that he could live in the Townships? Her husband's illness had been gradual; tests followed by more tests, then the terrible news about the cancer. Then the false hope that things would get better, that he'd make a miraculous recovery. It all came flooding back and she realized there was no magic cure. Life wasn't like that. Cancer, brain injury, there were no miracles. Maybe there was still something she could do for him.

***

Helene told Lacroix she wanted to visit Alan's cottage to look for clues as to where his daughter might be. Even though Lacroix thought it was a long shot he agreed to take her there anyway.

Lacroix hadn't bothered to check Davis's belongings that were in police custody, and he didn't have a key to the cottage. He needn't have worried: The back door was unlocked.

The simple two-bedroom cottage said a lot about Davis. It was spartan. Very rustic, old furniture, no television. A worn leather armchair near the fireplace. It was clean and tidy, no dirty dishes in the sink. *This place needs a woman's touch*, Helene thought.

She was drawn to the books lining the small bookshelf. This was a part of Alan she knew nothing about: his interest in philosophy and psychology. Lacroix was methodically going through the drawers in the small desk that looked out onto the front yard. The top of the desk was empty; the drawers contained bills and correspondences. As he looked through the letters, he noticed a couple of them were unopened.

The addressee on both envelopes was a Miss Lauren Davis and the address was somewhere in Burnaby, BC. Stamped across the front of the envelopes were the words "No longer at this address." He showed them to her and said, "This must be his daughter."

She looked at the top of one of the envelopes and noted the neat handwriting where Davis had written his return address.

"Shall we open them?"

"No," she said. "The letters are private. When we find his daughter, she can read them herself."

***

Helene visited Davis every day. Despite there being no change in his condition, she wasn't giving up hope. On the twelfth day, shortly after she arrived home after visiting him, the phone rang.

"It's Lacroix. The RCMP in Vancouver just called, they've been in contact with Alan's ex-wife and daughter. The daughter is booking a flight to Montreal and is expected to be here tomorrow. I don't know if this is something that you're comfortable with, but it might help if you were able to meet her when she arrives at the hospital. I'm sure she'd be grateful for some female company and to be able to talk to someone who knew Alan."

Helene didn't know what to say. She put herself in the girl's shoes and realized how difficult it would be. She'd need a place to stay as well.

"Of course, let me know what time you want me there."

She wondered if she was getting too involved. Alan had literally turned his back on her a few months ago and now suddenly she'd been dragged back into his life.

Her kids were excited when she told them the story about Alan. Suddenly he was a hero. They said they had no problem with Alan's daughter staying with them. Helene didn't quite see him as a hero and knew there was more heartache still to come. Lauren could lose the father she had last seen when she was a toddler. She probably had no memory of him. It would be like meeting him for the first time.

***

The following day, Lacroix walked Lauren into the hospital waiting room and introduced her to Helene. Helene stood up, and for a moment the two strangers just stared at each other, both unsure of what to say. Then Helene noticed the young woman's eyes. She had the same dark brown eyes as her father. Helene gently put an arm around her. "I'll take you to his room," she said.

When Lauren looked down at her father, she began shaking, trying to come to grips with the fact that the father that she couldn't even remember and never knew was unable to move, talk or even open his eyes. She had so many questions, so many things she wanted to say. Her mother had not been keen for her to come out, but she had persisted. She wondered where she got her stubbornness from. Her mother knew.

"You must be exhausted," said Helene. "Why don't we go get a coffee in the cafeteria?"

Ten minutes later, the two women were seated in the busy hospital cafeteria with paper cups in their hands. Lauren was pale, and she looked lost.

She looked across at Helene and asked, "How do you know my dad?"

"I run a bistro in Bromont. He came in one day for lunch, and we just started chatting and soon became good friends."

"What's he like?"

Helene laughed. "At first, he was shy. He wasn't used to small talk, and I got the sense he was lonely. Then he started to become a regular. I'd say he's kind, funny, thoughtful. As I got to know him, he opened up. He talked about you a lot, and how he regretted what had happened."

Lauren set her mug down and leaned forward. "What did he say exactly?"

Helene smiled. "I never got the whole story. I understand years ago, when you were a little girl, things weren't great between your mom and your dad. Together they decided that you and your mom would both be better off without him. He always talked about you and how he looked forward to the day that he would see you again."

Lauren wiped a tear from her cheek, and Helene reached over and took her hand. "Has Corporal Lacroix told you anything about your dad and what he was doing?"

"Only that he was helping them with some operation."

Helene nodded. "Your dad worked undercover in a gang, going after some bad people. As I understand it, he risked his life to get them in jail. You should be very proud of him."

Chapter 49

The police throughout Quebec had been on the hunt for Pigeon. His picture was in every Sûreté station. Until recently there'd been no sightings of him. Then a report had come in to the Estrie Sûreté from a resident not far from the town of Bromont, complaining about a vagrant living in an abandoned cottage. The duty officer that day noted that the description was of a male between five feet seven and five feet ten, scruffy appearance, several days' growth of beard and wearing a hoodie. He considered it such a vague description that it could fit most of the homeless population of the city of Montreal. He filed the report away, noting that no further action was required.

Primeau and Lacroix had received a few responses from the public. However, they had all proved to be dead ends.

Pigeon is keeping a low profile, not staying in one place long, thought Lacroix. And he probably has a vehicle. Lacroix figured the gangster might try to make sure Davis was dead. Chances were good that he'd avoid the city though. More likely he'd contact someone in the gang that he trusted to get news of Davis. Maybe he'd keep an eye on Davis's cottage if he thought he was still around. There were plenty of old cottages in the Townships, and many were unoccupied in the fall. He didn't know it was Pigeon for sure. If it was, he hoped that he would show himself sooner or later.

And there was always the remote possibility that he would show up at the hospital if he knew Davis was still alive. Lacroix shook his head. He realized he was becoming paranoid. While he believed Pigeon was the most likely person to have shot Davis, it could have been someone from another gang.

***

Lacroix arrived at the hospital just as Helene was leaving.

"I have some news for you," he told her. "We've had a couple of sightings of an individual we'd like to question in connection with the shooting."

"You think you might know who did it?"

"Let's just say we'd like to talk to the individual."

"Is Alan at risk?"

"We think it's highly unlikely. I'll let you know as soon as we've found the individual."

"These sightings … Were they in Bromont?"

"Don't worry, we have someone watching your house as well as the bistro. We think this individual is unlikely to attempt to contact you or go to the hospital in Montreal. He probably doesn't know Alan's condition and assumes that he's dead. We suspect that he knows we're looking for him and is trying to get out of town. As soon as we have news, we'll let you know. Don't worry, though, you're safe."

Lacroix didn't want to worry her, but the truth was he was concerned; they'd yet to apprehend Pigeon. He'd finally convinced his boss that they should leak the story that Davis had recently been shot by a known gangster and had died in hospital. At first his boss didn't believe that it would make any difference to Pigeon. Lacroix argued that it would have the effect of ensuring that Davis would be safe at the hospital, and would make Pigeon decide to leave town as soon as possible. They discussed the possibility that Pigeon might attack Helene and her family. Vincent pointed out that it was by no means certain that the assailant was Pigeon. Until such time as Alan Davis woke up and was able to tell them who the assailant was, or they apprehended Pigeon, they might never find out who had attacked him.

***

A few days later, the same elderly resident of the small village just outside of Bromont complained yet again of a homeless person using an abandoned cottage. This time the old man wanted to know what the Sûreté had done about his first complaint. The keen young officer on duty that day decided to look into the matter and read the earlier report that had been filed. He was aware of the hunt for Pigeon and wondered if the two were connected. Initially he was going to check it out on his own, but he decided to contact Primeau and Lacroix first.

***

By the time Lacroix and Primeau arrived at the Sûreté it was 5:30 p.m. and already dark. The young officer they met could have been Lacroix's son. They'd brought a two-man firearms unit from the RCMP with them. The young officer rode with Lacroix and Primeau; the firearms unit followed behind. The officers parked their cruisers down a lane and slowly approached the cottage on foot. From a distance of thirty yards, they could see a flickering light coming from one of the broken windows. As they arrived at the cottage, the light went out. The firearms officers decided to enter the cottage from the front door. Lacroix, Primeau and the young officer waited at the entrance.

The firearms officers drew their weapons and flicked on their flashlights, then the lead officer gently leaned on the door. It was unlocked and creaked loudly as it opened. They both entered the cottage, guns and flashlights in hand. One pointed to the other as he scanned the room with his flashlight. In one corner, lying on top of a sleeping bag, was a dishevelled-looking man. One of them shone his light in the man's face, causing him to open his eyes. "This is the police, identify yourself!" he shouted.

The man blinked but didn't respond. The officer repeated the command. The man stirred, sat up slowly and appeared to reach for a bag lying nearby.

"Don't move, stay where you are."

The man rubbed his eyes and then grabbed the bag and reached inside.

"I said don't move! Stop or I'll shoot!"

Both officers were shouting, their guns and lights pointed at the man's head.

The man pulled something out of the bag. Before they could tell whether it was a gun, a knife or even a pair of glasses, the first officer pulled the trigger and shot him in the chest from less than ten feet. The man slumped sideways.

Primeau and Lacroix rushed in as soon as they heard the shooting, their guns pointed in front of them. The two firearms officers were standing over a body, guns still drawn. Lacroix noticed a handgun on the floor beside the body. In the poor light he had trouble identifying the body.

***

Forty minutes later, crime scene investigators had arrived and both firearms officers' handguns were seized. Each officer was interviewed separately and told that in accordance with standard procedure, they'd be put on desk duty until the investigation was completed. The body was shipped to the Montreal Morgue for identification and an autopsy even though Primeau and Lacroix knew who it was.

The following morning, they paid a visit to the morgue. Although neither had ever met Pigeon, they'd seen enough mug shots of the man. The two tattoos located on his right arm were identical to those described in his police record. He looked smaller than five feet seven.

They brought Vincent up to speed. Lacroix knew that they still needed to match up the bullet that went through Davis's head with the gun found on Pigeon. Lacroix said he suspected the ballistics would confirm that the bullet had come from Pigeon's gun.

Chapter 50

Over the next few weeks, Davis's condition started to improve. The doctor said that it was still early days, but that given the trajectory of the bullet and the fact that it didn't hit any major structures within the brain, there was no reason why he shouldn't wake up at some point. He cautioned that there were no guarantees.

The news was welcomed in Helene's household. She wondered whether it had been the stimulation of her and Lauren's voices that he'd heard on a regular basis. Lauren had taken to talking to him as if he was wide awake, explaining who she was and how her life had turned out so far.

At the end of that week Helene told Alan about how his daughter was staying with them and how all three kids had gotten up early that morning to go fly fishing. Suddenly, she noticed his eyelids flicker. She looked at the monitor and saw that his heart rate had jumped. The heart rate came down just as quickly. She held his hand and carried on talking to him. It was so faint that she might even have dreamt it, but she thought she could feel his hand gently squeezing hers.

No one was ever sure what prompted the change. Over the next few days Davis continued to improve and one evening, as the doctor was checking him and doing more tests, he finally opened his eyes.

When Helene and Lauren visited him, he appeared weak and tired, but alert. Helene gave him a hug. He smiled and then looked at Lauren.

"Alan, this is your daughter, Lauren."

He looked at Helene, confused, and in a soft, croaky voice, he said, "I don't understand."

Lauren walked over to him and stood by the side of his bed and said, "Daddy, it's me, your daughter, Lauren."

Helene explained, "Alan, you were shot, you've been in a coma for over two weeks. Corporal Lacroix was able to find your daughter."

Alan smiled again.

The nurse came in and said they should let Alan rest. She told them that they could come back tomorrow morning. Waiting outside the door, Lacroix was anxious to have a few words with Davis.

As Lacroix entered the room the nurse turned on him and said, "I think he's had enough for one day. Can this wait till tomorrow?"

"This will take thirty seconds and it's urgent."

"Okay, you've got thirty seconds, and if he gets stressed in any way, you're out the door, understand?" Lacroix walked over to his bed. Davis appeared to have fallen asleep. He quietly called his name, "Alan, if you can hear me, please nod."

There was no response. He tried again. "Alan, was it Pigeon?"

Davis opened his eyes, nodded, then closed his eyes.

"We got him, Alan. We got Pigeon."

***

Lacroix knew that the elimination of Pigeon wouldn't necessarily mean the end of any threats to Davis. Rival gangs interested in taking over the port might still want him gone. Since Davis's name had already been mentioned in the newspapers, his plan was simply to have the RCMP release a report denying rumours that the recent death of a homeless man in an abandoned cottage in the townships was gang-related and the speculation that the individual was none other than Walter Pigeon. They would also refuse to comment on the recent death of another gang member by the name of Alan Davis.

Experience had taught Lacroix that whenever police denied rumours, the rumours were usually true. Whether this would satisfy the Montreal gangs vying for control of the port remained to be seen. He hoped that the reports would put an end to speculation that Davis was still alive.

Epilogue

Davis had been moved to a private nursing home north of the city under an assumed name. Lauren and Helene visited him regularly. He made a steady recovery and used the time to discuss the future. He'd made up his mind to move back to Miramichi in the Maritimes. Lauren talked of going to college at Mount Allison in New Brunswick, or maybe Acadia in Nova Scotia. Despite several attempts, her mother had yet to talk her out of it.

Alan and Helene took many walks in the gardens of the nursing home, which had originally been a small country estate. They both knew he could never live in the small, isolated communities of the Townships, where everyone knew everyone else's business and there were no secrets. They said they'd stay in touch, and once a year meet up somewhere, maybe a resort in the Townships or even Miramichi. But they both knew in their hearts that once he left, they'd never see each other again.

When he'd gone into witness protection all those years ago, he'd never expected to meet someone he cared about. When it happened by chance, at first, he couldn't believe his luck. In his heart he knew it would never last, that his past would always be there and would one day catch up with him.

Davis was never one for long goodbyes. All the possessions that he needed were packed in the back of his truck. He and Lauren were headed off to the Maritimes. He hoped to get a job at one of the fishing lodges. Helene's kids were there with her when she said her goodbyes. There were tears in Helene's eyes. She wondered if she'd ever see Davis again.

Davis didn't tell Lacroix and Primeau where he was going. He knew they'd find out where he was, sooner or later.

Sean Dunphy moved to Regina with his ex-wife and kids. After two months, missing the good life and bright lights of Montreal, the ex-wife walked out on him and the kids. Dunphy started to become the parent he never had been. At ten and twelve, the kids were still young enough for him to become a positive influence. He started attending his son's baseball and hockey games, and his daughter's volleyball games. The transition was tough at first, but he knew he'd been given another chance, and he wasn't going to mess it up. He was surprised at how quickly the kids adjusted to the transition. He never explained the reason behind the move or why their mother left. Maybe one day he would, when they were older.

Landry had fled to Germany and never returned to Canada. Attempts by various police agencies to bring him back were futile. There was no extradition treaty with Canada, and Landry was able to claim German citizenship, since his mother had been born there.

Investigations into the gang's financial affairs showed links to various companies based in Vanuatu. Located in the South Pacific some two thousand kilometres northeast of Australia, it was a tax haven for wealthy individuals and their companies. Any company incorporated in the Republic of Vanuatu could move money in and out of the country without consequence, and its privacy laws prevented any foreign government or law enforcement agency from forcing the company to disclose any information about its financial affairs or ownership. RCMP investigators had suspicions that Landry was behind a scheme to divert millions of dollars of his and the gang's money to the island. Years of investigation proved fruitless, and they eventually gave up their efforts to go after the money and Landry. As long as he stayed in Germany, he remained beyond the law.

Auryse De Riggi still lived in the same house in Saint-Henri that she'd shared with her husband for twenty years. Even though De Riggi knew that his wife's evidence had led to his downfall, he finally showed some compassion. He had his lawyer negotiate a clause in his plea bargain that meant that, although he had to give up all his assets, his wife was allowed to live in the family home for as long as she lived. Auryse got a part-time job working at a jewellery store in downtown Montreal, and continued to attend church every Sunday while at the same time cleaning the church four evenings a week to help supplement her income. She had no contact with her husband, making it clear she never wanted to see him again. She found all she needed in the Church and God, realizing that she'd been trapped in a bad relationship for too long. Her friends at church didn't shun her when they found out who she'd been married to and continued to be a great comfort.

Josie Chouinard moved to Quebec City and helped set up a shelter for abused women. She also got a job in a boutique hotel in the city and eventually met a man who reminded her a little of De Riggi. At close to fifty, she knew she wanted security and companionship, things she'd thought she'd found in De Riggi. She didn't love the guy, but he cared for her, treated her like a lady, and that was enough. She told him about her past. He said he didn't care and promised he'd take care of her. He had his own home and wasn't short of money.

De Riggi had a tough time adjusting to life after running the gang for so long. He found rural Alberta slow compared to the bustle of the big city he'd lived in all his life. He'd had little choice in where they'd relocated him.

He tried to settle in and hold down a job working on a construction site. He found normal life difficult. It wasn't just the menial tasks he had to do as a labourer. The guy running the site was thirty years younger than he was and always telling him what to do. After a few weeks he lost it and decked him. Eventually he found other work in construction, but his temper got the better of him and he ended up headbutting one of the site foremen on another job.

He started drinking more than usual and made the mistake of getting into an argument with a guy in a bar while playing pool. The guy tried to smack De Riggi over the head with the pool cue. De Riggi lost it and ended up throwing the guy through the bar window out onto the street.

A night in the cells and warnings from his parole officer didn't help. Within a few weeks he was back in prison. He didn't last thirty days and was stabbed to death while working in the prison laundry. There were no witnesses, and, as the warden explained to the police, De Riggi was very unpopular with the inmates and the guards alike, easily took offence at the slightest thing, and tended to keep to himself. He wouldn't be missed by anyone.

After returning to Miramichi with his daughter, Davis realized the remote fishing lodge life was no place for a young girl who was heading off to college soon. He and Lauren toured the Mount Allison University campus in Sackville, New Brunswick, and quickly fell in love with the place.

Lauren's mother back in Vancouver was worried about her only daughter travelling three thousand miles across the country to go to college. She pleaded with her to go to school somewhere nearer home. Lauren was having none of it, saying that at least her father would be nearby. She didn't tell her that her that he was thinking of moving to Sackville to live. When her mother complained that it'd take her the whole day to get to Sackville, and even then only if she got a good connecting flight in Toronto, Lauren smiled.

"Mom, think of it as an adventure. I'll be seeing a part of the world I've never seen before. And Dad won't be far away."

Her mother finally acquiesced, realizing there was no way she'd be able to change her daughter's mind. And she had to admit that when she travelled back with her when she started college, although she was put off by the eleven-hour trip involving two planes and a thirty-mile drive, she could see why her daughter had fallen in love with the place. The quaint old village with the 1950s movie theatre, neat old-fashioned coffee shops, small bakeries and used bookstores reminded her of the BC interior where she'd grown up. This place also had beautiful beaches nearby and the lovely rolling countryside. The small hotel that she stayed at, called The Marshlands Inn, was originally built in 1850 and renovated in the early 1900s. It was a delight; the beautiful quilt covering the four-poster bed, the antique furniture and the open fire reminded her of a bygone age. It was as if she'd travelled back in time. The service and food were excellent. She didn't want to leave.

Davis avoided any contact with his ex-wife. Somehow Lauren must have made it clear that she planned to spend some time with her dad. He had yet to decide where to live, and he found the city of Moncton reminded him too much of the drab smaller towns in BC that appeared to have been designed around the railroads with little care to how the place would develop and attract people that would want to live there and raise a family.

He gave his daughter a month to settle in and then went to see her. The few times he'd visited Sackville he liked it. Maybe a bit too quiet, but that's what he needed. He'd have to play it by ear. At least he was alive and his daughter had come back into his life after all these years. He'd try and be there for her now.

Acknowledgements

My thanks to all those at Iguana who made this happen, especially to Paula Chiarcos for her patience and guidance, Toby Keymer for his thoroughness and Cheryl Hawley for being the steady hand.

www.ingramcontent.com/pod-product-compliance
Lightning Source LLC
Chambersburg PA
CBHW020359030726
47496CB00007B/2215